PRAISE FOR

THE MIZOQUII

"I was immediately drawn to Edin's journey to break free from captivity and discover secrets of his past. *The Mizoquii* is an easy read due to the quality of writing."

—DR. CHARLES CANTRELL, **Research Chemist**

"*The Mizoquii* combines the familiar with the fantastic in an underdog tale that draws the reader deep into the world of Edin Carvosa, a boy trapped in the lowest level of servitude on a smuggling vessel. He makes his bid for freedom on an unfamiliar planet only to end up in a deathmatch arena. Durden's characters come alive and make the reader cheer them on in the struggle to survive."

—TIMOTHY M. SAVAGE, **Author of** *Regard for the Dead*

"Imagination is a precious gift, and *The Mizoquoii* shows us that Caleb Durden has been gifted with astounding imagination. Readers will be quickly drawn into the life of Edin Carvosa. His story starts as a smuggler's whipping boy but ends as something spectacularly different. Each scene is virtually painted with words that bring the story to life."

—ENDY WRIGHT, **Author of** *The Omicron Six*

The Mizoquii

by Caleb Durden

ISBN 978-1-64663-628-0

Published by

 köehlerbooks™

3705 Shore Drive
Virginia Beach, VA 23455
800-435-4811
www.koehlerbooks.com

THE
MIZOQUII

CALEB DURDEN

VIRGINIA BEACH
CAPE CHARLES

CHAPTER I

Upon the cosmos, the starship carried the depressed crew. Countless weeks had passed since they last left the ship for liberty. The captain pushed them tirelessly to produce revenue by smuggling for a mysterious client, but in the compartments and the corridors, none of the crewmembers openly complained of the heavy workload. Overall it meant extra coins in their accounts, which entailed that their retirement arrived quicker. All on board were old-school smugglers who had grown accustomed to lengthy stretches away from civilization—except for one. Nobody wanted to walk on solid ground and breathe true air more than the boy.

Edin Carvosa knew he would be denied permission to leave the starship at the next spaceport, but the least he could do was ask. He held a special request form in his fingers while pacing a narrow passageway. With each step, his boots rubbed the skin on his heels. The friction had formed nasty blisters. Two layers of socks didn't stop the painful discomfort. He figured he would steal a larger pair from a crewmember when the chance arose since he lacked the credits for a new purchase.

He climbed the ladderwell to the level above. The higher he rose, the brighter the passageway's overhead lights grew, reflecting off the smooth floors and walls on the upper levels where the captain and the officers dwelled. Edin saw himself in the sleek steel, his emerald eyes glaring back. Gray paint stained his black coveralls and discolored his sandy-blond hair. He had spent the morning shift coating the lower decks, but the lower decks never looked this glossy.

The metal door for the main bridge was ahead. The small scanner on the ceiling studied him as he walked up. A green light above the entry flashed, and the heavy door rushed open. Anxiety welled up inside him. The captain despised being disturbed.

The main bridge was an unusually dark compartment, but some illumination rose from digital monitors and control panels at the working stations and from the hologram map in the center. Six officers sat behind monitors, engaged in their work. They glanced towards the door, then dropped their gazes back to the displays. Across the compartment, a wide window showcased the vastness of space.

Edin knew it would be better to turn around and leave.

"Carvosa! What the flip are you doing on my bridge?"

Rhygert Jameson, the captain of the *Saircor*, strolled out from behind the hologram. An electronic device for smoking hung from his lip. Its vapor lingered above his head, which was covered with slimy black hair that dropped beneath his shoulders, blending into a black leather jacket with frayed patches. His eyes were deep brown, and so were his teeth.

"Captain, I have a request," Edin said.

The captain snatched the yellow paper out of Edin's hand, and the officers in the room looked at the boy and the captain with curiosity. Grimacing, the captain examined the document. Edin felt his stomach getting heavier. *This was a mistake*, he thought. *But I have to advocate for myself.* The captain placed his hands on his hips and gave the boy a stern stare.

"Really? This is the reason behind you coming here during working hours?"

"Yes, Captain. My apologies for the inconvenience. But I haven't been off the ship in three years. I have heard rumors of Lathas and its beauty. I am unsure when I would ever get the opportunity to visit again," Edin said.

The captain lifted the paper to Edin's face and tore it in half. "This isn't a flippin' cruise ship, boy."

Edin felt himself growing smaller as he looked into the eyes of the man who owned him. He was too intimidated to cry, show emotion, or even walk away. He just stared back and waited for the captain to speak again—this person who had plucked him off a dying planet and claimed to be his savior.

"All you do is complain about your shifts and ask for time off. This isn't a game. We all have jobs to do. You don't even know what's in the cargo hold, do you?" the captain asked.

"No, sir."

"Exactly. I'll tell you when you're authorized to get off this ship. Never come to my bridge with one of these stupid request forms. No one is getting off on Lathas except those on the assignment. What makes you special? We're touching down, dropping off the shipment, and leaving. It's foolish to think so selfishly."

"My apologies. I didn't know."

"For this act, you're not getting off on the next spaceport either."

"But, Captain, it's been three years," Edin said.

"I'll make it thirty! If it wasn't for me, you'd still be stuck on Rhytru, begging for water. This is a smuggling vessel, and the assignment always comes first. Not freedom. Not liberty. Not whatever future fantasies you have in your head."

"Roger that." Edin pivoted on his foot to leave.

The captain said, "I'll make sure you're standing watch during the next liberty port. Don't make any plans, boy."

Edin had nothing to say and left with his head down. The door slammed shut behind him as he walked out of the bridge and limped down the passageway. He felt guilty for putting himself through that. Hatred for the captain stirred in his heart. The captain wanted to turn him into something other than a child—a dull machine for labor and nothing more.

In an hour, Edin had to report to the galley to serve food to the crew. It would be best to get off his blistered feet for a while. He went down multiple ladderwells and headed aft. The dual hyper-engines produced violent volumes of clanks and clatters. He reached in his pocket and pulled out two hearing-protection devices, placing one in each ear.

The small space he inhabited was a storage locker on the other side of the engineering shop, below the engine bay. He arrived at the oval-shaped door with its rusty hatch and twisted it open.

The compartment was cramped. A hammock was strung up by thin rope tied to two bolts on the bulkhead. The pillow and blanket had been stolen during his time working in the laundry room. A hamper for clothes and a small copper nightstand stood next to the hatch. In the corner, a small bookshelf held volumes of historical literature. When he had free time, he enjoyed reading about the civilizations of the old galaxy.

A large red toolbox rested underneath the hammock. He knelt and placed his thumb on the digital lock. It unbolted, and he lifted the lid. Old coins and a necklace with an emerald charm lay on top. Pushing them aside revealed a purple pill bottle next to a plasma pistol. The gun had never been fired, by him at least, and he was scared to ever use it.

He grabbed the pill bottle and unfasted the cap. Inside was one white, diamond-shaped pill, all that was left of a six-pill prescription of tentezine, an opioid painkiller, given to him when he had his wisdom teeth removed many moons ago. He had saved the last one for an emergency. To numb the blistered heels soaking his socks in blood, he popped the pill in his mouth, even though the pills had made him sick before.

Catty-corner from the bookshelf, Edin sat on a plastic crate and propped his legs on the hammock. *I must find a way to get off this ship*, he told himself. He needed to research life on Lathas. *Maybe desertion is worth the gambit.*

Warm from the painkiller and refreshed from his break, Edin ambled into the ship's galley. His feet hurt but weren't throbbing like earlier. He changed out of his paint-covered black coveralls and pulled on the ones he served food in. The culinary specialist, Forlingo, would be irate if Edin showed up unclean.

The galley was a level below the main deck. The scent of fresh bread filled the corridor outside. Inside, grills and ovens were welded against the bulkhead, and pots and pans hung from metal hooks in the ceiling. A serving booth separated the kitchen from the mess deck where the crew would eat.

A thick stew was boiling in a large steam kettle. Edin grabbed an apron and approached the freshly prepared stew and bread behind the glass wall of the booth, anticipating that he would be the one giving out rations.

"Not today, Carvosa," Forlingo said.

Forlingo was a descendant of an ancient species called the kenjenk. He was around sixty standard years old and had large black eyes and orange skin with no hair. He looked fairly human besides the bloodred tendrils in a stripe on his head and his sharply pointed, red ears.

"What?" Edin asked.

"I need the dishes cleaned. I'll be serving today."

Edin looked over the kenjenk's shoulder and saw piles of dirty plates stacked to the ceiling, then let out a breath of frustration. This was one of countless disadvantages to being the only junior crewmember. "Alright."

He pulled on two rubber gloves as the water in the sink started running hot. *How long has it been since the dishes were washed?* He lacked the desire to discover the muck in the bottom of the basin. It already smelled foul. *This is a job for a machine or a droid,* he thought. The captain had always been too tightfisted to invest in embedding technology in the ship, believing that old-fashioned man power held the most reliability. At the moment, Edin wished he had the nostrils of a droid.

The crew filed into the galley. There were only thirty-four people on board to feed: the captain, six division officers, six engineers, thirteen maintenance personnel, four technicians, two ordnancemen, and two loadmasters. Forlingo wouldn't need any assistance. He was one of the few individuals on the ship Edin respected. The culinary specialist worked tirelessly to feed the crew a warm meal, always on time. But Edin's admiration didn't run sky high; after all, the old kenjenk had only managed to become a chef on a smuggling vessel—probably because he got in some sort of legal or financial trouble with the royal dynasty. Everyone on *Saircor* was an outlaw, except for Edin, whose life was held under bond—a self-described outcast amongst outcasts.

The painkiller numbed his feet, but his mind roiled at the thought of being arrested. If he got caught on the ship while they were transporting contraband, he would be sent to the dreaded prison planet, Harchment. *I have to get away and make something of myself,* he thought. He dried off another plate and stuck it on the clean pile.

By the time the crew had eaten, Edin was halfway done with the dishes. Forlingo told him it was time for a break and fixed Edin a bowl of stew with a grilled cheese sandwich. They sat down in the mess deck and finally ate their lunch. Edin dipped the grilled cheese in his stew until the bread became soggy. Peas and beef floated like buoys in the brown broth. After a few bites, his stomach cramped and his face began to sweat. *Tentezine doesn't mix with grease,* he remembered. He failed to eat the second half of his sandwich.

"Has the stew gone cold?" Forlingo asked.

"No, I have a slight stomachache. It's delicious. Thank you," Edin said.

"I heard you requested permission to get off on Lathas."

Edin looked down at his bowl. "Yeah, I tried."

"I might have some good news."

Edin raised his head. "What?"

"I'll need assistance getting rations for the next underway. You might be able to come with me. It would be good for you to get off. The marketplace in the capital is a marvel."

"Don't get my hopes up. The captain isn't going to approve. It will only make my situation worse."

"So, you don't want me to ask?"

Edin pondered the possibilities of leaving the ship with Forlingo. It would be easy to escape from him in a crowd. But someone had to stay behind and watch the ship, and the captain would insist that be Edin.

"I'm not getting off," he said.

"Well, I'll make sure you get off at the next spaceport, then. It's unhealthy to stay stowed away like luggage," Forlingo said. "The captain should realize that."

"His childhood was no different."

"Yes, but I fear you'll turn out different than him."

"Why do you fear that? I have no desire to be a smuggler."

"You could end up worse."

"Worse. Really?" Edin laughed.

The door to the galley slammed into the bulkhead with a sharp clink. Rendall Sawyer, the officer for the avionics division, paced up to the two. He wore black coveralls and stood just below six feet. His freshly combed but unwashed black hair held enough grease to fry meat.

Rendall looked down at Edin with a frown. "We got a dilemma on board."

Edin rarely spoke to the officers. It was unusual for one to approach him with a problem. They typically had someone else delegate him to a task. He wondered if he had gotten himself in more trouble. Maybe someone found the plasma pistol or the coins that he had stolen. *No. No one goes down there. Can't be.*

"What is the dilemma, sir?"

"Lester Krebs has died in the control room for weapons delivery. Seems to be of natural causes. Anyways, I need someone to get rid of the body."

That was the last thing Edin was expecting. "Uh . . . sure. I'll get to it right away. There's an airlock on the deck, so it shouldn't be an issue." He stood up.

"That's why Krebs didn't make it to lunch. That's disappointing," Forlingo said.

"He was the oldest person on the ship. Everyone knew it was just a matter of time," Rendall said.

Edin walked towards the door, trying not to stagger on his numb legs.

"Carvosa," Rendall called. Edin glanced over his shoulder. "Make sure you clean up the scene before you leave."

"Roger that."

Edin felt spacesick as he headed to the weapons control room. He tried not to limp or wobble. Sweat trickled down his neck to his stomach. He descended three ladderwells, the ship growing warmer. In the corridor, rusty pipes clung to the ceiling and leaked heated steam out of exhaust valves.

Edin passed two people from the maintenance department, Kintink Rah and Trent Sling—both middle-aged humans. Kintink was tall and had reddened skin. Trent was slightly shorter with light-brown skin. Rumors had spread that they were wanted for stealing a priceless portrait from the ancient house of Heiros, who were the monarchs of the galaxy and the spearhead of the royal dynasty. They glanced suspiciously at Edin; his face felt colder than a frozen moon and was probably just as pale. He gave them a quick nod and carried on. The spins were getting faster. He didn't want to admit to them or even to himself that he was about to throw up. The two continued forward and snickered.

He could have walked normally if it weren't for the boots constricting his heels. *Must get there soon*, he thought. His stride quickened despite the pain returning to his feet. Reaching the door of the weapons control room, he twisted the hatch, burst inside, and threw up in the garbage chute.

The compartment smelled dreadful. Edin shut the door to the room, closed the chute, and picked himself up. He wiped his sleeve over his mouth to clean the saliva and residue off. Control monitors and panels covered most of the steel bulkheads. Towers of electrical components stood in the center. The corpse of Lester Krebs lay sprawled out beside a black desk with a ripped-apart wiring harness resting on top.

Edin hobbled over to the desk. A yellow case contained crimping pliers and other wiring repair tools lay open. From the looks of it, Krebs had been inserting wires into a new cannon plug. The old man had died while trying to hold a steady hand. *What component was he working on?* Edin wondered while he stared down at the body. Krebs appeared even more fragile in death. His limbs had shrunken terribly, and craters developed where his skin had rotted. Patches of white hair dotted his scalp. The wrinkled face displayed a grave and deep depression, and the lifeless eyes appeared to be on the verge of dropping one last tear. *Time is everyone's adversary,* Edin thought.

This was not the way Edin wanted to be remembered. Left to die on a smuggling vessel, merely to be expelled out of an airlock like litter into the black hollow of space. Edin felt pity for the corpse. Krebs wasn't a horrible person; he never said much of anything besides singing soft tunes while pacing the passageways. But Krebs was the same as every other crewmember on the *Saircor*. He'd broken so many laws in the galaxy that fleeing to further crime was his only way to survive.

Edin knelt at the feet of the corpse. He untied the black boots and pulled them off the dead man's feet. They were two sizes larger than the ones he had on. He put them on and walked around the control room. The bloodied heels had space to breathe. His lips curled into a smirk; then he dragged the limp body to the airlock in his new boots.

CHAPTER 2

After two days of walking in the new boots, his feet started to heal up. Scabs formed over the heels where the open wounds once tormented.

The *Saircor* would arrive on Lathas in three days. Edin had yet to form an escape strategy. He had no idea where each crewmember would be stationed or how long they would be off the ship. But he happened to be working in the galley at the prime hour to discover that information.

Midrats were served at midnight when the night crew came in to get a meal from the day's extra rations. Forlingo had gone to bed early that night, so Edin was the only one on kitchen duty. About ten people picked up their portions of fried kulliben and noodles saturated in a creamy garlic sauce. They ate on the mess deck in no hurry. The night shift was far more laid back, considering the captain and the higher-ranking officers slept during this time. Edin fixed himself a plate and grabbed a glass of water, then exited the kitchen area and sat next to Kintink and Trent on the far end at one of the silver tables.

The two glanced at him, chewing their food, and then continued to eat. Edin twirled the fork in the pasta and took a bite. The kulliben, white meat from a domesticated fowl, remained appetizing even after being reheated.

"It's malarkey we're only on Lathas for one day," Kintink griped.

"Cuz of those daggum warheads we're carrying. Can't believe the captain got us hauling atomics," Trent responded.

"Warheads?" Edin asked.

"Yeah. You didn't know?" Trent said.

"No. The captain told me the cargo hold is off limits. Told me not to go in there until everything is out."

"It's for your own good. The captain didn't want you to snooping around. Probably better if you didn't know anything," Kintink said.

"Who's buying the atomics?" Edin asked.

"That's a question for someone with a little more rank on their shoulder," Kintink said. "I did hear a rumor it was the Sheeban Syndicate. But that's just mess talk. Don't go around saying you heard that from me."

"The Sheeban! If the royal dynasty found out we were giving atomics to terrorists, we wouldn't even have the honor of being sent to Harchment," Edin said. "We'd be executed on sight."

"We reckon there's a large bounty for this haul," Trent said. "Everyone thinks the captain wants to retire in a few years, and atomics is the fastest way out the game. Can't be smuggling forever."

Edin shook his head and took another bite of his food.

"I'm not even mad about the ordnance," Trent said. "I just want to get off the ship."

"You and me both," Edin said.

"*I'm* worried. Smells of a setup," Kintink said.

"Do you know what you'll be doing once we land?" Edin asked.

"A large crew is going to the rendezvous. Whoever is left will go with Forlingo to the marketplace and assist with the stores onload," Kintink said. "I'm assuming you'll be on the watch to help refuel this old bird."

"Most likely, yeah. Do you know how many will stay behind with the ship?"

"Not many, three or four at most. You only need two to fuel. Why?"

Edin shrugged. "Just wondering."

"Too bad you're not getting off on liberty, Carvosa." Trent lowered his fork and wiped his mouth. "Lathas has an open gauntlet. The fights are pure entertainment and madness."

A gauntlet, Edin thought. His ears perked up and eyes narrowed. "Like a fight-to-the-death type of gauntlet?"

"Yeah. It would be fun for you to go, view the kids your age raging in battle. Most have trained their entire life for it, and some say that winning the third match is the highest honor in the galaxy. Aside from a campaign medal from the liege pharaoh himself, of course."

"What happens after the third match?"

"A handsome sum of prize money and almost guaranteed acceptance into any academy. Tuition is fully covered," Kintink said. "Most victors study somewhere in the First System at one of the high academies. They go and do whatever educated people do."

"Dang," Edin said. "Sounds like a good gig."

"Either you live and become a legend, or die and become forgotten. It is more tragic than heroic for the families who invest so much."

"Yeah." Edin's mind raced with the possibility of entering the gauntlet. He looked at his plate and wanted to be alone. "Well, I've got to get to bed. Supposed to do laundry in the morning."

"Alright. See ya around, kid," Trent said.

After Edin left his plate in the sink, the walk back to his compartment was mostly silent and dark. Lights were cut off throughout the ship during these hours to simulate night. But the passageway outside the galley had an extremely wide, transparent wall; that morning the ship had shifted to parabolic speed, and when flying at this rapid pace, the stars and planets were indistinguishable, cosmic radiation altering the blackness of space into a pulsating and beautiful blue glow. Edin stepped up to the cold glass.

He decided that he would attempt to enter the gauntlet. What did he have to lose? He would train for it relentlessly. He clenched his fist.

This had to be the path: ditch the smugglers and achieve things they only dreamed of. If he graduated from a high academy, he could work for the royal dynasty. One day, he could even be a galactic agent hunting down outlaws like these lousy backplanet pirates. Maybe even maneuver his way into politics or start a business, start a legacy that he could pass down to generations after his death. He eyeballed his reflection in the barrier. *How long will they actually look for me on Lathas?* After selling the warheads, the captain would have no option but to leave in a hurry.

Edin was snoring loudly in his hammock when a fist pounded against the steel door of the storage locker. He jolted upwards as the hatch flew open and crashed against the bulkhead. The captain stood in the entry.

"Carvosa!"

Edin's heart thumped fast, his eyes wide, and he sat straight up with his back pressed to the steel wall. The captain never entered this part of the ship.

"Captain, what's wrong?"

"You're an hour late!"

Edin moved his head under the hammock to look at the digital clock. It read 0630. His small bed started to shake beneath his knees. He gripped the cloth edges as he tried to maintain balance. Too late. The hammock flipped over, and he crashed on the hard metal flooring in nothing but black boxer briefs. His cheekbone and elbow throbbed as he stood.

"What is wrong with you?" the captain asked.

"Uh, nothing. I was up serving midrats last night." Edin smiled nervously. "Must have forgotten to set the alarm."

The captain stepped up to him, chest to chest. Edin could see the oil in the captain's unwashed hair. Edin looked up into the mad eyes and was unsure of what to do or say.

The captain raised his calloused hands, placed them on Edin's shoulders, and clenched them with great intensity, white fingers digging into each deltoid. The captain's eyes inflamed. It felt as if time had frozen, until the captain slung Edin by the shoulders into the bookshelf. One of the oak shelves splintered in half against his back. The books came tumbling down on his head, and he lay there in the collapsed wood, glaring up at the captain.

The captain brandished a small device. "Do you know what this is?"

Edin studied it from the ground. It appeared to be some sort of metallic cylinder. Three small red lights flashed on the side, and stainless steel gripping fingers protruded at the end.

Edin shook his head. "No."

"It's a flippin' tracker. It was in the airlock that you ejected Krebs out of."

"I didn't notice it."

"Boy, you need to keep your foolish eyes open," the captain spat. "We shifted to parabolic with this flippin' tracker on board."

"Who is tracking us?"

"I don't have any flippin' idea! Could be the dynasty, bounty hunters, or other smugglers! But daggum, boy, you were the last one down there, and your worthless self couldn't keep a watch out for your own ship. This is your house. You live here," the captain growled. "If we're being hunted, so are you."

Edin stood and brushed the debris off his skin. As he stepped over to his clothing hamper, he knew the captain was staring at him with anger. Edin took out a pair of coveralls and slipped his leg into them.

"You're pathetic," the captain said. "Can't even wake up on time." He turned and slammed the door. The clanging of metal filled the compartment once again.

Edin zipped up the black coveralls and slipped on a pair of wool socks and the black work boots. *That could have been a lot worse,* he thought. He studied the area before leaving the cluttered compartment. The hammock was coiled up into a corkscrew shape, and the bookshelf appeared to have been blasted with a shotgun. He shook his head. He shut the door behind him and tightened the rusty hatch.

The laundry room was a level above and in the forward section of the ship. On the early-morning walk, Edin's eyelids drooped, begging to close. Four hours of sleep was not enough. He staggered with his head down.

He wondered who was tracking them and when the tracker had been placed on the ship. Perhaps on Genaught or Ethar. They docked on both planets for a few days. One of the grunts with the hangar crews might have attached it to the wall in the lower airlock. *How did I not see it when I ejected Krebs?* Everyone would be after the *Saircor* if they knew the ship was hauling atomics. A bounty must have been organized against the captain and his crew.

Edin climbed a corroded ladderwell. It was going to be a long shift, but the anticipation of landing grew. Even if another ship pursued them to Lathas, they should still have time to land and take flight if needed. The chaos might assist him in his scheme to escape. Nothing would benefit him more than the attention of the captain and the officers directed towards an unknown foe. He smirked.

The quiet passageway ended at a shuttered door with white paint chips peeling off. He twisted the hatch, and it squeaked open to reveal a small room. Six large machines awaited the crew's laundry, which was bagged up in nylon bags on a wide shelf spanning the entire wall.

He opened the washer furthest from the door and dumped a bag of coveralls inside. The smell of grease, sweat, and oil invaded the space. He threw a detergent pod in the machine and closed the lid. He pushed the start button. Nothing happened. *No water*, he thought.

He left the laundry room and walked to the engineering room for environmental systems, two levels down. From there, Lakada Oteftt could enable water and air supply to the washing units.

He knocked on a red metal door. Strange music played inside. A circular window opened, and Lakada peeked out. He was a kenjenk like Forlingo—orange skin with red tendrils on his flat head. Edin figured Lakada was the younger of the two but had never spoken much with him.

"Let me guess." Lakada examined Edin. "You're doing laundry today?"

Edin laughed. "Yeah. Can you send me some water?"

"Sure." Lakada opened the door and stepped into the passageway. "But first, what's up with this news about a tracker on board?"

Edin's cheeks reddened. "No idea. The captain woke me up and he was hotter than a comet this morning. He said it was in the airlock. But I didn't see it when I was there."

Lakada scratched his chin. "Odd."

"I know."

"It would be hard to miss something like that."

"You think someone on boa—"

"Obviously," Lakada interrupted. "But who and why?"

"You don't think I'm a suspect, do you?"

"You're the most likely."

Edin looked down. "That's why the captain was all riled up. It looks like I'm the one who placed the tracker there."

"Don't worry. You're also the most likely to be set up," Lakada said. "And the captain realizes that."

"What do you mean?"

"If the captain thought you were the culprit, you would already be dead. He's blaming you momentarily while he has time to interrogate the rest of the crew." Lakada looked up and down the passageway. "There's a spy amongst us. Keep your eyes open these next few days, and let someone know if you see anything."

"I will, Lakada," Edin promised.

Lakada grinned. "Also, try not to think about getting arrested, hunted, or any other nervous nightmares that raise worry. The captain has a reputation for being crafty in similar situations. Doubt anything will happen to the *Saircor* while he's the skipper."

"You're right. Can't forget there's a reason he's in charge."

Lakada nodded and stepped back inside. Before closing the door, he said, "Water should be on by the time you return. See ya, Carvosa."

The door latched shut. Edin returned to the laundry room, feeling refreshed after speaking with Lakada. Even though the captain was eccentric in his leadership, he was the type of untamed and uncontrollable individual anyone would want on their side in a skirmish. The captain would make sure they were safe. But had someone on board really planted the tracker?

Why am I even worried? He wanted off and away from everyone. His only desire was to disappear. The captain was an undomesticated ogre, not a born leader. It would be best to not get jammed up in this tracker problem.

He washed the coveralls and uniforms throughout the morning. He viewed this chore in the same manner he viewed washing the dishes; the ship should have had droids on board to handle the tedious errands. But the captain's dated philosophies disagreed with the use of droids. "Machines will overtake mankind one day if we're not careful," he would say frequently. Edin knew the true reason the captain avoided droids: cheap ones were easily hackable and programmable. The captain would never have full control over the ship if robots were marching around.

Edin bounced a rubber ball against the wall while waiting for the loads to finish. No one bothered him for two hours.

After the clothes were folded, Edin returned the laundry to the staterooms and the berthing areas. While walking the upper decks where the passageways were silver and polished, the tactical officer, Atam Fitz, asked him to check the oil and fuel in the vehicles in the hangar bay. They had to be ready by the time the ship landed.

Edin ate an early lunch on the mess deck. Forlingo had fried kulliben and soaked it in hot sauce and prepared mashed vegetables as a side. He nodded to Edin as the boy shuffled through the galley line, and Edin could tell by Forlingo's stressed expression that the kenjenk wished he had some assistance that day.

Edin sat and devoured the meal in minutes before anyone could speak to him. He didn't want anyone else questioning him about the tracker. The small crowd on the mess deck seemed preoccupied with their own conversations anyway. He dropped off his silverware on the shelf next to the sink and walked out.

The hangar bay was at the front of the ship on the lower levels, directly starboard of the cargo hold. They were the two largest sections aboard. Before entering the hangar bay, Edin stopped at the door for the cargo hold. He glanced down the long, smoggy corridor, checking for crewmembers, and then snapped his head back to peek through the small square window. There were fifteen pallets stacked high and covered with black vinyl over the atomic warheads.

"Holy insanity," he whispered.

Edin spent the rest of the day doing maintenance on the vehicles. The hangar was a spacious compartment with a very high ceiling where hydraulic lines and electrical wires interweaved like spiderwebs. Yellow toolboxes lining the starboard wall held every tool one would need for simple repairs. In the front, the large hangar door stood tall.

The ship possessed two types of small ground transports—windcycles and glidecars. The windcycle, an aerodynamically engineered bike, hovered aboveground instead of using traditional wheels. The ship carried six. They had chrome bodies with hints of corrosion and wear alongside the antigravity engines. For Edin to change the oil in these, he had to remove the black leather seat to access the maintenance area.

The glidecars were old and stubborn hovercrafts, red paint and orange rust coating their wide bodies. Eighteen feet long, their main function was to haul payloads in the flatbeds or on the floating platforms attached to the rear. Edin inspected, oiled, and cleaned the eight vehicles until late in the laborious night.

Streaks of grease dampened his coveralls. His lower back was sore and bruised from the captain's early-morning violence. He stretched his back out, gazed at his dirty hands, and smeared them along his tired legs. *One more working day until we land on Lathas*, he thought.

He walked the entire length of the *Saircor* to return to his wrecked living area, grateful the day was over. Time to finally rest. When he twisted the hatch, his eyes widened in shock. The padlock was shattered on the red toolbox, and the lid had been ripped off.

He dropped to his knees and searched the metal box he used to hold his dearest belongings. *No, don't be gone; please don't be gone*, he thought. His hands moved faster. *Where are you? Where are you?*

Relief washed over him when he spotted the emerald charm glimmering off the golden necklace. He clutched his only sentimental belonging and brought it to his chest. *But what did they take?* He rifled through the old coins and found that the only thing missing was the plasma pistol.

He would need the weapon if he planned to escape. He kicked the toolbox with rage and slammed his fist in the wall. He knew who stole it and why.

CHAPTER 3

"Brace for deceleration!" the intercom screamed through the ship. "I repeat, brace for deceleration!"

Edin sat on a chair attached to the bulkhead and buckled the safety belt. He was in the back of the ship, near the fuel storage tank. The ship would confront turbulence when decelerating out of parabolic. He gripped the red straps that tightly clutched his torso.

The intercom began to countdown.

"Five! Four! Three!"

This is going to be rough, he thought.

"Two!"

He closed his eyes.

"One!"

The ship yanked downwards ferociously, pitching and rolling uncontrollably in the bridge's attempt to regain control. The straps dug into his flesh as his body jerked around the seat. Even with his hearing protection, the sound of clanging metal and dying engines hammered his eardrums. White knuckles maintained a firm grasp over the fastenings securing his bony torso. Ten seconds it lasted.

Then the ship returned to stability.

Edin unfasted the straps and stood. He wore a fresh pair of black coveralls and the black leather boots he'd polished the night before. His blond hair was cleaner than it had been in months from the shampoo he stole while returning laundry to the officers' staterooms. He made sure his white skin was dirt-free before exiting the shower that morning. Today was the day he was going to escape from the captain and the *Saircor*. He had to look presentable.

He raced up the ladderwells to the main deck to get a glimpse of Lathas from space, passing a few maintainers in the passageway. He gave them a smile and a nod. They smiled back. Excitement drifted through the stale air. Everyone was fatigued from floating across dead space. It was always refreshing to see that life and civilization and hope existed within the galaxy—even if you didn't have permission to go out on liberty.

But arrival wasn't the only reason for his grin. The sly plot to ditch the crew gave Edin an all-important secret over them. And then his thoughts slid to the small but useful plasma pistol stolen from his toolbox. The weapon would have tripled his chances of escaping successfully.

He knew the captain was the culprit—that the captain had noticed the locked box that morning when he woke Edin and decided to return to the compartment when Edin was working in the hangar. The box must have looked suspicious with the bright-red paint and the digital padlock. If the captain had concerns about Edin being the traitor who planted the tracker, then there would be no other option besides rummaging the tiny chamber.

Edin reached the main deck and walked up a spiral stairway that led to the catwalk. Located between two of the upper decks, the catwalk was a footbridge enclosed by a tube of transparent glass that provided a wondrous sight. The view was far more glorious than he had dreamed.

Lathas glowed below in a strange spectrum. Jungles spread over the two largest continents with bright-orange flora and ranges of fields alternating between yellow and red. The third and southernmost continent had countryside and verdant mountains. The oceans grew deeper blue farther from the coastlines, and purple auroras swayed over the iridescent planet.

The intercom had yet to call out any signs of danger. The rest of the crew were supposed to be at their battle stations due to the threat of the discovered tracker, but Edin saw no other ship in the vicinity—no vessel chasing them out of parabolic.

A metal satellite orbited the planet in front of them. It zipped by, and he wondered at the speed. For ten minutes, he stood on the catwalk, waiting and watching for more silver satellites to pass. The planet would become his home, whether he entered the gauntlet or not; this was where he would begin anew.

The intercom speaker crackled, then loudly screeched when it came online.

"All clear. We will be landing on Lathas shortly."

The ship shivered before accelerating down to the planet. Edin left the catwalk and headed for the hangar bay.

After they landed, the crew turned the engines and computers offline. Power came from a backup generator to light the passageways and mission-critical compartments. A group of officers walked the exterior of the *Saircor*, checking to see if the outer shell picked up damage on the voyage. Edin followed them with a leather notebook and wrote down any discrepancies they mentioned. There were a few small dents and scratches along the hull. Grime and smudge smeared the exhaust ports. Nothing of significance. The officers ordered him to wash, repair, and repaint as much as possible when they left for the rendezvous.

Outside the ship, he swiveled his head and gazed at their environment. The spaceship was settled in a yellow meadow where the surrounding plants stood tall and swayed with the warm breeze. In the distance stood the jungles he had seen from orbit. Trees towered up to three hundred feet. They had dark-gold trunks and thick branches that dipped low and forked sporadically, the leaves a rich orange he had never seen before. That was where he would journey when the opening to depart provided itself. They would never find him in those woods.

He walked to the front of the ship; the metal structure looked awkward compared to open nature. Beads of sweat rolled down his neck and into the coveralls. He was surprised they hadn't landed at a docking station or on a reliable tarmac. *It must be because of the contraband.*

The ramps for the cargo hold and hangar bay were lowered to the ground. The glidecars were already out of the hangar. Most of the crew stood outside and watched the loadmasters load the freight onto the beds and the floating platforms. They used a small drivable machine, a quiklift, to lift the pallets with mechanical grippers and placed them down gently.

Edin could tell by the nervousness in the crowd and from the loadmasters that this was not a typical shipment. Atomic warheads could explode with a simple mishap in operation, a slip of a mechanical finger, a random accident. It was madness. He had never been a part of a smuggling operation this tense.

Captain Jameson strolled through the hangar and wandered down the steel ramp to the yellow grass. His long black hair was pulled back into a ponytail. He put the electronic cigarette to his mouth and inhaled deeply, exhaling a dense cloud that covered his stretched face. His lips twisted into a smirk while he watched the last atomics being unloaded from the empty cargo bay. He noticed Edin standing by himself and marched towards him.

Not now. Edin had hoped he wouldn't ever have to speak to the captain again. Jameson stopped in front of him and slowly pulled the plasma pistol from the pocket in his black jacket. He spun the pistol on his finger until it was a blur, then tossed it skywards and caught the gun with his finger while maintaining the rapid spin.

"I got fancy tricks," the captain said, the smoking device hanging from his lip.

Edin tried to show no emotion, no reaction. But he burned with fury. He wanted to snatch the pistol away.

"Ain't fancy enough to know who planted that tracker," Edin responded.

The captain scowled. He stopped spinning the gun and returned it to his jacket. He spat, "You're lucky there are people out here, junior. I don't do that talking-back nonsense."

Edin stood motionless, unsure what to say next. He had surprised himself with that remark, considering the tracker was the gravest insecurity in the captain's head. It was a direct shot at Jameson's competence as a skipper—especially if someone on board was plotting against him.

Edin shook his head and said, "Alright."

They stared at each other. The captain broke eye contact and spat a wad of brown saliva on the grass. He opened his mouth to speak but instead turned and walked to the glidecars, shouting in a raspy voice at the horde of misfits awaiting orders to get their foolish selves in the vehicles; it was time to go.

Sunbeams glistened on the shiny metal of the ship and the vinyl covering the pallets. Edin wiped the sweat from his brow with his sleeve. The two glidecars situated in the back were empty of passengers and cargo until Forlingo and Lakada hobbled down the ramps of the hangar bay and situated themselves in the driver seats. Their orange skin was bright under the sun. Edin remembered they were headed to the capital, Kosabar, to get food and other perishables in the marketplace.

A blue spacecraft flew over them. Everyone outside studied it as it whizzed by, headed south towards the capital. It vanished under the orange tree line. Edin failed to recognize the body or any designations on the ship that hinted at its purpose. It was too tiny and too fast to characterize. *Hopefully not a patroller or a hunter.*

Captain Jameson shouted at the crew to hurry up once again. The crewmembers cranked the engines on the glidecars, dark smoke puffing out of the rattling exhaust pipes. They were all operational and hovering two feet above the earth. A few of the officers cranked up the windcycles and showboated by whipping around in tricky turns. They hovered a foot higher than the glidecars but were significantly smaller.

The troop of floating transports began to move forward, away from the starship. The windcycles zipped around and in between the glidecars. The tall warheads, concealed by the black covering, stood vertical on the flatbeds and on the trailing platforms being towed. They were strapped down with automated ratchet straps. Edin thought the cargo looked unevenly secured. Even though the atomics weren't wobbling, they appeared to be tilted.

Most of the transports headed north, opposite of Kosabar, with thick fumes rising behind. Forlingo and Lakada headed for two large openings at the southern end of the meadow. Edin was never told of the meeting points but knew all parties were expected to return by nightfall.

"Carvosa!" someone yelled as Edin watched the transports dissolve into the horizon. He pivoted to face Atam Fitz, the tactical officer. Atam was a short, flabby human with a noticeable limp. His two petite legs were bent like they had once been broken and never healed properly. His hairline dropped back to his awkward ears. Of course he would be the one they left behind.

"We're fueling here in a minute. I already called up the local station, and they're sending a replenishment oiler," Fitz said. "It's probably on the way."

"Roger that," Edin said.

Atam trailed behind like a slow child while they headed back to the stern of the ship on the starboard side. Humming to himself, he opened up the fueling station panel. Edin leaned back against the hull and stared off into the clear sky.

It would be easy to escape from Atam. The man was not physically or mentally equipped to catch Edin. However, Atam would use one of the radios to transmit to the captain if anything irregular happened. *How to avoid this? Sabotage the communications systems? No,* Edin answered himself. Then he remembered the airlock.

The fueling station was one of the systems that ran on the backup generator. The airlock system did too. After they finished fueling, Edin would try and convince Atam to walk through the airlocked entrance and then secure the door behind him before Atam entered the second door, entrapping him within. Edin would simply tell him that the switches were malfunctioning, that he would go to the bridge to unlock the door at the backup control panel. But instead he would sprint to the hangar. He had counted the windcycles as they left and knew at least one remained on board.

They waited at the fueling station for forty-five minutes. His thoughts circled around the upcoming escape; he wondered if the anticipation anxiety would go away.

Edin heard the large replenishment oiler before he saw it. Towards the east, the bulky ship gradually came into view above the tree line. Titanic and shaped like a rectangle with a superstructure on top, it moved so slowly that it seemed to float instead of fly. The hull was painted a dark gray with lime-green trimmings. With each passing second, the volume of its engines grew in earsplitting intensity. The oiler eventually made it over the open meadow and landed roughly a hundred feet away from the port side of the *Saircor*. It kept its loud engines online.

Edin inspected the ship while waiting for a fueler to exit. The name was stenciled near the stern: *Guadacanoe*. A door on the bottom level burst open, and a man in purple coveralls emerged. He opened up a large access area containing a control panel and a thick hose wrapped around a bronze reel. He grabbed the hose and dragged it across the yellow grass. Edin decided to meet the fueler halfway. In the middle of the meadow, the fueler handed the hose to Edin and gave him a crooked smile. The engines were too loud for them to speak to each other. Edin wondered why the old man seemed so happy during a fueling operation.

The hose was heavy and hard to grip. He heaved it over his shoulder and felt his thigh muscles strain. Once he got to the *Saircor*, he connected the hose to the fuel port. He turned around and saw the fueler at the other ship, waiting by the control panel. Edin raised his arms and gave a hand signal that confirmed the connection and then a thumbs-up. The fueler returned the thumbs-up, and Edin felt the hose jerk. Fuel was flowing.

The *Saircor's* tactical officer stood in front of the opposite control panel and watched the monitor displaying the fuel levels. He had to make sure they reached over 95 percent capacity before they halted the operation. Edin waited with one hand on the hose, feeling the fluid surge into the tank. Another warm breeze brushed over his nose. He gazed to the south, to Kosabar. He lost himself in a vivid daydream of fighting in the gauntlet, winning in glorious triumph, the spectators of the arena rising and chanting his name in a rhythmic chorus.

Minutes later, a hand waved in his line of sight. He snapped out of the trance. Atam was giving the "kill it" hand signal; he dragged one finger across his throat like a blade. Edin acknowledged, then waved across the field to the fueler to get his attention. He gave a thumbs-up signal to cut off the pump. When fuel halted, Edin disconnected the hose and crossed over the grass to the other spaceship, where the fueler spun the reel that was gathering the tube.

The fueler gave Edin a fist bump when the hose was secured. Then he closed the panel and went inside the *Guadacanoe*. The ship lifted off the ground as Edin walked away. The force of the takeoff produced a gust of wind that pushed against his back. He spotted Atam shutting the panel for their fueling station. Now was the time. The replenishment oiler had disappeared behind the orange trees when Edin arrived in front of Atam. The escape plan entered the first phase.

"Hey, sir," Edin said. "I was wondering if you could help me with something in the engine control room."

Atam looked puzzled. "With what?"

"I have to do some periodic maintenance while the engines are shut down," Edin lied. "I'll need someone to pass me up a torque wrench after I climb up one of the shafts."

"Oh, okay." Atam nodded, sweat trickling from his balding forehead. "We might as well knock that out now."

"Yessir. I would just throw the wrench up there before I climb up. But I don't want to mess up the torque wrench or damage something on the engine. You know how the captain is."

"No problem, Carvosa. I understand."

"Thanks."

They circled the stern of the ship to the starboard side. Edin led and Atam wobbled behind. The nearest entrance to the engine control room was the lower airlock that Krebs had been ejected from. Edin picked up his pace and reached the airlock first. He pressed a sequence of numbers on the keypad, and the door hissed open. He entered the ship and walked through the second door of the airlock. A second later, Atam came strolling around the corner. Edin hoped that Atam was naïve and didn't think this was intentional.

As soon as Atam entered the first door, Edin pressed the keypad to disabled the airlock's inner control panel and to shut the two metal doors, leaving the tactical officer trapped inside.

CHAPTER 4

"Carvosa! Let me out!" Atam slammed his fist against the metal door.

"The system must have malfunctioned!" Edin formed his best worried frown through the glass window. "I swear, I only tried to close the outer door!"

Atam's flabby face reddened with anger. "Well, go up to the bridge and fix it!"

"Roger," Edin said sympathetically. "I'll be back in a minute."

"Hurry up! I don't have all day!"

Edin spun around and sprinted. He sprinted all the way back to his little compartment near the engine bay. He swung open the hatch and grabbed the black backpack. It was heavy and contained all the golden coins he had kept locked away, the emerald necklace, and two books of fiction that he had yet to read. Hoping the coins might be worth something in the city, he left the dreadful storage locker for the last time.

He raced up the ladderwells with quick hands on the rails and feet striking the steel steps. His legs pumped quicker and quicker while he accelerated through the passageways and prayed that no one was returning anytime soon.

How long would Atam remain in the airlock? Edin considered whether there was any way for the tactical officer to communicate with outside parties, the captain or Forlingo. He hadn't noticed Atam in possession of a radio set while they fueled. And the airlock was only capable of internal communications. Atam should be trapped in there for a while. *Hopefully.*

When Edin arrived, the hangar bay was empty besides the one windcycle. The last hovering vehicle looked to be the oldest one the ship possessed. Edin knew the fuel and oil levels were on point, but he had no idea about the operating efficiency. There must be a reason it was the only one left behind. The door to the outside remained open, and the ramp to the ground had not been removed. All he needed to do was jump on and take off. But there was a problem.

Edin had never operated a windcycle. He learned all the routine maintenance procedures about the craft, but he was never given the chance to drive one. He hiked his leg over the black leather seat, sat down, and gripped the handlebars before starting the antigravity engine. A heavy breath escaped his lungs.

Let's go, he told himself.

He flipped a red switch on the left handlebar. The windcycle vibrated between his legs, which were wrapped around it like a rope. The engine pulsated as he was levitated off the steel floor. He placed his feet on the foot pedals and used his left foot to push the shifter into reverse. With his right hand, he turned the throttle. The windcycle jerked back rapidly, and his hand clenched the throttle harder until the cycle slammed brutally against the bulkhead on the other side of the hangar. His body was launched into the air, and his head crashed against the metal wall.

Feeling dizzy, he stood up with the backpack. The windcycle, still on, hovered like a fluttering bird. He jumped on the seat, snatched the handlebars, and shifted out of reverse. There was no time to waste. If he couldn't figure this out, he would have to run on foot. And he truly did not favor his odds running through the jungles with no weapon. He slowly turned the throttle. The cycle leapt forward. He maintained his grip without increasing speed. He twisted the handlebars to the right. The windcycle surged into the meadow.

He scanned the yellow field, and his jaw dropped at the sight of what was emerging from the horizon. The glidecars that had gone with the captain were returning at full speed. Gloomy smoke trailed from their exhaust pipes. *What perfect timing,* he lamented. They were under two miles away. He was unsure if they had spotted him yet or why they were coming back so soon. Had Atam broken out and sent them a message? Had the transaction been smooth?

He sharply turned the windcycle to enter the jungle in a clearing three hundred yards to the right. While turning, the cycle rolled over and sent him crashing into the ground. He landed on his back. The blow knocked the breath out of his rattled lungs. He pushed himself up with his skinny arms and looked in the distance. The glidecars were on the verge of entering the yellow meadow, and Edin assumed they had noticed him by now. But there was something utterly alarming about what he witnessed: the drivers and passengers were not looking ahead but behind them.

The passengers in the glidecars shot plasma rifles at somebody on a windcycle trailing them. *Is that the traitor?* He sprinted back to his cycle and hopped on with his eyes still focused on the gunfire headed towards the ship.

Chaos ensued.

A massive green energy beam emerged from the trailing cycle and struck a glidecar, which instantly exploded into a spiral of flames. The detonation echoed across the flat land while fire whistled over the steel frame.

Edin sped towards the tree line, constantly glancing over his shoulder to see. He swore his eyes told a lie.

None of the other windcycles returned with the party. The meadow contained only the five glidecars, with all the atomics already unloaded, and the unknown assailant that followed. Edin assumed whoever it was had disposed of the other windcycles. But the green energy beam seemed to come from the assailant's hand, not a gun or weapon.

Three more glidecars burst into balls of fire after being struck by the light. Edin reached the jungle as the last two were approaching the hangar. He hovered behind a thick tree on the edge of the meadow. Far away, the assailant on the windcycle wore a long black cloak, and his hair looked silver in the sunlight. He wasn't a crewmember of the *Saircor*. Edin guessed the stranger was a bounty hunter hired by an underground criminal organization.

But the green energy—how is he doing that? And where are the warheads?

Two additional glidecars entered the meadow. Forlingo and Lakada were driving them, and they were hauling no cargo. The captain must have radioed them before they even reached the city. Forlingo and Lakada fired the forward cannons at the rogue windcycle. The assailant spun around and dodged the plethora of red beams with clever maneuvers. He zipped across the meadow and raised his right hand. Two green orbs of energy manifested, and he hurled them with frightening velocity.

It felt like a fist to the gut when Forlingo's glidecar exploded; Edin gasped. Lakada's exploded next. They were no match for the cosmic wizardry. The black cloak swayed behind the assailant as he whipped between the fires and back to the *Saircor* to assassinate the last of his victims.

The four remaining crewmembers exited the two glidecars and marched towards the ambusher. A technician and an ordnanceman led an officer and Captain Jameson. All four held plasma rifles in their arms as they approached certain death.

Edin realized the assailant was a manipulator—someone who possessed the ability to manipulate cosmic energy, a power referred to as the Gift. The Gifted were a unique and rare class of mortals. Edin wondered why one would become a bounty hunter. Typically, the Gifted had advanced schooling and were hired by a lucrative firm in the First System or an agency with the royal dynasty. This man appeared more savage than sophisticated in the way he killed and progressed to the next. It was the first time Edin had seen a manipulator. He never wanted to see one again.

The Gifted assassin leapt from the speeding windcycle and miraculously landed on his two feet. The captain screamed, but Edin was too far to distinguish the words. A part of him wanted to move closer to get a better view of the captain's last stance. The captain and the other three charged, firing plasma rifles. Purple blasts rocketed across the soft air, but the assailant backhanded one of the purple beams and sent it soaring over the jungle. *That's not possible*, Edin marveled. The other flashes of violet missed badly. The assailant lifted both hands. Four green orbs of swirling energy materialized from nothing. He slung his arms, and the glowing spheres rained down upon his prey, causing an eruption of smoke, dirt, and body parts.

"He's dead," Edin whispered. "Captain Jameson is dead."

The dark cloud climbed into the clear sky. The yellow grass was charred black and showed no signs of life. The assailant brushed the filth off his legs and shoulders. He was walking back to his hovering windcycle when he twisted around and stared intently at Edin.

How can he see me? That's impossible. Edin stared back. He did not know what to do. The assailant broke the glare, sprinted, and hopped on the windcycle.

"I'm in trouble."

The assassin had completed his mission—kill Captain Rhygert Jameson.

Others died, others who might not have been involved in the betrayal and thievery that the assassin's family had suffered. But after seeing the atomics that the smugglers handed over to the Sheeban Syndicate, he felt no remorse for the massacre. *No telling what planet the syndicate blows up within the next year. Not my problem.* His grandfather would be proud that these lowlife pirates had been exterminated, that the family had been avenged to an extent. Even if was impossible to even the tally.

In the meadow, fires flared around glidecars and windcycles and body parts. He brushed off his pants before walking back to the sole windcycle. He wanted to stay on the planet longer—visit the casino in Kosabar, maybe order a plate of fresh fish. But he knew local authorities would soon be investigating this nightmarish scene. Once they discovered it was the infamous Rhygert Jameson and the *Saircor*, they would inform other establishments within the solar system and possibly get the royal dynasty involved. The assassin had no desire to involve himself further in the scenario.

Before he reached his windcycle, he sensed another antigravity engine nearby. Instantly he snapped his neck towards the jungle, where his one robotic eye zoomed in rapidly, making out the features of a teenage boy. *Was he with the* Saircor? *It's not possible . . .*

The assassin leapt on the windcycle, turned the throttle, and sped towards the boy, who vanished amongst the massive trees.

Edin fled deeper into the jungle. At first, he could hear the other windcycle trailing. But the assailant never caught up with him and disappeared within fifteen minutes. Edin questioned why the unknown phantom left the pursuit, but figured there were more important things than chasing a fifteen-year-old. He spent an hour dodging trees at deadly speeds and glanced over his shoulder a million times before finally concluding that he was not being tracked anymore.

The jungle was filled with strange sights. The golden trunks twisted in odd shapes, with gnarled branches overlapping one another and vines snaking from limb to limb with razor thorns. Orange leaves swayed in the thick canopy, but the dead leaves on the floor turned bloodred. Sunlight rarely reached the damp ground.

He stopped to pee in a thicket. It was refreshing to get off his rear and stretch his legs, but Edin kept his head on a swivel with scouting eyes, just to be safe. His stomach growled. He wished he had packed snacks in the backpack.

To Edin, being hungry and lost on Lathas was better than slaving away on the ship. The wilderness felt alive. This was freedom; this was living—breathing real air, standing in real gravity. All he had to do now was make it to the city, find housing, and earn some coins. Then he could study the dynamics of the gauntlet. He would enter if a chance of victory existed.

But he did feel remorseful about the entire situation. Even the captain's death had a bittersweet taste. The captain had never admitted it, but Edin knew the captain thought Edin would grow into a smuggling elite one day and had discretely attempted to render the boy his heir. That was the major conflict Edin had with the skipper. Edin resented his future being predetermined. He wanted to create his own path and forge a destiny outside of the smuggling profession. He held a clean record with the dynasty and every solar system within the galaxy. There was no firm reason to pursue a life of lawlessness.

From what he gathered, the gauntlet provided an opportunity unlike any other. He hoped everything he heard was true. *Fight for more than your glory and pride; fight for a future.* From a smuggling vessel to a high academy in the First System—imagine that.

After the short break, he spent another hour on the windcycle, riding south along the rocky embankment of a ravine. His knuckles were white on the handlebars. The leafy canopy split over the stream, and sunbeams refracted over the rushing water. His blond hair morphed into a frantic mess in the wind. Under his coveralls, currents of air dried the sweat.

As he pushed forward, he came across a steep waterfall plummeting into a rounded lake. He hovered at the height of the falls and looked below at the orange canopy and tiny birds fluttering. Narrow channels from the lake ran under the trees, eastward. On the far side, an old wooden dock extended in the calm water from a sandy beach. Behind the dock was a marina, and behind the marina was a little town. *It must be an outer community of Kosabar,* he thought.

The main street ran between two lines of brick buildings. In the middle of the town, a wishing well stood like a worshiped statue. White smoke escaped from the black funnels of a restaurant on the corner.

Glidecars were parked along the strip, and people walked from the road to the shops, unaware of the boy watching from above. It looked remote and peaceful. No signs of bounty hunters.

At the falls, the incline was too steep to drive down. He swerved into the jungle to find a safe path. While hovering to the lake, he realized anticipation kept intensifying since landing on Lathas. He was going to speak with new humans and different species. Maybe he would even talk to a girl. His face reddened at the thought. While stuck on the all-male *Saircor*, he had not seen a girl in three years. How would he speak to one?

After navigating the path, he sped past the lake and the small marina. The town was named Corbson, according to the bronze plaque standing beside the wishing well. Four timber columns hoisted the shingled roof of the well over a gray cobblestone base, and a bucket dangled on a hempen rope tied to a crossbeam. He dismounted the cycle and peeked inside the rustic well. Dark nothingness. He reached inside his backpack, grabbed a coin, and flicked into the abyss. He wished for triumph in the gauntlet.

He rode the windcycle down the main strip. The brick buildings were old, and some were even empty. Most of the traffic was in front of the diner and the general store. He spotted a family, two adults and three kids, leaving the diner with bright smiles. He wondered if he'd spent his coin on the wrong wish and felt an awkward mix of jealousy and sadness. He'd remained shy and quiet on the *Saircor* because he never felt he fit in. Perhaps a stray child was a better match for the smugglers than for law-abiding citizens. He knew nothing of traditional family.

At the end of the strip was a crossroad and a large concrete building with a glowing sign; the purple lettering read *Corbson Hoverparts*. Edin parked his windcycle in front and walked through the sliding glass doors. Inside, the shop was overly bright and spacious. It smelled of fresh metal and leather. The tall shelving held parts he never knew existed on ground transports. He glanced down the row for hydraulics.

"Hello, sir. Need any help today?" asked a squeaky voice.

Edin spun around and saw nothing until he looked down. The question came from a ball of black-blue fur. The small creature had canine ears, a pointed snout with a wet nose, and stood on two legs with wolf paws. His hands were paws too. He wore denim overalls and moon-shaped spectacles over icy-blue eyes.

"Um, actually, yeah, I have a question," Edin said. "Do you guys purchase windcycles?"

"Of course we do."

"How much could I get for one?"

"Depends on the model and condition."

"Well, I have one outside. I would like to get an estimate."

Edin followed the little doglike creature, who bobbed on his paws while walking. He told Edin his name was Chapster and that he was six years old in human years but around twelve in worefann years, his species. Edin did not know what to tell Chapster about himself. What would he say? That he was fifteen and running away from a bounty hunter who had the Gift and who already killed the other people he was fleeing from? The less shared, the better.

Chapster inspected the windcycle and scribbled notes on a white pad. He muttered under his breath while checking the antigravity engine. He nodded and licked his chops with his long pink tongue.

"Alright, just got to get to the computer, punch in the numbers, and get your total," Chapster said. "But why are you selling her?"

"Um . . ." Edin paused. "I just need the coin."

Chapster laughed. "Don't we all."

They walked back inside and to the old computer next to the cash register. Chapster entered numbers on the keyboard rapidly while staring at the thin monitor. The coin drawer unlocked and slid open. Edin received five thousand dynasty credits—black coins with red outlines. They felt fresh in his hands and weighed significantly less than his old gold coins. He asked Chapster if he knew anything about the pre-dynasty coins that he possessed. The ball of fluff said they might be exchanged for dynasty credits at a pawn shop or by a collector in the capital. He told Edin to set up an account with a bank for digital currency; it wasn't smart to carry that many coins on one's person.

Before they wished each other a farewell, Chapster called a taxicab to pick up Edin and take him to Kosabar.

CHAPTER 5

The cab driver was an android, a skeleton of dark steel with red wires running underneath. Two ruby lights glowed from his metal skull like eyes. He stated his name was A-Veetwo when he picked up Edin in the old glidecar.

"Can you take me to a hotel in the midtown area?" Edin asked. "Somewhere very cheap."

"Yes," A-Veetwo said. "I have the perfect place."

The voyage to the capital was quiet. The android didn't speak a word while he gripped the steering wheel and glared ahead with lifeless eyes. Jameson had always talked about artificial intelligence negatively, but Edin had no experience with the machines to pass his own judgment. He tried to conceal his discomfort by inspecting the small towns they passed.

The towns grew wider and busier. Eventually the android drove through a sprawling suburb that led to a four-lane highway. Horns honked from surrounding ground transports. Edin smiled when he spotted a sign marking Kosabar city limits. The silhouette of the skyline appeared ahead. The red sun dipped below the summit, making the heavens look as if they were painted with pastel colors. In the darkening sky, spaceships zipped to and from the glass towers and outer space like insects swarming a crowded hive.

They turned down a street packed with taverns and lounges. Loud music flooded the concrete sidewalks. The bright hues of digital billboards and business signs illuminated the jazzy scene. Not only humans but also foreign species in various shapes and sizes and colors entered and exited buildings. *This is already much better than being stranded in space*, he thought.

"How much further? And where exactly are we going?" Edin asked.

"I am dropping you off at the Pebble Inn," A-Veetwo said. "It is across the bridge in the midtown district. Right now, we are in the university district."

"Oh, okay."

"Don't worry. It is inexpensive. And I personally know the owner. You will be satisfied."

"Alright." Edin wondered how an android knew anyone *personally*.

They drove over a silver bridge hoisted by thick cables. The bridge inclined to a high point that lingered on a spectacular view of the city. It was his first time seeing the Kosabar Arena, the stadium for the gauntlet, which was built of brown stones with an open roof bordered by rising battlements.

The bridge dropped back down, and the dark water running beneath reflected all of the scattered lights. After crossing the river, the glidecar turned sharply onto a narrow road. It was shadowy and dead silent. Streetlamps flickered and faded. Edin felt anxious. Alleys empty of people and music produced inverse vibes to the environs on the opposite side of the bridge. They drove for a couple more minutes in the darkness. Then the android halted the vehicle.

"Here we are, Mr. Carvosa." The android pointed a finger out the window. "That is the Pebble Inn."

The six-story hotel leaned to the left like it had been damaged by an earthquake and never restored. Black shingles draped the gabled roof, creeping vines concealed the mysterious windows, and dark-gray bricks and mortar molded the walls. The wooden double doors of the entrance were lit with torches held by crumbling gargoyles.

"Are you sure there isn't a better place?" Edin asked.

"This is as close to midtown you will get for a cheap fee," A-Veetwo said. "It is the perfect place for you."

"I'm sure it is." Edin shook his head. "Thanks for the ride."

The backpack hanging from his shoulder, he opened the door and stepped on the dirty sidewalk. The street was silent besides the humming exhaust of the glidecar driving off and leaving him by his lonesome.

The Pebble Inn, vacant of guests and nightlife, looked like an abandoned hideout for runaway criminals. Edin walked up the concrete stairs, past the gargoyles, and approached the daunting doors. Hopefully the silver-haired bounty hunter would not find him here. But Edin doubted that the assailant was still on the planet. *Probably on his way to collect the reward for the hit on the* Saircor.

Edin wondered if he should knock or just walk in. He raised a hand to the metal knocker shaped like an owl, then pulled his hand back and resolutely twisted the doorknob, pressing against the door with his shoulder. The hardwood floor creaked beneath his foot as he entered.

Lit by antique sconces, the lobby was a small and unoccupied space. Oak columns rose to the cobwebbed ceiling. The floor continued to creak as he shuffled forward and the door shut behind him. He pivoted around in alarm, expecting to see something, but saw nothing. Turning back, he spotted a marble reception desk with no receptionist. He walked up to it. Paperwork and stationery cluttered the top of the desk. Behind it was a white door. He inspected the desk and spotted a bronze service bell. He slammed his palm on it. The sound ricocheted loudly.

Surprised shouts came from behind the door. He heard someone moving around, and then the door opened. His face went cold as the blood rushed out. It was a girl.

There was a confidence in her stride. She wore a blue housekeeping dress, and her dirty-blond hair was tied in a ponytail. Her freckled cheeks glowed pink over tan skin. He had no idea how to introduce himself.

She smiled. "Welcome to the Pebble Inn. Do you need a room?"

"Um." He stared at her. Somehow, he forgot to move his lips.

She tilted her head and narrowed her eyes. "Can I help you?"

"Oh . . . yeah, I'm sorry. I need a room, for me. Just me, no one else."

She laughed. "Any preferences on the bed or room size?"

"The cheapest room you have . . . for a standard week."

"We have a room for 315 credits per week."

"That's fine."

"I just need some identification, and I can get you checked in."

"I don't have any identification. Been in space all my life."

"That's fine; just fill out these papers."

She handed him a manila folder and started whistling to herself. He scribbled his signature on the documents in the folder without reading the print entirely. He closed the folder and smiled nervously. She picked it up and looked inside.

"Mr. Edin Carvosa. You should be ready to go. I just need the payment."

He slung the black backpack around, opened it, and grabbed enough credits. He placed them on the counter. "That should be 315."

"Not paying with digital currency?"

"I don't have an account."

"You're too old to not have an account."

"I'll get one soon."

"Good. Probably should get some identification too."

"I will."

She counted and nodded in approval, then opened a drawer and pulled out a transparent keycard. She handed it to him with a piece of paper that had *Room 607* jotted on it.

"Looks like you're all set." She grinned. "If you don't mind me asking, what brings you to Kosabar?"

"Well . . ." He tapped his hands on his pants. "I'm going to enter the gauntlet."

"Wow, you're funny for a spacer." She snickered. "Well, my name is Vanya. If you need anything, don't hesitate to ring the front desk."

"My name is Edin."

She pointed at the folder. "I know."

He entered the hallway to the right of the reception desk. Relief rinsed over him. He hadn't spoken to a human girl since he was a child and didn't remember much about the conversation. Talking to females was a weakness he would need to improve upon. He contemplated why she had laughed at him when he mentioned the gauntlet. Did she think he was not capable enough to compete? Would he be dwarfed by the competitors? Was he a joke to her?

Quit questioning yourself.

He pressed a circular button, and the elevator doors split open. He stepped inside and let out a deep breath. The day had dragged on forever.

The elevator smelled like burnt toast. It jerked roughly and then moaned all the way up to the sixth floor. He slid the keycard in the slot at 607, and the door unbolted. The room was dim even with the overhead light turned on. A small bed with a striped comforter was pushed against the brick wall. A digital display hung over a writing table. An armchair and a floor lamp conquered an entire corner by themselves. The grimy window gave him a view from the backside of the Pebble Inn. He looked outside only to see another dark alleyway. He turned the bedroom light off.

He slipped into the bed, but before going to sleep, he heard a rodent scurrying in the ceiling.

The next morning, he made it to the Eastern Marketplace on foot. He needed clothes and items for the upcoming week. The bazaar was loud and crowded with various species, humans in the majority. Vendors shouted from behind their wooden booths, promoting local fish or imported vegetables. The smell of frying conch fritters smacked him in the face as he finished making his purchases. He wanted nothing more than to follow his nose inside a little cantina with a straw roof. But he had his hands full and needed to return to the Pebble Inn.

He walked along the cobblestone pathway following the river. The veins in his forearms swelled as he gripped seven different paper bags. He'd spent four hundred credits on all the items: a brown leather vest, clean undershirts, wool trousers, bronze boots, toiletries, sandwich meat, and bread. Ground transports whizzed by him, and spaceships roared overhead. The blazing sun signaled it was midday. He hurried along because he had another errand to run before sundown. He was going to officially sign up for the gauntlet.

The walk back was three miles. For the first time, he deeply considered what had happened the day before. All of his old crewmembers were now dead—unless Atam Fitz found a way to break out of the airlock and flee to safety. But the bounty hunter probably raided the *Saircor*. And Edin guessed the ship had already been stripped of its parts by local scavengers. Most of the gizmos and gadgets on board could be sold, and the rising smoke from the exploding glidecars would have drawn attention to the area. No telling who or what had already visited. Part of him wanted to go back and look around, make sure of Atam's fate, but he knew it would be fruitless.

When he returned to the Pebble Inn, he labored up the concrete steps. He was unsure of how far he had traveled that morning, but he could tell his burning legs were not prepared for the gravity on Lathas. He pushed his shoulder against the oak door and entered the ghostly building. Behind the reception desk, Vanya was writing something down. She looked up when he entered the lobby.

"Went shopping, I see."

He wobbled up to the desk. "You could say that."

"Need any help with that?"

"No. But could you call me a cab? I need to go to the Casino of Lathas."

"Yeah. I'll have one here in no time." She studied the bags in his hands. "But you probably shouldn't be gambling if you're staying in this hotel. Not to get in your personal affairs, but you've already been shopping today. You might need to save some money."

"I'm not going there to gamble."

She tilted her head. "Then what are you going for?"

"I told you last night. I'm entering the gauntlet, and I must speak with the gamewarden."

Her jaw dropped. His eyes widened. They stared at each other.

"What?" he asked irritably.

"I thought you were kidding. You know you will die, right? The gauntlet is suicide."

"You don't know anything about me." He turned to leave. "Just call a cab."

Edin changed out of the coveralls, showered, and donned the new clothes. His stomach growled. He fixed a sandwich and ate quickly. The receiver box rang, and he pressed the yellow button to receive the transmission. Over the intercom, Vanya told him that the cab was outside.

He rushed to the lobby, but Vanya was no longer at the reception desk. When he stepped outside the double doors, he was surprised to see the same android picking him up. A-Veetwo was in the driver seat of the old glidecar they'd ridden in yesterday.

"You again?" Edin asked after opening the door.

"I believe so, Mr. Carvosa."

Edin jumped inside, and the glidecar sped down the empty street.

"Do you have a contract with the Pebble Inn?" Edin asked.

"This glidecar and I are owned by Mr. Waldrip."

"Who is that?"

"The owner of the Pebble Inn. You have met his daughter—Vanya Waldrip at the reception desk."

"I was wondering why a pretty girl worked there." Edin covered his mouth. He snapped his head towards the droid and pointed a finger at it. "Don't tell her I said that."

A-Veetwo laughed mechanically. "I won't mention it, Mr. Carvosa."

As they drove deeper into the metropolis, the buildings grew taller and wider. A few skyscrapers disappeared into the low-hovering clouds with spacecraft buzzing around them. Hovering buses and taxis weaved between lanes. Cafes and condos and shops crammed every corner. He spotted young children bouncing a rubber ball against the walls in a backstreet. He admired the city's contrast between ancient and modern when noticing a wooden seven-story pagoda.

"What is that old temple for?" Edin asked.

"It is a museum now. It was built millennia ago as a holy place for the old religion called the Order of the Oracles." A-Veetwo changed lanes. "They believed all of the Gifted were abominations, and they frowned upon the dynasty. They challenged House Heiros and were eventually wiped blank."

"I've heard of the oracle religion. Didn't think I'd see a shrine on Lathas, though."

"Oracles ruled before the dynasty. Their constructions and sculptures are still standing on many planets in the fringes."

"Interesting."

They drove south towards the ocean. Eventually they arrived on Blue Street, the most frequented tourist area in the city. Large pubs and saloons faced each other on either side. Lively songs drifted out of tiered balconies and lingered over the boulevard. Drunkards roamed from one side to the other with drinks in hand while dodging the floating traffic. The glidecar turned on Blue Street next to the Kosabar Arena.

Ahead stood a glass tower with *Casino of Lathas* engraved in golden letters on a bright sign. The casino comprised a crystal cylinder held by steel beams rising from the egg-shaped foundation. Sunbeams rebounded off the wraparound windows of the condos on the upper floors. The glidecar neared the marvelous structure, then halted at the curb by the entrance.

"We have arrived, Mr. Carvosa. What time should I expect you to be done?"

"Meet me back at this spot in thirty minutes. I shouldn't be long."

"Will do."

Edin opened the door and stepped out. He felt fresh. The new vest and boots looked spiffy, and the undershirt and pants were far more comfortable than coveralls. He hurried around a large fountain methodically spraying water in the air. The entryway was a revolving glass door boasting two security guards on each side. They all carried plasma rifles. Edin felt jittery at the sight and held his head down as he passed the guards and advanced into the casino.

Entering the spacious a lobby, he looked up. Columns towered from the marble floor to a high ceiling trimmed in golden plasterwork. His mouth hung open. Between the trimming, the ceiling exhibited a mural of the jungle under a night sky with a violet aurora. The aurora lingered over the rainforest, and the twinkling cosmos drifted above them all. It was the most masterful piece of art he had ever seen on display, and in the last place he expected to see such art. The phenomenon appeared more magical than natural. He snapped out of his gawking reverie.

The backdrop music merged with shouts from excited and frustrated gamblers. An overabundance of card tables covered in black felt stood to the left. Hustlers flocked to the busier tables and smoked their electronic cigarettes and drank their fancy cocktails. On the other side were slot machines with hologram displays hovering above the floor. He noticed a group of older ladies, various species, perched in front of the machines on floating stools, their eyes cemented to the holograms spinning their fortunes.

He strolled deeper into the casino where the music and shouts grew in volume. He felt the increasing warmth of the gaming floor and noticed some of the card players dripping with nervous sweat.

A short droid rolled in front of him. The blue machine had three rubber wheels for legs and a triangular torso. It carried a serving dish crammed with drinks and fried appetizers.

"Droid," Edin called.

The small droid halted its wheels. "Yes. How may I be of service?"

"Where is the gamewarden?"

It freed a mechanical arm from under the platter, then pointed. "In that back corner is the sporting quarter. The gamewarden can be found there."

Edin glanced in the direction and nodded. "Thanks."

He maneuvered around betting contraptions producing a spectrum of beeps and chirps and honks. They weren't just slot machines; they held a diversity of games he hadn't known existed. He had never been in a single room so large. It didn't feel like an indoor space at all but rather a blooming ecosystem, irrigated by rich dreams.

CHAPTER 6

I n the sporting quarter was a horseshoe bar and an expansive lounge. Video screens hung from the roof, live feeds of sporting events from across the galaxy streaming on each display. Humans and nonhumans sat on the floating stools and sipped their carbonated ales.

Beyond the bar, built into the wall in the far corner, was a workstation with a glass window. Glowing letters on a neon sign broadcasted, *The Gamewarden*.

Edin walked up to the transparent barrier. Behind the glass, a gray creature sat on an office chair, reading an article from an electronic tablet. The nonhuman had multiple layers of muscle on his shoulders and four long arms. It looked up at Edin, its black eyes bulging like a bug's.

Edin hesitated, then said, "I need to speak with the gamewarden."

"You are speaking with him now." The gamewarden flashed a smile of sharp teeth. "What do you need?"

"How do I register for the gauntlet?"

The gamewarden shifted in his chair. "You're here to register for the gauntlet tournament?"

"Yes."

"Come in through that the door." He pointed to his right, at a cutout in the wall with a shiny handle. "There's a lot we have to go over."

Edin entered through the sleek entrance. The room consisted of cubicles and walls painted white. Paper and stationery littered the desks. It was dull and depressing compared to the thriving energy of the gaming floor. The gamewarden stood and used one of his four gray arms to shake Edin's hand. The creature's skin glimmered like hardened steel, but the hand was soft and slimy.

The gamewarden pointed to a chair. "Have a seat."

Edin sat and waited for the processing to begin. He was ready to sign this life away with the hope of receiving another one in return.

"First off"—the gamewarden brushed his dress pants and took a seat—"do your parents even know you're here? I don't want anyone dropping out of the tournament the week before. This is the biggest event of the year. We like to have the contestants named and ready to go. I'll be extre—"

"I don't have any parents."

"Guardians?"

"Dead."

"Okay. Are you from Kosabar or Lathas?"

"I've been in space my whole life."

"Ah, a spacer." The gamewarden scratched his chin. "Don't worry; we've had some space urchins in the past."

Edin sat motionless with his hands in his lap. "So, I'll be able to sign up?"

"Certainly, this year we have a high need of contestants."

"Why?"

"Do you have any knowledge about the gauntlet tournament on this planet?"

"I arrived on Lathas yesterday. I heard rumors about the gauntlet in the galley of my ship. I asked someone in the Eastern Marketplace how to register, and they told me to come and speak with you."

"Yes. Speaking with me is the first step. But this is a lot more than just a swordfight in a coliseum. Especially this year."

"What is special about this year?"

"Cane Nazari. He's fighting."

Edin leaned closer. "Who is that?"

The gamewarden shook his head. "You don't have any idea about House Nazari, do you?"

"Never heard of them."

"They're the richest and proudest family on Lathas. Along with the oracles, they ruled this solar system before the dynasty claimed everything as their own. However, House Nazari still has a lot of power in this solar system."

"So? He's just a kid that comes from money and an old bloodline."

"It's not that simple." The gamewarden stretched his lower two arms. "House Nazari has won the tournament nineteen times. And they have lost a match only once. They have great trainers and nearly unlimited resources. Their entire lives are spent in preparation for this. When a contestant with their blood enters the gauntlet, the others flee."

Edin sighed in frustration. "It sounds like you're trying to talk me out of it."

"No. I just want you to be aware of the scenario before you get your hopes up."

"I still want to register," Edin said, his tone flat. "My decision is final, and I will go through with it."

"Great." The gamewarden grinned with a bit of hesitation. "But I must inform you on the rules before you sign any paperwork."

"Okay."

"There are three main rules every contestant must acknowledge. The first rule regards what is used in combat. You shall not wear any shielding, and the only weapon you are allowed to bring into the pit is the hyperblade you are given prior to the match. You will be examined by an official before entering at every match, so it's an automatically enforced rule, but folks will try to sneak anything into that arena when their life depends on it. Do you know what a hyperblade is?"

"Ye— . . . yeah." Edin knew what a hyperblade was, but he had never used one nor seen one in person.

"That wasn't the most confident answer."

"I've never used one," he admitted.

The gamewarden rolled his eyes. "That's not something I would go around confessing when you're a gauntlet contestant. Everyone else competing will have been trained in sword-to-sword combat. And most have experience with a hyperblade as well."

Edin felt worried. "Okay. I'll practice . . . or something."

"I'll go over the details. A hyperblade is just a hilt when retracted. You flip the switch, and the adamantine blade extends out around three feet." The gamewarden raised his two upper arms to signal the length of the sword and then dropped them back at his sides. "The metal blade has a band of infinity plasma running along the cutting edge. It can cut through nearly anything other than adamantine. If you're wondering why we use hyperblades, it is because of the next rule."

"Which is?"

"To win, you must kill the opponent. There is no draw. If the two contestants refuse to fight, they both will be executed on-site. Using the hyperblade makes the kill much quicker and cleaner for our competitors. You see, the audience loves a competitive sport, but they don't want to see a child hacking away at another child using a primitive weapon." The gamewarden laughed. "We're not that heartless."

Edin shared a fake laugh. He didn't find the statement humorous.

"Now it's time for the final rule. I'm sure you won't have a problem with this one."

"Hit me with it."

"Absolutely no manipulation in the pit. We typically don't have Gifted individuals enter the gauntlet anyway. But none of that sorcery or magical malarky is permitted. I'm sure you understand why."

"I knew manipulation wasn't allowed and I understand why. But I don't have the Gift."

"Great. Well, those are the three rules about combat. Do you still want to proceed with registering?"

"Yes. Like I said before, my decision is final."

"That is logical, knowing your circumstances. Just don't quit on me before the tournament starts." The gamewarden smirked. "I get a commission for recruiting."

The gamewarden handed Edin a stack of white papers and a fountain pen. Edin scanned the tiny print and scrawled his signature upon every blank line he came across. *It's actually happening*, he thought. Eagerness gave speed to his fingers, and he handed the completed documents back.

"All done?" The gamewarden grabbed the papers and flipped through them.

"Should be good to go."

The gamewarden place the forms on the desk, then looked at Edin. There was a brief tension between the two, like they had just conspired on a subversive plot. The gamewarden broke the stale silence.

"Now all you have to do is show up to the gauntlet drawing ceremony." He handed Edin a blue folder with a pamphlet and booklet in the pockets. "That has all the information you need for the drawing. It's where you find your seeding in the tournament and meet the other contestants. The drawing should be . . ." The gamewarden looked at a calendar pinned to the wall. ". . . in three days."

Dang, too soon, Edin thought. He snatched the folder. "So, I'm registered and everything is cleared?"

"Yes, Edin Carvosa. Welcome to the gauntlet tournament."

They shared smiles and shook hands, which was awkward at first because Edin was unsure which one of the four to reach for. He stood and headed for the door.

"Hey, Carvosa."

Edin spun around. "Yeah?"

"Good luck. I'm praying you don't draw against Cane Nazari first."

"Pray for his sake, Gamewarden."

Edin walked out into the sporting quarter. The bar and lounge had doubled in crowd size and loudness. Everyone there appeared to be twice his age. It was time to leave the casino. He wanted to get back to the Pebble Inn and call it a day. He traveled into the massive maze of gaming machines and tables on his way to the entrance and hoped that A-Veetwo was waiting outside.

But then he felt a disturbing presence—an unexplainable sensation that irritated his consciousness. Somebody was watching him. He felt their eyes burning into his skin. He snapped his head to the left, towards a card table, and his pulse rocketed at the sight.

The nameless bounty hunter sat with cards in his hands. The silver hair gave him away. They locked eyes momentarily. Edin guessed the man had been tracking him, just like he tracked the *Saircor* and killed all of the crewmembers. Edin noticed something in the stare-down that he hadn't noticed from a distance on the windcycle: the bounty hunter had a mechanical eye built of dark steel. He was some sort of cyborg.

Edin ended the stare-down. He paced faster than normal. Then he panicked. He sprinted across the marble floors, dodging gamblers and staff. Why was the assailant still on Lathas? *What did Jameson do to this guy?* He turned and saw the bounty hunter had left the card table and was weaving between two rows of slot machines; the killer was coming after him. Edin rushed to the entrance, flung himself into the revolving glass door, and surged outside.

The four guards stood with their plasma rifles. They observed Edin as if he were a crazy kid playing with the door. He looked back through the glass to see if he could spot the bounty hunter coming after him. The glass was too cloudy.

He turned around and ran past the large fountain. Gripping the folder close to his heart, he sprinted into the traffic and across Blue Street.

The sun disappeared, and two moons rose into the heavens. Everywhere, lights flashed from digital billboards, spiraling towers, and blinking spaceships. Edin made sure to stay within the shadows on the walk back to the Pebble Inn. A singular question ran through his head: *Is Vanya safe?* For some reason, the thought of her kept recurring.

He had to go back and make sure she was unharmed. If the bounty hunter killed everyone on the *Saircor*, then he would surely kill Vanya.

He got lost in a neighborhood with no businesses around. The apartments were made of red brick. Washed laundry hung from thin wires, drying in the heated breeze. Edin spotted the outline of a young lady on her balcony.

"Hey! I'm lost. Do you know how to get to the Pebble Inn?"

The lady turned. No facial features were discernable in the blackness. She shouted down, "I'm not familiar with that place. But if you take a right on the next side road you come across, you'll be headed straight towards the river!"

"I think I can find it from the river. Thanks!"

He hurried up the street and eyed the alleyway he had to pass through. It was very narrow. As he entered, he spread his arms out and was able to touch both walls. All light disappeared midway through. His heart quickened. Darkness. Silence. Both surrounded him.

He pictured the bounty hunter dropping down from the rooftops and landing in front of him with two glowing orbs of cosmic energy. This would be the place to kill someone and leave the scene a mystery, he knew. But he heard and saw no one on his way to the other side.

Streetlamps brightened the promenade edging the river. A few other foot travelers were enjoying their night by the water—a couple with interlocked hands, a boy younger than himself with a feline pet. As he continued, he discovered a group of boys around his age. He counted eight of them. They were playing on an abandoned bridge with old railroad tracks laid over decaying wood. Underneath the tracks was a platform, suspended by steel wires, that they climbed down to. Edin saw the two blue moons reflecting upon the swift water and figured the boys made the climb for the view. He wondered what childhood would be like growing up in the city with other children, and the possibility of real friends.

In some ways, the crew of the *Saircor* had been like friends— maybe even family, but a distant kind of family. They were bonded by experiences. But he doubted any of them wanted to see him discover success, become something other than a smuggler. Jealousy was the trait most exhibited amongst the older crew. Now he felt a twinge of jealousy watching the boys play together on the bridge, knowing they had families waiting for their nightly return home.

When he reached the Pebble Inn, he inspected both sides of the slanted building and the backside where there was a large dumpster with a rotten odor. No one was there. He went back to the front and snuck up the steps, past the gargoyles holding torches. It didn't look like anything had happened in the area. He opened the oak door.

Vanya was standing behind the reception desk. She looked up at the sound of the door. He felt an instant relief that she was there, alive.

"Where have you been?" she asked. "A-Veetwo waited an hour for you. He looked up and down Blue Street for another two hours."

Edin rushed up to the desk. "I have something to tell you."

"You signed up for the gauntlet?"

"No. Well, yeah, I did. But there is something else I have to tell you."

"What?"

"First, let me ask, have you seen a gray-haired cyborg in a long black cloak around the hotel in the past day or two?"

"No. And if I saw a cyborg with gray hair, I'm sure I would remember. Why?"

"I think I'm being tracked. But don't worry; I don't think you're in danger."

"You don't think I am in danger," she said flatly. "What does that mean?"

"I just think someone is looking for me, that's all," he lied and grinned. "No worries."

"This cyborg is the reason you left Blue Street."

"Yeah. He was just staring at me in the casino. It weirded me out."

"He can't do anything to you now."

Edin scrunched his eyebrows. "What do you mean?"

"You're enlisted in the gauntlet. You're property of the Lathas government. If he messed with you, then he'd anger everyone on the planet. The tournament is serious, Edin. I don't think you realize what you have got yourself into." She shook her head. "It's too late now."

"I'm sorry."

"Don't apologize. It was your dumb boyish choice."

"I know, but it's what I have to do."

"Whatever you think is best for you." She flipped her hair. "Anyways, I'm glad you're safe."

"Thanks." He left the reception desk and stepped in the direction of the elevator. "I'm going to go to bed now."

While walking down the hall, loud coughing from a room took him by surprise because he had yet to see another guest in the hotel. At least he wasn't the only person staying in this eyesore.

Upstairs, he paced to his room, and the sense of quietude calmed him. Even though the Pebble Inn was grungy, it was also cozy and felt more like home than the *Saircor* ever did. He would have been devastated if he had come back to find a dreadful scene.

The door handle to 607 appeared to be untouched. He swiped the keycard and walked inside the dark room. The light switch did not work. At first, he thought it was odd. Then he felt a shudder of paranoia. In the darkness, he ran to the floor lamp and flipped the switch. Illumination dispersed. By the window, the silver-haired cyborg stood, his mechanical eye locked onto Edin.

CHAPTER 7

The mechanical eye was welded above scar tissue. His other eye was covered by bangs. His face showed a mature young man, around thirty standard years old—too young for an entire scalp of gray hair. He wore a black hooded cloak draped over a platinum breastplate, armored sleeves leading to platinum gauntlets, and dark pants tucked into platinum boots.

The assailant stood completely unafraid, and there was a look to his stare that made Edin assume his death sentence had arrived early.

"Do not move and do not scream," the bounty hunter said.

Edin instinctively backed towards the door. The bounty hunter raised an arm, and a glowing green orb materialized. "I said do not move, Edin Carvosa."

Edin froze. "You know my name."

The bounty hunter lowered his arm and the orb vanished. "Of course. I came to Lathas because of you. We need to talk. I swear I did not come to hurt you."

"I'm sorry, sir." Edin trembled. "But I really don't want to talk to you."

"Don't call me sir. That's strange."

"Why?"

"Because I am your cousin. My name is Ithamar Avrum, prince of the Mizoquii."

Edin shook his head in confusion. "What did you just say?"

"My name is Ithamar Avrum, prince of the Mizoquii."

"No, no, no." Edin shook his head again. "Before all that."

"I am your older cousin."

They stared at each other momentarily as if both were unsure what to say to the other. Edin opened his mouth to speak but only stammered incomprehensible words.

Ithamar nodded. "It is true. We have been looking for you for a long time."

"Whose we? Are my parents still alive? And why did you kill everyone on the *Saircor*? What did they have to do with anything?"

"Your parents are dead." Ithamar sat on the foot of the bed. "As I said, we need to talk."

Edin perched uneasily on the leather chair. "How am I supposed to trust you? How do I know you don't want to kill me?"

"Calm down, and listen to what I have to say. If I came to kill you, I wouldn't have a conversation with you. I would just kill you."

"Okay." Edin shook his head. "I'm listening."

"Do you know anything of the Mizoquii?"

"Only the stories I've read in history books. All I remember is the Mizoquii were a civilization in the Second or Third System. An old warrior race. Didn't know they were Gifted . . . or bounty hunters."

"I'm not a bounty hunter, and history books are written and published by those in control." Ithamar scratched his head. "The Mizoquii are a race from the Second System that was banished during the Odieux Era and never allowed to return to Morhaven under the Order of Oracles. There was unimaginable warfare between us and the colonizers from the First System. Supposedly, we lost in a swift war."

Edin leaned closer. "I still don't get what's so important about the Mizoquii. Who cares what old bloodlines I have running in my veins?"

"Every Mizoquii is Gifted, with transcendent potential."

Edin sloped back in the chair. "I have never shown any signs."

"It must have something to do with you being in space for so long. You should have awakened by now."

"I'm sorry. This is too much." Edin stood and started to pace. "What in cursed moons is going on?"

"You need to leave with me. You must speak with our grandfather, and meet the rest of us, on our planet."

"I can't just leave. I'm a contestant in the gauntlet tournament."

"You'll die. No manipulation is allowed, and you have no combat experience. Why would you even think about signing up?"

Edin glared daggers through Ithamar. "You killed everyone I knew on the *Saircor*, and now you're sitting in my room asking me why I entered the gauntlet tournament?"

"I killed them for revenge."

"Revenge for what?" Edin demanded loudly.

"Your dear Captain Jameson was paid to transport a baby to our planet, Morhaven IV, fifteen years ago. The lying imbecile never came." Ithamar looked down to his feet. "Reshef Avrum, our grandfather, the sapa khan of the Mizoquii, has had a bounty on Rhygert Jameson ever since he failed to show up with you. Everyone thought you were dead after such a length in time." Ithamar looked up at Edin. "When I saw you on that windcycle, I questioned if you were the lost boy. But your eyes are way too green for an ordinary human. That is a Mizoquii trait."

Edin sat down quietly. His lip quivered. "What happened to my parents?"

Ithamar remained silent for a moment, rubbed his chin, and then spoke. "They were killed in a raid by the royal dynasty. The liege pharaoh's very own guards, the Jovian Escort."

"And why would the royal dynasty be hunting the Mizoquii?"

"This is why I must speak with you." Ithamar narrowed his eyes. "When the dynasty was rising into existence, the Order of Oracles warned House Heiros that their end would come by the hands of the

Mizoquii. Strangely, the old religion prophesied we would at least be involved in some type of rebellion; maybe it even means we are next in line after the dynasty."

"And that's why Zalor Heiros destroyed the entire order before establishing the royal dynasty," Edin guessed. "He didn't want a prophecy to catch fire and spread."

"Your assumption might be correct. You need to be returned to your people, your home."

"I can't just leave Lathas. The gauntlet is serious. If I leave, the entire galaxy will label me a runaway coward."

"I can't let you die on this planet. You're one of us."

"Train me."

"What?"

"Train me in combat. You must be skilled beyond just manipulation."

Ithamar sat in silence, contemplating.

"C'mon, Ithamar. Let's do it for the Mizoquii. Then I'll visit our grandfather."

"No."

"Yes."

"No."

"Please."

"If I train you, and you win, then you're leaving this planet with me immediately."

"Deal," Edin said. "But I still want to go to an academy in the First System."

"Let's focus on winning this flippin' tournament first." Ithamar shook his head. "Can't believe I'm doing this."

The next morning, they planned to leave the city of Kosabar.

Ithamar's starship was parked on the roof of the Pebble Inn. Before leaving for the night, he told Edin to come up whenever he was ready.

They would spend the morning in search of a training ground outside of the capital, in some remote area.

Edin had a hard time sleeping. How could he fall asleep? He had met a blood relative. He knew who his kin were. Now there were so many questions spinning inside his head. *What if I actually do have the power of manipulation?* There was no evidence he had abnormal abilities. He passed out with sheepish doubts that he would ever be considered Gifted.

Sunshine slipped through the long curtains, irritating his eyelids. He yawned and stretched his thin arms above the sheets. He looked out the window and figured it was time to get up. He slipped on his boots, pants, shirt, and vest.

The staircase at the end of the hall led to the roof. He sprinted up the dark stairwell. The wooden door creaked as it closed behind him.

The starship was painted royal blue and trimmed in silver. It had two forward-swept wings with mounted minicannons. In the front was a cockpit with sleek windows. In the back were four exhaust thrusters. A steel ramp led up to the cabin from the center of the craft. Edin figured the cabin was the size of a bedroom. He paced across the hotel's grimy roof and up the ramp.

Ithamar stood at the airlock with a mug of steaming liquid. He smiled.

"Ready to go?" Edin asked.

"Yeah, come on in and check out the old dirty bird."

Edin stepped past Ithamar and into the cabin. "Dirty bird?"

The cabin had walls and ceilings built of flat metal soundproofing, but the floor was blanketed by beige carpet. It had a small kitchen area with a sink, digioven, freezer, and cabinets. The top bunk protruded from the bulkhead with untidy sheets dangling. There was a door to the cockpit in the front. And towards the back was a door with red lettering that stated, *(Danger! High Voltage!): Maintenance Access Room.*

"Yeah, I call her the dirty bird," Ithamar boasted. "The only Riskplay left in the galaxy."

"Oh, so this is a Riskplay?"

"Yeah, you've heard of 'em?"

"No."

Ithamar laughed. "They're pretty old, but shifty little fighters when in a jam."

"Cool." Edin looked around the messy cabin. Dirty laundry, food wrappers, and random books were laid out on almost every open space. He asked, "Do you know where we're headed?"

"Yeah. Let's get into the cockpit. I have the coordinates loaded in the computer."

In the cockpit, control sticks and pedals faced two gray leather seats. The dashboard had instruments, dials, displays, and buttons. The roof boasted an array of levers and circuit breakers. Edin took a deep breath, trying to take it all in. He had never been inside the cockpit of a smaller spaceship. It was inviting yet intimidating at the same time.

"Sit down," Ithamar said, taking the pilot's seat.

Edin sat in the copilot seat while Ithamar pressed buttons in a chaotic sequence. The power turned on, and the engines rumbled. For a brief moment, the ship hovered above the hotel. Ithamar pressed forward on the cyclic stick. Then the ship rocketed over the river and zipped between two towers. Edin was forced back into his seat, shocked they were moving so quickly at such a low altitude. Buildings and starships turned to silver blurs, and the terrain through the windshield shifted into a distorted haze.

"Are you sure we should be going this fast?" Edin asked.

"Yeah, we're already out of the city."

As if by magic, the terrain below changed from gray to bright orange. They were soaring above the canopy of the rainforest. Edin relaxed into the seat. There was no reason to stress. Not a single starship flew within their view. Only the open wilderness lay before them.

"Where are we headed?" Edin asked.

"I searched the network this morning and found an old training camp near the mountains about two hours north." Ithamar stared ahead. "I figured we'd go check out the spot, and then after drawing day we will stay there until the days you fight."

Edin felt bummed by this news. A part of him wanted to see Vanya at least once a day. It was nice to speak to someone around his age, particularly since they had already gotten past those awkward beginning stages of getting to know someone. He remembered how nervous he was when he first checked into the Pebble Inn.

Ithamar said, "High-altitude training will be good for you. All the other contestants have been prepared in strict environments. We will need to accelerate your fitness as well."

"Understandable." Edin turned towards the pilot. "So, do you have this whole thing planned out already? You think you can train me enough to win the entire tournament?"

Ithamar kept his gaze forward. "I don't know."

Edin frowned and looked ahead at the orange and yellow countryside.

"But I do have something planned," Ithamar said.

"What?"

"To make sure you're prepared enough that when you step in the arena, you fight smart and admirably."

"I guess that's all I can ask for."

One question burned in Edin's mind, but he was nervous to bring it up.

"What were my parents like?"

"I don't know. I never met them. And the rest of our family doesn't speak of them much."

"You never heard any stories? I mean, like, nothing at all?"

"Not really. They weren't on the same planet as us when you were born. I'm not sure what they were even doing. The sapa khan doesn't speak on the topic much."

"Oh."

"But people claim your mother was beautiful, and your father was brave."

"Everyone says that about men and women who die; that's not specific."

"Yeah, I know." Ithamar scratched his chin. "Your mother was the daughter of the sapa khan. Your father was the son of a navigator. They were young when you were born. Not sure if our grandfather approved of the arrangement or even knew about it. That's all I really remember hearing about them."

Edin nodded, then decided to switch the conversation. For the rest of the flight, they chatted on and off about the gauntlet. Once they reached the mountains, Edin perked up. The ship decelerated and glided above rocky cliffs and lofty trees. He spotted a concrete landing pad next to a wooden bungalow.

Ithamar lowered the collective stick at his side, and the spaceship came to rest on the concrete. He pushed an assortment of buttons. The engines hissed to a halt, and Edin followed him out of the ship.

A breeze brushing through the woods produced a ghostly whisper. Hair rose on Edin's arm, and goosebumps prickled. This place wasn't as creepy as the Pebble Inn, but it was just the two of them in seclusion. Edin wondered if Ithamar planned this trip to kill him. What if the man wasn't his cousin and was truly a bounty hunter? Edin felt gullible. Maybe he believed everything Ithamar said too easily. *The connection to the Mizoquii seems like an elaborate, made-up story.*

He tried to push those thoughts out of his mind. Ithamar had already had plenty of opportunity to kill or kidnap him and was his only shot at winning this tournament.

The bungalow was made of yellow wooden logs with a sod roof. Two steps led to a wide veranda that wrapped around the entire house, and old chairs sat underneath the gable shading the entryway. The square windows were covered with dark curtains. Edin looked around the scene. Trees encircled them in every direction, with a few openings to narrow trails. A bird flapped its wings and soared off a branch, disappearing into the deep jungle. Nothing else moved besides the breeze.

They stepped onto the veranda, and Ithamar opened the timber door without knocking. Inside was chilled. The first floor was one large room, a combination den, kitchen, and dining area. The furniture was dated and boring. There were no video displays or computers or advanced electronics.

"Doesn't seem like much in here," Edin said.

"Yeah, it's perfect," Ithamar said. "No distractions."

They were back in Kosabar by midafternoon. Ithamar rented the remote bungalow for the entirety of the next two months via the network. After drawing day, the two of them would head back north for training. It meant that Edin had tonight and all day tomorrow at the Pebble Inn.

Perhaps Vanya would get dinner with him. He decided to ask upon returning. When they landed on the roof of the hotel, Ithamar started the shutdown procedure, and the volume from the engines died down. "So, what's the point in staying here? We could get a room somewhere else for our time in the city. I'll pay for a nicer place."

"Nah, I like it here. It's quiet and you don't have to deal with the public that much."

"Are you sure? This place looks haunted. It doesn't even stand up straight, like it might fall over if a rogue wind blew by."

Edin laughed. "Don't worry. The Pebble Inn grows on you."

"Well, did you have any plans for tonight? Maybe we could go to a show downtown or walk around Blue Street. Get familiar with the area before everything happens."

"Um, I think I'm going to go walk on the river with a friend."

The statement felt weird leaving his mouth, like he was asking permission—like Ithamar was now his legal guardian.

"Oh, that's fine." Ithamar fell silent for a moment. "Who is it?"

"Just this one girl that works here," Edin admitted.

Ithamar smirked and punched Edin in the shoulder. "Now I know why you want to stay at the Pebble Inn, little trooper. Well, tell this girlfriend of yours that she's not allowed at the training camp. Girls are distractions. Always remember that, no matter what you do in life. Girls are nothing but evil distractions."

"She's not my girlfriend." Edin's cheeks reddened. "We're barely friends."

"Sure. Well, since you're busy, I'm going to head to the casino and see if I can dig up some secrets on the contestants. But I'll leave the ship up here. Don't want to fly after I've had a few oortbrews."

They unstrapped their seatbelts, stood, and disembarked. Ithamar went directly to the lobby and left for the casino. Edin stopped by his room to shower before going downstairs to ask Vanya to dinner. *It isn't a date*, he told himself. He was only looking for friendship.

After making sure his sandy-blond hair was combed perfectly, he left the room and took the elevator to the lobby. When he reached the reception desk, no one was there. He rang the bell. Shouts came from the office. The door flew open.

Vanya walked out in her housekeeping dress. When she saw Edin, she smiled. He smiled back and told himself not to get tongue-tied.

"Hey, Edin, what's up?"

"Hey." He paused, not on purpose. "I was wondering if you wanted to get some food."

"Um, I'm at work, and I'm not dressed to leave."

"Oh, well, as you know, I'm entering the gauntlet, and I'll be training outside of the city after drawing day, so I was just wondering as just friends or whatever."

Vanya smiled. "You're saying I'm your best friend in Kosabar and you want to go eat before you train for your suicide?"

"Yeah, I . . . that's what I'm trying to say."

Vanya nodded. "You should've called down the office, and I would have gotten ready when you did. I can get A-Veetwo to watch the front desk tonight. But it will take me a few minutes to get showered and changed."

"That's fine. I'll just wait here in the lobby."

"Okay, Edin. I'll be ready in twenty minutes."

It took nearly two hours for her to return to the lobby. Edin had fallen asleep on the sofa and felt something push against his shoulder. He opened his eyes and saw Vanya standing over him in a blue skirt and a white top. Her legs were tan and intimidating. His skin paled in comparison, to the point of embarrassment. He stood and noticed her hair wasn't in a ponytail anymore. Her eyes had some sort of purple makeup on them.

"You look nice."

"Thanks. Are you ready? You look tired."

"No, I'm fine. Let's go."

He held the door for her as they walked outside.

CHAPTER 8

"You didn't even try to kiss her?"

"No. I told you it's not like that."

"You took her to eat gyros and went to the riverwalk, and you didn't even think about making a move?"

"No, stop asking."

"I remember the younger years."

Edin and Ithamar rode in the back seat of the glidecar driven by A-Veetwo. It was nearing noon, and they were headed to the Lost Quarter to shop for an outfit for drawing day. Ithamar had convinced Edin that he must look neat in front of the crowd, in order to win fans.

"What did you get into last night?" Edin asked. "You weren't in the ship by the time I got back."

"Oh, you know how the casino goes—an hour feels like seconds. The tension on the card table has a way of distracting me from time."

"Did you win any coin?"

"No, I lost three thousand credits."

"Three thousand credits! Why didn't you stop playing?"

"I never said I was good at gambling. I only do it for the thrill."

"Wow, the thrill."

"It's not an everyday habit. Just for fun. You need to loosen up, kid. I think space took the fun out of you."

"Sorry that my parents were murdered and I was raised by a smuggler who treated me like a galley slave. I don't know much about fun."

"I can tell. You volunteered for a gauntlet tournament."

The glidecar turned down a street bordered by elegant houses built centuries ago: wooden homes in colors ranging from gray to lavender and, further along, mansions of brick, stone, and steel. Colorful trees decorated the gated lawns, and behind the leaves he saw fountains and fishponds. Columns rose from porched entryways to upper balconies with ritzy outdoor furniture.

"Who lives here?" Edin asked.

"Old money," Ithamar said.

A-Veetwo said, "We are nearing the Lost Quarter Bazaar."

They passed a few more houses, and then tall shops appeared ahead, and the glidecar hovered onto a wide boulevard inside the shopping district. The droid parallel parked in a tight space. Edin opened the door to the sidewalk.

"Mr. Carvosa, I hope you will be returning this time," A-Veetwo said.

Edin was halfway out of the glidecar. He turned to the driver. "Yeah, I shouldn't have a bounty hunter chasing me this time."

Ithamar lightly pushed Edin out. "You never had a bounty hunter chasing you."

"I'll remain parked here. Don't forget," A-Veetwo said.

Edin and Ithamar left the droid and strolled the sidewalk. The Lost Quarter Bazaar consisted of boutiques crammed next to each other like books on a shelf. A boulevard separated the two rows of shops and created a spacious outdoor venue packed with many species. In the median, giant sculptures stood at attention like marble gods.

Restaurants and cafes released appetizing odors into the warm wind. The shops they passed blared diverse genres of music from the windows and doorways. The tunes resembled the themes of the unique merchandise sold. Edin saw a group of human girls around his age. He tried not to make eye contact with them.

"There's a men's clothing store up here." Ithamar walked with a confident stride. "We'll get you something to make you look like a gentleman."

"Wanna get food first? I'm starving."

Ithamar shrugged his shoulders. "Sure, why not? Have you seen somewhere you want to stop?"

Edin pointed forward. "That place up there has a patio facing the street. It's a nice day out."

The two cousins stopped for lunch at Gálanoir. They sat in iron chairs at an iron table in the shade of a burgundy awning. A young waitress dropped off two laminated menus and asked them what they would like to drink. She had deep-blue, hairless skin, an athletic build, and was taller than both of them. They ordered hot plumdine tea, and she returned inside.

"What kind of species is she?" Edin asked.

"I don't know." Ithamar kept his head down, scanning the menu. "I never really bothered to learn all of them."

"I heard that one hundred and seventy-three intelligent species live on Lathas. And there are twelve thousand within the galaxy."

"Seems like a plausible guess."

The waitress came out with two mugs of scorching-hot tea. She placed the mugs on the table and asked, "Have you two chaps come to a conclusion on what you're going to order?"

"I'll go with the red fillet with mustard sauce, and a fried spud," Edin said.

"Yeah, I'll go with the same," Ithamar said.

"Brilliant choice," the waitress said before walking back inside.

The cousins people watched on the patio while sipping the plumdine tea. It tasted sweet and bitter, like drinking warm berries.

"Last night, you didn't tell the girl about the Mizoquii, did you?"

"No, I didn't. We only talked about the tournament. I told her my cousin was training me. Why do you ask?"

"Because no one must find out. You will receive a lot of attention in the tournament if you begin to win matches. You don't want rumors to spread that a Mizoquii is battling in a gauntlet tournament."

"You think the royal dynasty would hunt us this far out?"

"They might send a unit from the Jovian Escort. But I doubt they're worried about the Mizoquii right now. We are assumed to be extinct."

"Alright. Well, I didn't tell Vanya anything about the Mizoquii, but she is mad that you're parking on the roof."

"You told her I parked on the roof?"

"She saw you walking in the lobby on the way to the casino. Not many guests are currently at the Pebble Inn. She figured you were with me."

"I don't want to move the Riskplay."

"You don't have to move your precious ship." Edin smiled. "She's just going to charge you rent."

Ithamar shook his head. "Whatever."

The waitress walked out the door with two white plates that she dropped off at the table. "Anything else I can assist you with?"

"No this should be fine," Ithamar said.

She strolled back inside. Steam rose above the food. Red juices leaked from the fillet, charred with a pink center. The spud was sliced into thin crispy pieces. A golden sauce smeared the entire plate. After the first three bites, Edin considered it the best meal he'd ever had. The flavor, the tenderness, the warmth—perfection.

Ithamar paid for the meal. They left Gálanoir and continued down the crowded sidewalk, weaving between foot travelers and passing boutique after boutique. *Flawless weather*, Edin thought. Not a cloud in sight. Starships flew amid the crystal skyline and the red sun, which was warm but not extreme.

"The store is up here," Ithamar said. He quickened his stride and cut away from the street and closer to the shops. A green sign hanging from a steel bar above a glass door read *Henton & Henton*. Racks of discounted clothes squeezed near the front of the shop. They walked under the sign and through the door where they were greeted by a woman at the cash register.

The floors, walls, and ceiling were golden hardwood. On both sides of the shop were towering shelves of the same color. The shop was narrow but deep like a tunnel. Jackets, vests, and overcoats hung around the entrance. Ithamar proceeded towards the back and Edin followed. They passed a section with watches, belts, glasses, flasks, and wallets.

The next section boasted mirrored walls. A man with dark hair and glasses stood in obvious anticipation.

"How can I help you gentlemen?" the man asked.

Ithamar put a hand on Edin's shoulder. "We need to get this kid a drawing day outfit."

"No problem. Was there anything in particular you had in mind?"

"He's a contestant in the gauntlet tournament. We need something special."

The man gasped. "A contestant . . . wow. Usually, contestants have their outfits tailored months prior."

Edin stood quietly, embarrassed. He never assumed drawing day would be such a big affair.

"We're a little late. Is there anything you got for us?" Ithamar asked.

The man smiled. "My name is Tom Henton, and I am the owner of this store. If anyone in Kosabar can find a contestant a drawing day outfit the day before, it would be the person you're talking to."

Ithamar grinned back. "Well, Mr. Henton, let's get to work."

Tom looked at Edin. "What exactly is the theme you're going for? Is there any family crest or home colors you'd like to draw inspiration from?"

Edin hesitated. "I'm a spacer and I don't have a family crest. Maybe just a hint of emerald."

"Ah, so you're a spacer with an eye for emerald. I'll see what I can find." Tom walked towards a mirror and opened it like a door, walking into a stockroom.

Ithamar said, "Where did you get the idea for emerald?"

Edin pulled the gold chain from under his shirt. The emerald charm sparkled under the chandelier lights. Ithamar grabbed the stone and examined it.

"Do you know where this came from?" Edin asked. "I've had it since I can remember."

"No clue. Maybe your mother decided to send it with you. Our house colors are black and green."

"Ah, maybe."

Tom marched out of the mirrored door with a black garment bag. He hung the bag on an empty hook and unzipped it. Within was a ceremonial black suit—a silk coat with a standing collar and emerald buttons aligned diagonally, and matching trousers in black silk. Edin scanned the garments up and down. It was a formal and sharp outfit. He had never seen any clothing like it in person and assumed it would be worn by royalty to weddings, rituals, or political affairs.

Tom also held an emerald stole. "What do you think?"

"It's amazing," Edin said.

"If you think this is the one, we have a body scanner in the back that can take your measurements. I can go ahead and get it fitted for you," Tom said.

Ithamar looked at Edin. "Are you sure you don't want to look at others in the store?"

"I trust Tom's judgment," Edin said. He started to walk towards the back.

"Don't trust too many strangers," Tom warned. "Lathas can be deceitful to contestants."

Drawing day arrived the next morning. Edin rode the elevator down to the lobby of the Pebble Inn with Ithamar. The ceremonial suit, fitted to exactness, had raised his confidence. He felt like a different person, an aristocrat with important dealings on his agenda. He tried to hide the excitement and nervousness twisting in his gut. All he could think about was the chance to scope the competition for the first time.

Ithamar brushed off the shoulder pads on Edin's suit like they were dusty. Edin felt uncomfortable because he knew the shoulders were clean. Ithamar had developed the tendency to treat the connection between them more like that of a parent and child than of two cousins. Of course, Edin needed the mentorship. He'd witnessed the brilliance of Ithamar's abilities. And the Gifted cousin was his secret advantage over the other competitors. They would assume Edin was just a lowborn spacer. But he was a Mizoquii who would be trained in combat by the prince of the Mizoquii.

A-Veetwo stood behind the reception desk. Vanya waited by the entrance in a dark-green formal dress swinging to her calves. The straps along her shoulders had silver studs, and she wore a silver necklace. Her light-blond hair was braided intricately.

"You two take so long to get ready. I've been waiting for the past hour," Vanya said.

"Nobody said you had to come," Ithamar said.

"Don't mind him," Edin said. "This is my cousin, Ithamar—the one I told you about."

Vanya greeted him with a handshake. "Wow, your eye really is mechanical."

"Clearly," Ithamar said. He twisted his head at Edin and mouthed, "Distraction."

Edin shook his head. "Let's go."

The three walked out of the lobby and into the midmorning breeze. A parked glidecar hovered by the sidewalk. Vanya got in the driver's seat, Edin sat next to her, and Ithamar slid into the back seat.

"We're really going to let her drive?" Ithamar laughed.

Edin smiled. "Yeah, have you ever driven in the city before?" he asked her.

Vanya's face reddened. "I'm sure you two can get out and walk if it comes down to it."

"Hurry up; we're running late," Ithamar said.

Vanya pressed a button on the dashboard, and the engine came to life. She slammed on the pedal. The glidecar jerked forward and sped down the empty street. Edin gripped a handle on the door, and they glided into traffic on a wide avenue. Horns honked as they switched from lane to lane at a blistering pace.

The drawing day ceremony was held on the Toujo River, the major channel cutting through the city of Kosabar. Behind the Kosabar Arena, on the riverside, an outdoor amphitheater with a grandstand faced the water where the wooden stage floated. The amphitheater had been built recently, many years after the neighboring coliseum and the casino on the other side of Blue Street. While it lacked the height and width of the other two structures, it was still an engineering marvel of impressive proportions. The seating area stretched into the sky, packed with eighty-eight thousand spectators. Vast banners swayed in the stands, and loud chants reverberated throughout. In the river and on the piers, watercrafts anchored or moored themselves within hearing range. The tallest boats enjoyed a view of the stage.

Edin Carvosa parted with Vanya and Ithamar. They went into the stands while Edin proceeded to the thin bridge that led to the floating platform where people were already standing. He guessed they were tournament officials on standby, waiting for the contestants to arrive. Before the bridge was a steel gate and two guards dressed in blue uniforms with plasma rifles in hand. The guards examined the crowd with attentive eyes. They looked down at Edin when he approached.

"What do you want?" the skinny guard on the right asked.

"I'm a contestant, Edin Carvosa."

"Got paperwork?"

"Yeah." Edin pulled out a verification document with a barcode. The fat guard on the left snatched it and scanned it with a device that beeped. The fat guard gave a thumbs-up to the skinny one, who then opened the steel gate.

"Good luck with your draw," he said.

Edin grinned. "Thanks."

He walked onto the bridge. Cyan water relaxed beneath the planks of wood. However, nothing else about the amphitheater was at ease. The grandstands roared at the sight of another contestant strolling towards the platform. Amongst thousands, he felt vulnerable and lonesome. The confidence from this morning had vanished. He kept his head forward and refused to glance at the spectators. Too many eyes would be looking back at him.

The gamewarden stood where the bridge connected to the platform. He wore a long white robe with embroidered sleeves. When he spotted Edin approaching, the four arms of the massive gray creature all raised in unison.

"Mr. Carvosa! You didn't bail on me!"

Edin reached the floating stage. "I told you I was coming."

"You never know with spacers."

"I guess. Is it about to start?"

"Yeah, we just have a few more contestants that need to arrive, and then the ceremony will begin." The gamewarden put a hand on Edin's shoulder and pointed with another arm. "Just go stand over there with them."

"Alright." Edin headed off to join the others.

"By the way, you look sharp, Carvosa. Most spacers don't know how to dress in public."

Edin turned his head back. "Not sure if that was a compliment, but thanks."

Five contestants stood in a row. Behind them, the tournament officials chatted with each other. The contestants and officials all wore formal attire in various colors and styles. Edin noticed the other contestants staring at him, and he nervously looked away. He stopped at the beginning of the row, pivoted on his foot, and faced the crowd.

The grandstand was a madhouse. Thousands of spectators jumped up and down in wild excitement. Flags with familial crests waved in the uppermost regions. Chants rose in volume and floated down to the water. Edin wondered, *If the fanatics start a riot, who will be able to stop them?*

The next two contestants to arrive were twin brothers. They both had shaved heads and athletic frames. The gamewarden greeted them by the bridge, and then they strolled on the platform. They waved at the crowd and seemed unfazed at being visible to a plethora of onlookers. Edin lacked that natural self-assurance. The twins stood next to him at the end. They were now waiting for only one more contestant. Edin looked in the stands to find Vanya and Ithamar, but it was impossible to identify anyone in the blurry mass of bodies.

Strangely, the crowd calmed down. The loud chants turned to low whispers, which eventually turned to a long silence. *Who are they waiting for?* Edin wondered. Then he remembered the gamewarden's warning.

A drum sounded off in the distance.

It thudded faster and faster, building to a climax. In the grandstand, canisters gripped by various spectators dispersed thick layers of purple and yellow smoke. The clouds swarmed over the raging fanatics. A majority of the amphitheater began to chant in unity.

"Na-za-ri! Na-za-ri! Na-za-ri!"

CHAPTER 9

Cane Nazari walked like a man in full maturity. He paced the bridge with his chin up, chest out, and arms to the sides. His golden ceremonial suit was lined with purple pinstripes. Curly black hair ran down to his hulking shoulders. Admirers in the seating area went absurd at the sight of him nearing the platform.

He rivaled the gamewarden in size, only a few inches shorter. The gamewarden shook hands with Cane. Cane swaggered onto the open stage with thousands of eyes upon him. He reached the front edge of the platform and then gently bowed to the crowd.

Edin noticed the tournament officials behind him had quit their chatter. They applauded in admiration of the royal fighter sharing the stage with them. *The buffoon hasn't even accomplished anything yet,* Edin thought. He felt more jealousy towards this Cane Nazari, a person he never met before, than any other being he had encountered in his life, and he wasn't sure why. Perhaps it was due to the undeserved attention Cane was receiving. Perhaps it was due to his physical stature and the certainty that the gauntlet tournament had already been won. Perhaps it was Cane's fortunate circumstances of being born to a rich and noble family. Cane rose from his bow, turned, and glared at Edin with fire in his eyes.

Why is he staring like that?

Cane charged at him. Edin had no clue if the threat was serious or a trick to make him cower. Time sped up in the moment; it was fuzzy in remembrance. Cane pushed Edin to the ground Edin fell on his back and slid back, burning the skin on his spine. Cane stood over him with an ugly, brutish expression.

"Flippin' spacer, not even from this system and joining the gauntlet," Cane said. "Better hope you—"

Edin jumped to his feet quickly and was scurrying towards Cane before a mass of arms held him back. Instinct had taken over, and the only thought in Edin's head was revenge for the sheer embarrassment of being shoved to the planks. The other contestants had separated the two.

"What are you going to do?" Cane asked from behind one of the twins. "You're trash. You shouldn't even be here. You're going to get killed in the first round, and I hope I'm the one to do it."

"Flip off," Edin barked with flared nostrils.

The gamewarden intervened by stepping between them and guiding Cane to the end of the row of contestants.

"Space trash." Cane laughed and shook his head while walking away. "Pathetic."

Edin brushed his suit off and looked towards the grandstand, cringing in humiliation. *I shouldn't be here*, he thought. The purple and yellow smoke grew thinner as it drifted and lingered in the sky. The crowd was awkwardly quiet during the quarrel, but they reenergized when the contestants realigned themselves as before.

The gamewarden walked to the podium in the center of the stage, ahead of the contestants. The gray creature gazed over the crowd and made a hand signal with all four arms in an attempt to calm them down. He spoke in the microphone.

"Ladies and gentlemen of Lathas, I welcome you to the drawing-day ceremony for the 292nd Lathas Gauntlet Tournament!"

Eighty-eight thousand spectators erupted in such a frenzy that the vibrations created small waves in the water and rumbled the platform.

The gamewarden proceeded quickly. "Today we are here to discover the bracket seeding for the tournament in which our young contestants will fight until the death. It is the most prestigious and honorable sporting event our solar system has held the last two centuries." He paused to catch his breath and flashed a smile with daggerlike teeth. "This year we have a diverse group of contestants, including those from the noble houses on our planet and within our solar system. And we have some lowborn competing under their family name for the first time in history."

The gamewarden continued, "As most of you know, the seeding placement is generated by a computer using a third-party service."

There were shouts from the crowd: "Fraud!" "Fake!" "It's rigged!"

"I can assure you this tournament is not rigged," the gamewarden promised.

A massive hologram display emerged in midair between the grandstand and the stage, displaying a three-dimensional tournament bracket with humanoid avatars for the eight contestants. It was the largest hologram Edin had laid eyes on. He scrutinized the stage to find what contraptions were generating the visual effect but couldn't detect any projectors.

The gamewarden spoke into the microphone. "The seeding will be generated now."

The hologram shifted, and the avatars disappeared. Then they reappeared one by one on the eight-lined tournament bracket. Edin spotted his opponent. Their names were underneath the avatars in script. In the first match, he would face Finder Shaw.

Edin looked back down at the contestants. They all eyed each other in search of the person they would be fighting. He made eye contact with the boy named Finder Shaw. The kid appeared young and short and dressed down when compared to the other contestants. He wore a tan tunic and khaki pants. Combed-over brown hair lay over an average face that looked awfully sad when staring back at Edin. *Dang, kinda lucky*, Edin thought. Finder didn't appear to be a threat.

The gamewarden hushed the crowd. "Now that the drawing has been announced, you may proceed with your parties." He did an about-face and smiled at the contestants. "I'm sure our competitors will be too busy training to worry about partying."

Fireworks shot out of cannons from behind the stands and exploded. Rainbows of light sparkled in the sky. Smoke grenades dispersed dense clouds underneath the colorful bursts of flames. Multiple chants rang from various sections of the amphitheater.

Edin was ready to leave. There were too many people in one place. Then he noticed Cane Nazari approaching him.

"Don't take it personal, Carvosa. I just don't like anything about you. It's not your fault you had no other options in life and decided to use the gauntlet as a last resort," he said scornfully. "Finder Shaw will kill you, though. The little boy is a psychopath raised solely for this tournament. I can't wait to watch a hyperblade slash your throat."

"What's your flippin' problem?" Edin asked.

"My problem is that I have a useless spacer coming to my planet and competing in my tournament. You're not one of us. You're not from here. You were lucky the tournament needed another body."

"Leave me alone."

"Make me, space trash."

Edin stepped up to Cane. Their faces almost touched. The other contestants pushed them apart before either one raised a hand to strike. Once again, the gamewarden intervened by seizing Cane by the shoulder and walking him away.

The gamewarden shouted, "Carvosa, you need to leave. And the rest of you too. No point in staying on Blue Street with all the radicals roaming around."

Ithamar and Vanya were waiting in the glidecar by the time Edin arrived in the parking garage a few miles from the amphitheater. As he left the scene, the screams from the drunken spectators had declined to faint sounds in the distance, and the flamboyant explosions from fireworks faded like dying stars.

Edin entered the back seat of the hovering vehicle. The other two looked at him.

Ithamar said, "That didn't go very smooth."

"Cane has issues," Edin said.

"Clearly," Vanya said.

"He's royalty," Ithamar said. "What did you expect? Yes, the dynasty unified the galaxy. But the noble families on most planets hate outsiders for that exact reason."

"Fear someone else will come to their planet, conquer them, and further oppress," Edin said.

"Pretty much."

Vanya backed out of the parking spot and left the garage. Edin noticed she seemed different, worried. She must have thought he would die soon. For most people, the risk of the gauntlet overshadowed the reward. But the only choice he had was to proceed.

At that moment, Edin realized something about himself. He could have easily fled from the captain and the crewmembers of the *Saircor* and afterward found simple work in a field other than combat—maybe learn a trade or skill. But what drove him to the gauntlet was ambition. He imagined a future greater than working on Lathas for the remainder of his life or winging across space with lowly smugglers. He wanted an education in the First System, and a pathway to a meaningful profession. Winning the tournament would set him up with opportunity.

The glidecar entered a major highway in bumper-to-bumper floating traffic. Edin looked at Ithamar. At least he had someone on his side through all this. The tournament had yet to begin, but now he knew he needed Ithamar far more than he ever believed he would need anyone. Since learning of his family and the Mizoquii, he felt a change within himself, but had more questions than answers. Perhaps his ambition was fueled by ancient ancestry. If he somehow made it off this planet alive, he would be greatly indebted to Ithamar; he would pledge himself to the Mizoquii and to his grandfather, the sapa khan.

"It will be alright," Vanya said. "You can win this tournament. There's something about you. I think you have what it takes."

"With good training, he will be able to compete," Ithamar said. "Hopefully he makes it out of the first round."

"Do you know anything of Finder Shaw?" Edin asked.

"I searched the network and found some information about him. He is from the planet Worinth, the closest inhabitable planet to the sun in this solar system. It is a very poor planet, but Worinth tends to send savages to the tournament. The last person you want to be fighting inside the arena is someone who is not afraid to die." Ithamar wiped his nonmechanical eye with the back of his hand. "They're the hardest ones to kill."

"He seemed small on the stage," Edin said.

"Smaller might mean he's quicker than you. Also, there will be less space to target. He will be agile and well trained in swordsmanship," Ithamar said. "I think you can win. I just hope he doesn't cut one of your arms off in the process."

"That sounds brutal."

"It's the truth. Killing someone with a hyperblade isn't as easy as you think when the other person is trying to do the same."

Vanya said, "You better train him how to dodge."

Ithamar laughed. "I can train his feet to move quick, but dodging is instinct."

"So, I really can't come to visit you two in training? I'll be so bored at the Pebble Inn."

"No, we need to focus. Training is the only thing that matters these next two weeks. Every minute, every hour, he needs to be in the mindset of killing. His opponents will be ready. You saw Cane Nazari today. That's a dominant and violent mentality. I have to instill that into Edin."

"He won't be the same person with that mentality."

"Good," Edin said.

After navigating traffic, the glidecar halted at the sidewalk by the Pebble Inn. Ithamar went up to the Riskplay, giving Edin time to pack the things needed for the two weeks away from the capital. Edin assumed Ithamar left him alone to also say goodbye to Vanya. Before heading up to the sixth floor, he spoke with her in the lobby.

"Well, I guess this is goodbye for now," Edin said.

"Yeah, but you're keeping the room here, so I'll see you around."

"Only if I win the match. Ithamar is only letting me stay in the capital on the nights after a fight."

"You'll win. If you listen to Ithamar. He looks like he'd be a good instructor for this sort of thing."

"Yeah, hopefully. Take care of yourself while I'm gone. Are you sure you're going to be safe here by yourself?"

Vanya smirked. "I'll be fine. A-Veetwo has built-in protective functions in case I need a hero."

"Ah, okay. Well . . . I'll see you in two weeks with a bit of luck."

"Sounds like a plan. I'll try to meet Ithamar in the seating area. Maybe we can start a cheering party for you."

Edin smiled. "That would be nice. See you later."

"See ya."

As he took the elevator up, his brain buzzed. The truest part of him felt more comfortable at the Pebble Inn than anywhere else he had ever been. It was like a home, and Vanya was his friend. He knew leaving for training was the right decision and there was no other way. But buried deeply beneath the layers of truth and purpose and ambition, something wanted to stay instead of leave.

The Riskplay flew out of Kosabar at a tremendous speed. The spiraling glass structures of the city swiftly turned to the orange canopy of the jungle. Edin was less worried about Ithamar accelerating this time.

"There's something I want to show you before we go to the training camp," Ithamar said, staring straight ahead.

"What?" Edin's ears perked up.

"I want to take you to the location of the *Saircor* landing. To see what's left."

"Why?"

"I'm interested to see if any of the ship is still left. But also, I want you to have a glance at where you come from. So you know why you're entering this tournament."

"Uh, okay."

"We will start training early in the morning. I'll need you ready. This is meant to motivate you because I'm about to put you through the worst experience of your life."

"The worst?"

"I have to get you combat ready. Your life depends on it. These next two weeks aren't going to be fun."

The starship decelerated at a gradual pace. Trees that were once an orange blur became clear enough to see their leaves fluttering in the wind. The red sun melted into the purple horizon where thin clouds intertwined purposelessly. An open field bordered by trees unveiled the *Saircor*.

Parts of the hull had been stripped, but a significant portion of the frame remained intact. All the glass was gone from the catwalk and bridge. The hangar bay doors were still open to the air, and tall weeds edged the rusty underside. It was decaying and becoming one with nature like a fossil. The destroyed windcycles and glidecars were still scattered in the field. Ithamar lowered the collective stick, and they landed parallel to the larger vessel.

"There's probably some creatures living in there," Edin said.

"Maybe some homeless humans, or worse," Ithamar said.

"What?"

"Zombies."

Edin laughed. "Right."

The joke reminded him of Atam Fitz, the tactical officer.

"Actually," Edin said. "I locked someone in the airlock. Did you search the ship after you tracked me?"

"No," Ithamar said. "Why would you lock someone in there?"

"I told you that I planned to escape. He was the person they left with me to fuel."

Ithamar unbuckled his seatbelt and stood. "You just trapped him inside and walked away?"

"Pretty much."

Ithamar laughed. "It was really that bad?"

"I mean, I guess it could have been worse." Edin rose from the copilot seat. "But I wasn't going to stay forever."

"Understandable." Ithamar walked out of the cockpit. "Whoever scavenged the ship might have freed or enslaved him."

Edin followed. "I felt bad for him, honestly."

"Why?"

"He wasn't all there, mentally."

Ithamar didn't respond. They left the Riskplay and wandered onto the yellow meadow. A breeze pushed a chill underneath Edin's vest. They marched across the grass, examining the scene of destroyed transports. Quietly, they proceeded up the ramp leading to the empty hangar bay and entered the interior of the *Saircor*. The passageway was extremely dark, impossible to see ahead. Ithamar raised a hand, and a green orb of energy materialized.

"Be careful with that thing," Edin said.

"I control the Gift. Don't fear."

Ithamar pushed the orb forward, and the humming sphere led them through the passageway as if it had a mind of its own. Small white sparks crackled on the outer shell. Edin was more amazed than fearful. But he knew the damage the electrical projectile could inflict. Other than the orb and drops of liquids resounding against the steel floorings, the inside of the ship was eerily silent. Edin heard his own heartbeat.

A foul smell drifted into his nose, and he wanted to vomit instantly. *Repulsive.*

"What is that?" Edin asked.

"Something rotting."

"Well, let's not go forward." Edin pointed to a cutout in the bulkhead. "The catwalk is up these ladderwells here."

"What airlock did you leave that guy in?"

"Atam Fitz. Uh, I left him in the airlock back there, but we can go on the level above and walk to it from there. The galley is on this level, and I'm guessing the smell is coming from old food."

"Okay."

They took the ladderwells up to the catwalk. Edin remembered when he stood in the tube of glass while the ship hovered above Lathas—when he first laid eyes upon the planet and its mysterious jungles and purple auroras. Now the glass was broken into thousands of shards on the floor. He eyed the timberline as night approached. Ithamar stood next to him, and the green orb vanished.

"This place sucks," Edin said coldly.

"Was there anything you left?"

"No. I didn't have much. Let's go see what happened in that airlock and leave."

Edin led the way with a new green orb following above his shoulder. The passageways were entirely destroyed. Wires, expensive metals, and electrical components had been ripped from the bulkheads. He had never seen the ship this dark or quiet. They continued aft in the narrow passage until they reached a set of ladderwells.

"The airlock is down a few levels," Edin said.

"Alright."

Their boots against the metal steps produced noisy clinks. As they descended into the blackness, Edin worried about what he was going to see. They reached the floor of the airlock, and he stepped up to the closed door. He peeked through the dusty circular window.

Moonlight filtered in the airlock from the window on the exterior hatch. Inside, the decomposing body of Atam Fitz lay still as stone, dark-blue and green spots on his skin. His eyes were milky and bulging.

Edin gagged, then jerked his head away.

"Let's leave." Edin felt a spike of guilt, but he just wanted to put the entire situation in the past and forget what happened. "I never want to see this place again."

CHAPTER 10

Edin woke in alarm to pounding on the door and pushed himself up as it flew open. A figure glared at him through the darkness.

"Time to get ready! You're late! Training starts now!" Ithamar yelled.

Edin looked out the window and saw nothing but black. He threw the sheets off and changed into cotton training attire and athletic sneakers.

"Let's go! I don't have all day!" Ithamar's voice boomed in the shadowy room.

"I'm coming," Edin grunted.

The laces tied themselves robotically after he pushed his feet into the electric shoes. He stood and followed Ithamar out of the bungalow and onto the front porch. The morning sun had yet to show itself, and the air was cool.

"We're going on a run," Ithamar said.

Going on a run was an understatement, Edin thought a little before noontime. They'd spent an hour jogging through the trails before the first signs of sunshine peeked through the leafy canopy. Ithamar quickened his stride for the next hour. They had a fifteen-minute break at a mountain stream. For the next two hours they continued downhill at a slower pace until they eventually reached a walk because Edin could barely move his feet at this point. Sweat leaked from his body and dried up over and over again.

"What is the point in this?" Edin asked.

"What do you mean?"

"All this running."

"Endurance will be your ally in the arena."

"Yeah, but so will a hyperblade. When are we doing sword training?"

"Not today."

Edin shook his head. "Why not? I know nothing about using swords."

"The sword is only an extension of the swordsman, like the Gift." Ithamar paused. "You must train your body first. The art of the swordplay will come naturally, once you're conditioned physically."

"That's no fun."

"I told you this wasn't going to be fun."

Edin stared through the woods with a grimace. A bead of sweat dripped from his gray shirt to the red leaves on the forest floor.

Ithamar said, "We are running back to the cabin."

"Now?"

"Yes."

Ithamar broke into a steady jog. His legs were long, calf muscles flexing with each step. Today was the first time Edin had seen him in anything other than the silver suit and black cloak. His older cousin was beyond shredded, with veins swelling on his forearms and neck. Yes, he was a slayer with the Gift, but Edin realized Ithamar could also kill another man with his bare hands.

The warm day wore on, and Edin decided he wasn't built for this type of training. Ithamar kept slowing down to pace himself with Edin. They jogged for another hour, and the only thing running through Edin's head was the question of how far they had traveled. It was the furthest he had been on foot in a single day. *But there's not much room to run on the spaceship*, he reminded himself. Another hour passed.

No lunch.

That's what angered Edin the most. *Just run all day? What kind of training is this?* He felt like vomiting, but there was nothing in his stomach. His legs liquified more and more with each stride forward. They reached a hill with an extremely steep slope. Ithamar sprinted up it, dodging thorny vines and jumping over low bushes. He reached the summit and pivoted, then bent over, out of breath. Motionless at the bottom, Edin observed the hill.

"Sprint!" Ithamar screamed from the top.

"Holy insanity," Edin whispered to himself.

Edin charged the slope. Burning in his quads increased tenfold. He pushed forward, lunging at the earth. His thin legs injected the sneakers into the soil and rebounded to the air, only to strike the soil again. Harder and faster he charged. But it wasn't enough. He collapsed face-first into the ground. He got up for a few more strides. Fell again. He started to crawl his way to the top. Finally he reached Ithamar and lay flat on his stomach, on the red leaves.

"How much longer?" Edin muttered with his head in his elbow.

"One more hour and we're back. Get up."

Edin stood, and his legs wobbled like the land underneath was trembling. He tried to remove the pain in his legs with other thoughts. Edin wondered what Vanya was doing back in the city. He wondered about the training routine of Cane Nazari. And then his mind wandered to Finder Shaw. The thought of combat with Finder motivated him for the rest of the outing. He zeroed out the aching. They entered a path where the soil was hard, and they continued the jog until early afternoon.

When they reached the cabin, they didn't speak to each other. They both crashed on the couches in the den and were too busy chugging water out of large mugs to talk. Ithamar stood and walked into the kitchen with a slight limp.

"I'm going to heat up this kulliben, probably make some rice too."

"Alright, good. I've never been this hungry before."

Ithamar baked in the kitchen while Edin rested on the sofa. The smell made Edin's mouth tingle. He was tired as well, and his eyes grew droopy. Smoke spilled from the digioven when Ithamar opened the door. He prepared two plates and walked back to the den. Placing both plates on the table, he looked over at Edin, who was snoring.

The tenth day of training wasn't much different from the first: intense running through the high-altitude jungle. Sprinting up slopes grew easier. The first four days, Edin's body was sore to the point of passing out on the couch every afternoon, depleted of all energy. But he'd kept up with Ithamar in the past few workouts. However, Edin had yet to pick up any type of sword, and there were only three days left of training until they had to leave the remote bungalow for Kosabar.

Ithamar added calisthenics to the runs. Edin would do sets of pull-ups on tree branches until he fatigued, push-ups until his triceps quivered for mercy. Lunges across long distances were the worse of them all. But he made it to the tenth day without giving up, and he noticed his body transforming. He remained skinny as a twig, but there was definition to his muscles. He saw the veins popping in his forearms. His calves doubled in size from all the running. Also, his white skin grew a shade darker from the hours underneath the sun.

On the tenth day, they reached the end of the workout without any weapons training. They walked out of the wooded trail and proceeded to the bungalow.

"Ithamar, it's been ten days, and we've done nothing but run through this flippin' jungle. When do I start sword training? The gamewarden plainly told me the other contestants would be trained in swordsmanship. And that I must get comfortable with the hyperblade."

"Like I said, you must get comfortable with yourself first, physically and mentally."

"I don't understand, if the overall goal is to win in swordplay."

"We will work on swordplay tomorrow."

"Really?"

"Yeah."

Sunlight slipped through the curtain. It was dawn and the first morning Ithamar hadn't slammed his fist against the door to wake him up. The smell of fried kulliben eggs rose to the bedroom, and Edin was excited at the thought of food. He donned workout clothes and sneakers, then rushed to the kitchen for breakfast. Ithamar stood beside the digioven, sipping out of a white mug.

"There's some tea brewed," Ithamar said.

"Nice." Edin grabbed a mug and went to the kettle and poured. "Are we still doing combat training today?"

"Yes," Ithamar said distantly.

"Is something wrong?"

"Don't hate me after today. I've been pushing this off for a reason. I won't go easy on you."

"Okay."

After they ate the eggs and buttered toast, they walked into the yard, stretching their legs and arms. Ithamar strolled around the house and came back with two wooden swords. The blades were blunt, the hilts wrapped in cheap leather. He handed the training weapon to Edin.

"This is heavy," Edin said.

He steadied the blade and cut through the air in front of him. He imagined confronting a swordsman and moved his feet while pretending to parry an attack.

"I'm going to beat you with this wooden sword, and you're going to try to stop me," Ithamar said.

Edin stepped back. "What?"

"That's today's training. No offense. Just survival."

"But—"

Ithamar rushed forward and swung the sword, slamming it into Edin's as he raised it to block. The vibrations in Edin's arm never fully settled before he had to block another attack. Ithamar popped Edin's hand with the wooden tip. It stung.

"What the flip?" Edin asked.

Ithamar smashed Edin's hand again, the wooden sword slapping against the fingers. Edin's sword went spiraling and landed in the yellow grass. They locked eyes briefly before Edin sprinted to his sword. Ithamar whacked him on the back as Edin bent to pick up the wooden weapon. Edin pivoted and tried to block the next strike, but Ithamar landed a hit on his elbow. Each slap of the blade left lingering pain. Bruises would be forming shortly, he knew.

Survival.

Edin ran into the jungle, and Ithamar chased him like a deranged animal.

The next day, they trained for physical strength, and the day after that they completed another survival exercise where Edin ran for his life through the woods while Ithamar hunted him. Ithamar had called it a friendly scrimmage, but there was nothing friendly about the dark-blue bruises on Edin's back, arms, and legs. It was borderline torture. There were moments when Edin feared for his life. But Ithamar would only strike him once or twice with the wooden waster before letting Edin escape behind a tree or into a valley.

During their breaks, Ithamar showed Edin defensive skills: guarding, evading, distancing, parrying, blocking, and riposting. These skills were tested brutally during the following drill sessions. Edin never struck Ithamar once on a counterattack, and swinging at his mentor usually meant another bruise was coming Edin's way. But throughout the two days of survival training, he realized how much quicker and shiftier he had become since they arrived in the training camp and how evading and guarding developed naturally.

Ithamar waited until the very last day to train Edin on the fundamentals of attack. They woke late that morning and ate eggs and toast, then washed breakfast down with fresh tea. Together they walked outside, picked up the wooden swords off the porch, and strolled into the yard.

After much internal debate, Edin figured out the stance he would use in the first match and began to train with it against his mentor. He placed his left foot forward and slightly bent both knees. He held the sword low with both arms, guarding his left leg. Considering his next opponent was short and quick, this seemed like a good option. Also, Ithamar approved of the stance, saying it was a simple resting position that conserved energy. They trained all morning and afternoon—striking, thrusting, lunging, feinting, grappling, and disengaging. Edin discovered the purpose of the continuous lunging exercise he was forced to do during physical training. His jumping and striking speed must have triplicated. There was no way he'd have had this burst of strength when he arrived at the remote site nearly two weeks ago. Before the sun dipped below the timberline, they quit training for the final time before the first match. Now the worries and concerns of future combat haunted Edin, even more than the soreness from physical training.

Every evening after training, when Edin woke from his nap, they had watched footage of old gauntlet matches on a hologram in the downstairs living room. Ithamar would discuss tactics and the importance of distancing and positioning to strike at the right moment. On the hologram, recorded avatars quarreled with hyperblades above the wooden table while the two cousins studied and inspected every move, including the microscopic details of footwork, stances, and strike angles.

The fact Ithamar loved to expose was that most of the contestants defeated in the gauntlet had died from their own mistakes; rarely was there a swordsman so glorious with a hyperblade that he was impossible to defend against. However, they watched three matches starring Bognor Nazari, Cane's grandfather. Bognor slashed through the blocks and wimpy defensive attempts of his opponents with no fear. His hyperblade spun in a whirlwind of anger and assault. It was pure talent, the finest display of swordsmanship either of them had seen. Bognor killed faster than any other contestant, and he killed with flawless strike accuracy. Edin wondered if Cane had similar skills.

On the night before they had to leave for the capital, Ithamar played footage of contestants with physiques similar to Finder Shaw's. Ithamar pointed out the speed that Edin should expect to find in his upcoming opponent. He recommended counterattacks and even grappling, where Edin might have the advantage because of size. Ithamar told him to keep his guard low. Finder wasn't tall enough to strike from above because it would leave him exposed.

Edin skipped a nap during the day and went to bed early that night, but he had trouble falling asleep once he settled in the sheets. Winds hissed between the trees and the siding of the bungalow, yet it was the thoughts within his head keeping him awake. The arrival of match day was the main contributor to the anxiety. He visualized entering the arena with thousands of spectators chanting and colored smoke saturating the grandstands. Hyperblades clashed repeatedly in his mind like a broken hologram only capable of displaying one scene. He tried counting to get his mind off the fight, but his thoughts drifted to Vanya Waldrip. *What has she been up to in the past two weeks?* He remembered the night he took her out to eat. He prayed for the opportunity to speak with her the next day, after the fight. He hoped she would be in the stands when he triumphed.

As the night continued, his anxiety wasn't the only thing keeping him awake. His stomach growled like a starving predator. The clean diet combined with the rigorous exercise schedule left him hungry all the time. Ithamar promised he could eat all the greasy food within the city limits of Kosabar if he won his match. Edin thought about gyros with double portions of grilled kulliben. He thought about every kind of delicious food he had been deprived of while he tossed and turned in the sweaty sheets.

Eventually he fell asleep with a few hours to spare before the morning. The sleep was ridden by strange visions. He was alone, by himself, on an odd planet plagued by lightning and thunder and heavy rain. Ahead was the outline of an old castle in the storm. He floated towards the castle like a phantom in his own nightmare, unsure if he was a character in the play or just a camera for an unknown audience. Somehow, he teleported to the throne room where guards stood at attention, dressed in resplendent gray armor that covered them from head to toe. On the throne, a human stood up as the phantasmic Edin drifted to the seat of power.

The lord of the castle wore white chain mail with a golden breastplate. He was a tall but skinny middle-aged man with long brown hair and a simple face. Edin had no control of the events within the dream, and he raced up to the throne despite wanting to leave.

"Edin Carvosa, the boy I have waited years to meet," the lord said.

"Who are you?"

"You don't recognize your liege pharaoh? Everyone in the galaxy should."

"Liege Pharaoh . . . Zator Heiros?" Panic trembled in Edin's mind. His legs and arms shifted around in the bed as he tried to escape the dark reverie and return to reality. It was useless. He was trapped. "Why am I here?" Edin asked.

"I'm ordering you to die in the gauntlet tournament tomorrow."

"No."

"You must, for the fate of the galaxy. It will be a better place without you. If you live, Edin, you will bring destruction upon entire solar systems and murder millions in a failed rebellion against the royal dynasty. We are forever. The Mizoquii are an abomination."

"You don't know the fate of the galaxy."

The liege pharaoh drew near to Edin. "You will die in this tournament. Or you will die at the hands of the royal dynasty." The liege pharaoh leaned closer and whispered in his ear, "It wouldn't be the first time Carvosa blood poured on the marble of this throne room."

Edin jumped back. "What?"

The liege pharaoh raised an arm with extreme focus. Red energy emerged in a swirling circle that glowed brightly. He said, "Run and hide. That is what the Mizoquii are known for." The liege pharaoh launched the ball of energy, and it smashed into Edin's face.

He jolted upright in the bed, covered with sweat.

CHAPTER 11

Edin arrived at the Kosabar Arena two hours prior to the match, only to find that the locker room he was provided had no toilets and no benches and no lockers. It was a square room of nothing but pure concrete and a single lightbulb. A yellow piece of paper was stuck to the wall. Ithamar snatched it, pulling off a purple tacky substance along with the note.

"Looks like your friend Cane Nazari hooked you up with the dressing room." Ithamar handed the note to Edin.

Dear Space Trash,
I hope you enjoy your room!
Don't forget to wipe and flush, you turdpiece!
Your Prince,
Cane Nazari

Edin crumbled up the paper. "How considerate of him to send a 'welcome' letter."

Ithamar laughed. "He hates you. But it is pretty funny. This place couldn't be much worse."

"I'm not even fighting him yet and he's testing me."

"Take out your frustration on the opponent you will face. That's enough revenge for now."

"I wish it was Cane, not Finder." Edin spat on the floor. "I'm ready."

"Don't think about what you can't control."

Ithamar had brought a black duffle bag with him. He dropped it on the floor, unzipped it, and pulled out a gi—a lightweight two-piece outfit consisting of baggy, jet-black pants and a green jacket closed with a cloth belt. The design was simple, but the green and black looked refined and stylish.

"It looks like something a prince would wear," Edin said.

"Maybe not to the people on this planet," Ithamar said. "But you are royalty."

Edin changed into the gi. It felt loose and weightless. He paced the room, throwing punches. The warm-up continued with him performing simple footwork exercises and pretending to swing an imaginary sword at an imaginary foe.

"I think I'll make my way to the seating area now. I told Vanya I would watch the fight with her."

"Alright."

"The guard will hand you the hyperblade in the tunnel. It should be light compared to what we trained with."

"Alright."

"You good?"

"Yeah."

"Good luck, trooper."

"Thanks."

Not long after Ithamar left, there was a knock on the door. Edin stood, left the room, and entered the walkway. A tournament official was waiting for him. She was a tikkino, a birdlike species that stood on talons and had another set of claws beneath their feathered wings. She was taller than him and had white feathers and tan eyes. Her slim orange beak opened as she asked, "Mr. Carvosa, are you ready?"

"Yeah."

They strode through the web of underground corridors in taciturn silence. Guards with plasma rifles stood watch in stationary muteness at nearly every corner. As they traversed the labyrinth, more and more cameramen lined the cold block walls and aimed their gadgets at him. He tried to ignore the surroundings and concentrate on the imminent battle. He turned the final corner with the bird lady and saw sunlight entering from the pitch. *Don't think about it, just win.* They stopped a few meters away from the end of the tunnel. *Don't think about it, just win.*

"We still have ten minutes or so until you walk out," the tikkino said.

"Alright."

"Would you like the hold the hyperblade?"

Edin shrugged. "Yes."

The tikkino pulled a metal hilt from under her huge wing and handed it over. Edin examined the handle. It was a black apparatus with a silver button. He knew the weapon was made of pure adamantine, and it was the first time he had ever held the unbreakable element. It was lighter than he expected and looked freshly constructed, as if he were the first person to ever wield it. He was nervous to press the control that actuated the blade. He pointed the hilt ahead of him in open space, then activated the weapon.

The adamantine blade extended in three different shafts that narrowed and curved to a dangerously sharp point. After it lengthened, the razor edge started to glow white. Infinity plasma was the substance that turned the weapon from a simple sword to an intimidating marvel. He watched in amazement as the hyperblade transformed from metal to plasma. It maintained the bowed silhouette as before, but now it buzzed with vitality.

The hilt had warmed up in his grip. He sliced the hyperblade through empty air. It was beyond his imagination. Light, simple, and deadly. He carved up the space in front of him and wondered what the recoil would be like when two hyperblades collided. This was the weapon he was going to use to record his first kill. He lowered the sword and closed his eyes. He let out a heavy breath and waited for the fight to commence, the electrified hyperblade humming in his right hand.

Vanya Waldrip entered the Kosabar Arena in a walkway below the seating area. She paced through small crowds of humans and various other species until she reached the section beside the tunnel that Edin would use to appear on the pitch. She felt slight disappointment when she arrived in the stands and Ithamar was nowhere to be found. The match had also failed to draw the number of spectators that fights earlier in the day had reaped. A spacer and a kid from Worinth weren't exactly the highlight of the first round, she knew. But it should be a good match: two desperate contestants with nothing to lose and the galaxy to gain.

In the front row, she situated herself on the metal bench and waited for Ithamar to show. The stadium looked larger when it wasn't packed with wild hordes jumping together shoulder to shoulder. It was a quiet day, and the sun provided warmth, peace before a storm. Across the stadium, at the entry of the other tunnel, a mass of people from Worinth sat motionless in brown robes. They had come from their desert planet to watch their beloved Finder Shaw. Her section was bare in comparison to most of the stadium. Edin would only win fans and draw attendance by winning matches in this tournament and making bettors rich.

She pitied Edin. His death would surely happen in the tournament. There was too much competition. Even if he did make it to the finale, it would take a miracle for anyone to kill Cane Nazari. The noble houses had too much invested in their youth. Still, she admired Edin's ambition and hope for a future beyond the standard.

Ithamar entered the stands from the walkway. Vanya stood and raised her arm to seize his attention. The gray-haired man wore his black cloak and silver armor. His mechanical eye locked onto the waving hand in the front row. He strutted down the limestone stairs to sit beside Vanya.

"How are you, stranger?" she asked.

"Busy, busy, busy." He sat. "How has the city treated you?"

"Not exciting. But not much can compete with the excitement of having a contestant and a cyborg at the Pebble Inn."

"C'mon now. You got A-Veetwo."

"A-Veetwo isn't the most charming droid."

"You're hinting that Edin is charming now?"

"No." Vanya giggled. "How is he, though? You think he'll be able to hold up today?"

"The kid is dangerously fast, much shiftier and quicker than one would assume. It should make for an interesting match, considering the opponent."

"Is he ready to kill if it comes to it?"

Ithamar paused. "I hope so." He looked across the stadium at the crowd from Worinth. "He does lack striking accuracy and remaining hungry on the offensive. I'm hoping the arena provides him with the needed focus."

"You know Finder will be ruthless. If Edin hesitates, it will cost him his life."

"I know."

She noticed Ithamar's eyes wandering to the top row on their left. The glass skybox rose over the rest of the arena like a lofty spire on a castle. It consisted of ritzy lounges and a rooftop balcony with golden railings. The richest spectators and gamblers in the solar system watched from inside while occasionally migrating to the upper promenade.

"The noble houses are watching this fight," Ithamar said.

"They watch every fight." Vanya observed the skybox. "It is more than a tournament to them. It's about honor, pride, and tradition."

"Imaginary obsessions."

"You must have an imaginary obsession or two. Edin told me you

were a great fighter, and all great fighters are driven by something."
Vanya met his eyes. "What is your obsession?"

"That is none of your concern."

A hidden cannon fired an explosive rocket over the stadium. It burst
with a *BOOM* and showered dazzling light, signaling the competitors
to exit their respective tunnels.

Edin rushed onto the pitch, kicking up gravel. His heart thumped
madly, and he gripped the hyperblade with all the strength in his
forearm. Over the expansive terrain he saw his opponent running
headlong in his direction.

When the contestants met in the center of the pitch, neither one of
them went to guard. They both swung their blades wildly. The swords
smashed into each other and bounced back. Finder went to strike again
and Edin blocked it. Finder swung over and over, again and again. The
frantic speed was controlled, but he lacked the reach to find a soft spot
in Edin's defense. The blades flashed through the air in violent blurs.
Edin had yet to gain a position to attack.

He assumed he'd find an opening after he blocked a strike. He
attempted a counterattack by swinging for the neck, but Finder
stretched the sharp tip of his hyperblade forward, aiming for Edin's
gut. Edin halted his movement mid-swing and evaded the thrust with
a sidestep and a leap backward, then aligned himself to his trained
stance. The two contestants were out of striking range, breathing
heavily. He studied Finder and Finder studied him. The short boy's
eyes were frenzied and ravenous. His hair was windswept, and sweat
trickled from his brow and down under his collar. In the stands behind
him, a mass of spectators wore tan attire. In comparison, the rest of the
stadium appeared lifeless.

"You're surprisingly fast," Finder said.

"You're the one on the attack," Edin said.

"Eventually I will hit flesh."

"You haven't yet."

"Watch this." Finder took two quick strides forward and leapt with the hyperblade bending towards Edin. It was an easy evasion. Edin lunged to the side. Finder attempted a strike in the same manner again. Edin easily dodged it with another lunge.

"You're going to have to do better," Edin teased. "You have all your people watching."

"Quit running, coward," Finder growled.

They paced in a circle like two moons orbiting an invisible planet. The warm-up was over for Edin. His feet felt alive. His mind felt focused. He'd discovered Finder's weakness was his aggression. The speed was an advantage, but the conceitedness that came with the speed was a flaw.

"If you're faster than me, you should be able to catch me."

"Don't worry, Carvosa. I will. You really think I'll lose in the first round to space filth?"

Edin smirked. "I do, because I'm quicker than you."

Finder charged headfirst. "C'mon then!"

The blades collided with a thud. Finder continued striking, the hyperblades a fuzzy wave of plasma. Edin managed to block all the blows. He tried to parry with a counterattack intended for the shoulder, but Finder swung his blade low towards the legs, and Edin sprang back in panic. It was the closest either one had gotten. Edin realized his entire left leg could have been cut off.

Finder must have noticed the worry on Edin's face because he pounced with a flurry of swings. Edin displayed a defensive spectacle of technical blocks and lightspeed footwork against the bombardment, but Finder kept swinging faster and harder. Edin had to backpedal and wait for the moment.

Finder swung overhead recklessly and left his body exposed as if to tempt Edin into the counter. Edin blocked the strike, half lunged to the right, and feinted a parry. Finder's eyes swelled in excitement.

He quickly aimed his blade for the gut—just as Edin had predicted.

Edin lunged back to the left, evading the entire hyperblade thrust. With his free hand, Edin grabbed Finder's outstretched arm, clenched the forearm, and pushed it upwards, the hyperblade following suit. The body of the Worinth boy was left unprotected, and Edin drove his hyperblade into Finder's exposed gut. Red soaked the belly of the tunic. Finder groaned painfully, and his weapon fell from his hand to the gravel. In the stands, the mob of brown robes gasped in shock.

Edin pulled the blade out.

"Not to you." Finder dropped to his knees and clasped his stomach. "I shamed my family."

Edin bent down. "No, you didn't. I'll let you in on a secret."

"What?"

"I am a Mizoquii," he whispered.

"What the flip is a Mizo—"

Edin stood and decapitated the boy from Worinth. He turned and stepped away from the falling body, a fan of blood spraying from the throat. As he walked over the terrain, the bare seating area didn't display much affection for the victor. But two people in the stands above the tunnel were jumping and waving their arms in victory—Vanya and Ithamar, Edin knew.

He pressed the silver button to disengage the hyperblade, and it retracted into the hilt. He waved back at them in the stands and walked off the pitch and inside the dark tunnel.

Vanya made a reservation for three at a restaurant called Maypoes, located in the garden district. The restaurant nested on the top floor of an old hotel called the Coat Check. Vanya, Edin, and Ithamar were dropped off by A-Veetwo in the old glidecar. After the match, Edin changed out of his gauntlet wear and outfitted himself in a gray hoodie and blue sweatpants. Vanya remained in the seersucker minidress that she'd worn earlier.

She led the way through the sliding glass doors with a bearing of having been to the place a million times. They walked over marble floors and passed a massive reception desk on their way towards the elevator in an arched hallway. She pressed the arrow and they waited.

Edin examined the hall. "This is a nice hotel."

"Yeah, it's a cool hangout," Vanya said. "You'll like the rooftop."

"Fewer cobwebs than the Pebble Inn," Ithamar said.

Edin laughed. "True."

Vanya straightened her posture. "Maybe you can clean up the lobby tonight, since you stayed on my roof one night for free."

"Just me?" Ithamar asked. "You're going to need an army to clean that place."

"And that probably won't be enough," Edin said.

Vanya shook her head. "I don't know why I even try to be friends with boys. So inconsiderate."

The elevator pinged, and the doors opened. A young human boy exited. He eyed Edin with indescribable wonder.

"You're Edin Carvosa," the boy said. "You won today."

"Uh . . . yeah. I did."

"That was awesome! Someday I want to enter the gauntlet tournament!"

"Oh, okay. Good luck, I guess."

The kid smiled and ran into the lobby.

"Now we have to deal with the hero worship," Vanya said.

They stepped inside the carpeted elevator. It zipped up forty levels to the top of the building. Edin and Ithamar were surprised by the speed, and she giggled at Ithamar holding the railing.

"This thing took off like we were about to leave the planet," Ithamar said defensively.

The doors opened to an upscale restaurant taking up the entire top floor. As soon as they stepped out the elevator, a red-haired hostess greeted them from behind a glass podium. A busy bar lined the nearest wall, which was covered with a web of clear tubing connected to multiple mechanical contraptions producing an assortment of frozen cocktails.

"Now I know why you wanted to come here," Edin said. "There's every drink you could think of."

"Partially," Vanya said.

The hostess smiled. "Welcome to Maypoes! Do you have a reservation?"

"Yes, Waldrip for three."

The hostess glanced at a screen connected to the podium. "Ah yes. Your table is ready. Follow me."

They hurried through the dining area by the packed bar. Crystal chandeliers hung from the domed ceiling and produced dim lighting. The air held scents of grilled citrus and seafood. The booths and chairs had bloodred cushions and white tablecloths laid underneath ancient candles.

All eyes gravitated to the three of them as they followed the hostess. At the bar and the tables, the patrons twisted their necks to get a glimpse of Edin Carvosa. Even though the arena was empty earlier, most of the citizens in the city had viewed the match digitally—or at least glimpsed the highlights running nonstop on multiple channels. The dinner guests whispered amongst themselves. Vanya thought she heard someone say "luck" and another person predict Edin would be dead after the next round. She cringed and tried to ignore the low voices. Following the hostess, they exited the dining area onto the rooftop patio.

The patio provided a great view of the Kosabar nightscape. Light pollution radiated from bright billboards and towering skyscrapers. Spaceships zipped amongst the clouds and industrial pillars of civilization. They passed more tables and patrons and walked to the corner of the patio where there was a concrete staircase.

The hostess smiled. "Your reservations are for the private deck, up here."

"I guess we're important," Ithamar said.

"Not you, just Edin," Vanya said

CHAPTER 12

In the veranda, the hostess seated them at a lone sectional. She promised a waitress would be there shortly and then left. The three examined the view of the glowing skyline and the blinking dots of spacecrafts in the distance. A gentle wind brushed over Edin. Two rounded moons complemented the night. The city before him reminded him that civilization existed. He missed the busy excitement when training in isolation.

Ithamar glared at Vanya. "So, your parents just left you on Lathas by yourself?"

Vanya was looking at the skyline. She snapped her head towards him. "That's a random question."

"I was just wondering. Edin told me they were off-planet for business."

"Yes, they're acquiring hotels on another planet. Or something like that. I'm not fond of the family business and try to not concern myself with their affairs. I'm only at the Pebble Inn to help my grandfather."

"He's the one coughing on the bottom floor?"

"Probably him. There are three patients on the first floor."

"Patients?" Edin asked.

Vanya nodded. "We have three patients on bed rest. They pay all the bills so they don't have to go anywhere else. That's why the inn is so dirty. I'm tending to them most of the time."

"Dang. Why haven't you told me that?"

Vanya's cheeks flushed. "I thought you wouldn't want to stay. It sounds more like a nursing home than a hotel."

Edin sat speechless.

"Yeah, that's strange to know, in hindsight," Ithamar said.

"I was bored of having no one to talk to besides A-Veetwo. When Edin showed up for a room, I gave him one. I mean, the inn can still function as a hotel. It's just not many people travel that way or even think we're open."

"Why are you there by yourself?" Edin asked. "Don't you want to do something else?"

"Yeah, of course I'd rather be doing something else with my life. I have ambitions too. My parents promised to help me financially if I watched over grandpa while they were gone. They promised they'll put me through an academy—the best one I can get into."

"Do you think they're returning?" Ithamar asked seriously.

"Yes! They're my parents and I'm their only child!"

Ithamar laughed. "Sorry, but they did leave you on a planet to run a decaying hotel."

Vanya shook her head with a grimace. "I'm done with you."

The waiter arrived from the stairwell. He was a hairless creature with red skin and wore a spiffy black uniform.

"Gentlemen, lady, how are you doi—" The waiter paused. "You're Edin Carvosa! I watched your match today."

"Oh yeah," Edin murmured.

"This is crazy. I've never served a contestant after a match."

"We figured we'd spend the night in the city."

"Splendid idea. Maypoes has arguably the best outdoor patio in Kosabar." The waiter smiled with a toothless mouth and large lips. "What can I get you fine people to drink?"

"I'll take a Roltu cryptini with an orefruit twist," Ithamar said. "Shaved and very dry."

"Excellent taste. Well traveled, I see."

"I'll take the same," Vanya said.

"Excellent."

"I'll take a water," Edin said.

"Ah, no appetite for a buzz, I see."

"None."

The waiter smiled. "I'll be back shortly. The menus are on the table if you want to go ahead and look through those." He walked away.

"Have you ever had a Roltu cryptini?" Ithamar asked.

"No," Vanya said. "But you sounded confident when ordering it."

"It's strong."

"Good. Today has been quite the day."

Edin picked up an electronic tablet from the middle of the glass table. The other two picked up digital menus as well. The screen turned on automatically when Edin made eye contact with it. He scrolled through the long list of appetizers to reach the entrees. A note stated each signature dish was served with hot bread and a spread of peppered cheese. His mouth watered at the thought. The main courses consisted of seafood from Lathas, mainly. However, there were three cuts of fish from other solar systems. *Probably transported in a dumpy spacecraft while frozen for an eternity,* he thought. The price was outrageous at 176 credits each. He decided on the gourff legs in tauco soup. Gourff was a small and native amphibian of Lathas. He had never eaten amphibian meat.

"I think I'm going with the gourff legs," Edin said.

"Gross," Vanya said.

"Not a lot of meat," Ithamar said. "You don't want the halofish fillet?"

"Nah," Edin said.

"I might try the halofish," Vanya said.

"That's what I'm getting. Quit copying me," Ithamar said.

"I figured since you're so old, you have enough life experience to know what to order."

"I'm not that old. I was born with gray hair. I could still go out and enjoy a night in the city if I wanted to."

"I heard hangovers get worse with age." Vanya grinned. "They must be torture for you."

"I bet after two cryptinis you're in the bathroom puking while Edin is holding up your hair."

"You don't think girls can handle their liquor?"

"I know they can't. That's why Edin isn't drinking."

They laughed.

"I hate you," Edin said.

The waiter arrived with their drinks. The cryptinis came in two stemmed glasses with the green louche liquor saturating tiny shavings of ice and garnished with the lilac peels of orefruit. A glass of water was dropped in front of Edin. He watched the other two take the first sips of their cocktails. Vanya recoiled at the taste. Ithamar took a huge gulp while watching her wince.

"Wow, that's strong," Vanya said. "It's like I'm drinking disinfectant."

Ithamar chugged the rest of the drink and returned the empty glass to the table. "Cryptinis—the elixir of life."

Vanya took another baby sip. "You're an alcoholic."

The waiter was still standing by the table, watching them. "Um, are you guys ready to order?"

"Oh yeah, I'm sorry about that," Ithamar said. "I'll take another drink and the halofish fillet."

"I'll take the halofish fillet as well," Vanya said.

"And for you?" The waiter asked Edin.

"The gourff legs in tauco soup," Edin answered.

"Interesting choice. Alright, I'll put those in."

The waiter vanished downstairs. Edin eyed the cryptini in Vanya's hand.

"Would you like to try it?" she asked.

"Sure."

She placed the stemmed glass on the table. He picked it up and watched the fragments of ice floating amid the cloudy liquid. It smelled of matured honey and sour melon. He positioned the rim of the glass on his lips and took a swig. The cryptini tasted robust and bittersweet and provided a numbing aftertaste. He felt a hypnotizing warmth from the icy liquor and smiled spontaneously. He handed the drink back to Vanya.

"I've never tasted anything like that," Edin said.

"After the tournament, you can have all the cryptinis you want," Ithamar said.

Vanya took a sip. "Yeah, I think I'll pass on this next time."

"What's your preferred drink?" Edin asked.

"Nectardrop."

"Girly," Ithamar said. "But nectardrops are enjoyable."

"Alright, well, we will have to go out for cryptinis and nectardrops after I defeat Cane Nazari," Edin said.

"You have to beat Zokku Rellen first," Vanya said.

The table went silent. It was the first time anyone had mentioned the next contestant Edin would face since Ithamar notified them. After his fight against Finder, they left the arena, and Zokku dominated his opponent in front of a full crowd.

There was one major issue with fighting Zokku. He was the biggest contestant, even larger than Cane. A mountain of raw power. Oddsmakers considered him the second favorite to win the tournament, Cane the first. They sat in silence because no one was sure how Edin would fair against someone so massive.

"He will beat him," Ithamar said.

"Do you have a plan?" Vanya asked.

"I have thought of something, although it might be dangerous. Everything will be dangerous against Zokku."

Edin sat still and quiet with one arm in his lap and the other stretched to the end of the armrest. He wasn't sure what to think about the scenario. He had never competed against someone of such stature. He hoped Ithamar would know what to do and train him properly.

The waiter arrived carrying a tray with two cryptinis, two sizzling hot plates, and a bowl of soup. He dropped off the two plates of halofish fillet first. The white meat was seared and seasoned with verdant spices and herbs. Ithamar and Vanya beheld their meals in elation.

The waiter lowered the bowl of tauco soup in front of Edin. The roasted amphibian legs swam in the bronzed broth. It stunk like swamp water.

"Hope that you enjoy your meals." The waiter left the next round of cryptinis on the table.

Edin picked up the wooden spoon in the bowl and took a sip of the broth.

He didn't know what to think of the taste. There was something different. Something unknown. It wasn't the taste; it wasn't the texture. He was unsure of what exactly was in the soup, but he knew couldn't breathe. *There is something in that*, he thought. He coughed, then choked for air desperately. The other two stared at him with wide eyes. He was choking on nothingness, and his eyes began watering at the thought of his own death. It was poison. It had to be.

"What's happening to him?" Vanya gasped.

That was the last thing he heard before his waterlogged vision faded to an immense blackness . . .

Edin spent a week in deep sleep from the poison in his soup. He dreamed of planets scattered in the reaches of the galaxy. Rising visions crashed in waves against the shoreline of his consciousness. A war raged between two massive armies of battleships launching bright projectiles in dark space. He saw Gifted warriors battling each other on distant worlds. Rays of cosmic energy collided and exploded amongst the stars, entire planets destroyed in fire and ruin and death. He shivered in his sweat. His weak body lay in the bed, fighting the poison while combating the conflicts within his own twisted mind.

When he woke from the sleep, he barely remembered the dreams. He had no recollection of what happened before he tasted the poison. The last thing he recalled was killing Finder Shaw in the arena. His eyes creaked open, and he looked around a bedroom filled with natural light. He knew where he was. It was the upstairs bedroom in the bungalow where he stayed for training. He pushed himself into an upright position. His body felt stiff and fragile.

"Ithamar!" he shouted.

"Edin!" someone yelled outside of the room.

Footsteps clamored against the stairs. The door swung open and banged against the wall. It was Vanya, Ithamar behind her. They hurried into the room and regarded Edin with pity.

"How are you feeling?" Vanya asked.

"Alright, I guess. What happened?"

"Someone poisoned your soup at Maypoes."

"Who?"

"That's the question we don't know the answer to," Ithamar said.

"What is Maypoes?"

"It's the restaurant we went to after your victory."

"Oh. How long have I"—he paused and looked at himself in the bed—"been like this?"

"Nine days."

"So, I fight in five days."

"I don't think you're going to be ready," Vanya said.

"Yes, you fight in five days." Ithamar stared Vanya down. "He will be ready."

"How did I not die?" Edin asked. "If someone poisoned me, why am I still alive?"

"You didn't drink enough of it. And I have a poison kit in the Riskplay."

Edin swiveled his legs out of the sheets and stepped on the wooden floor. He stood for a second and felt the blood rush to his tingling toes. He was clumsy on his feet, but he made it down the stairs and sat on the couch in the den. Vanya sat next to him. Ithamar went to the kitchen and brought him a plate of hot food—yellow vegetables and grilled mountain fish.

"I thought no one would try to kill a contestant," Edin said. "Why would someone poison me?"

"Someone who was in collusion with Captain Jameson, I suppose. They might figure you know too much about his operations and clientele," Ithamar said. "If someone knows you were on the *Saircor*, and then they see you winning matches in the gauntlet, they may assume you'd rat them out. Or maybe you were even the one to kill the crew. Most likely, whoever did this has nothing to do with the tournament."

Edin took a bite of the fish and swallowed. "Geez, now I have a real bounty hunter after me."

"I believe so. Somebody outside of the arena has to want you dead."

"Well, why is she here?" Edin pointed at Vanya.

"What is that supposed to mean?" Vanya raised her voice.

"No girls are allowed at the training camp."

"We don't really know what is going on back in the capital," Ithamar said. "Whoever tried to kill you might go after Vanya if we left her alone. We figured she'd be safer with us, and we decided to let the droid run the Pebble Inn."

"A-Veetwo is going to burn that place down," Edin said.

"The Pebble Inn will be fine," Vanya said.

Edin started training the next day. Ithamar and Edin ran through the woods and through the morning, all the way into early afternoon. Even though they jogged next to each other for hours, Edin didn't speak much with Ithamar. They were focused on the task of physically preparing for combat.

On the run, Edin kept visualizing the upcoming battle with Zokku. His opponent was much taller and wider than him. The only way Edin saw himself winning was with a quick and evasive maneuver. Standing toe to toe with blades clashing would result in a defeat. Zokku, a machine of muscle, had strength and reach. Edin pictured himself sneaking around Zokku and jabbing a hyperblade in the gut of his foe.

They returned to the bungalow that afternoon. Both panted for air beside the porch after a long sprint.

"You're not ready," Ithamar said.

"I will be," Edin promised.

"No. It's too late."

Edin hardened his gaze. "What do you mean too late?"

"You're not going to be able to compete against him close-up. It would be too much of a risk with his size advantage and your lack of shape. You were moving way too slow on that run."

"Well, I have no choice but to kill him or die, so I don't get what you're saying."

"You're going to have to kill him from a distance."

"I don't have mysterious and magical powers like you. Even if I did, I couldn't use them."

"That's not what I'm talking about."

Ithamar walked across the yard towards the Riskplay. Opening the airlock, he vanished inside briefly. Moments later he exited with something in his hand. Edin eyed what appeared to be a hilt.

"You have a hyperblade!"

Ithamar smiled as he walked back to Edin and handed him the weapon. Edin held the hilt and inspected the adamantine steel. It was real, just like the one he fought with in the arena.

"Let me see it," Ithamar said.

Edin handed it back over. Ithamar pointed the hilt away from his body and pressed the button to actuate the weapon. The blade extended quickly and pulsated with life as the infinity plasma heated the edge of the sword. What he did next was something Edin wasn't expecting.

Ithamar threw the sword.

The energized blade rotated viciously, flying across the open yard in the direction of the jungle. It stuck into a very thick tree with a thud, followed by the hissing sound of burning wood. The hyperblade dropped and left a trail of black burned timber from the point where it entered the tree all the way to the ground.

"What did you do that for?" Edin asked.

"That's how you're going to kill him," Ithamar said. "You're going to send the hyperblade flying at his face before he even has the chance to swing on you. He will never see it coming."

"If I throw it and miss, I'm dead."

"You're not going to miss."

"What if . . ." Edin couldn't think of an argument. He was confused.

Ithamar walked towards the hyperblade and the tree. He picked up the weapon and brought it back to Edin. "Throw it."

Edin took the hyperblade and gripped the hilt. He slung it. The sword spiraled to the ground before making it half as far as Ithamar's throw. It started to singe the grass.

"Cursed moons, that was awful," Edin said.

"Good thing we have four days to practice."

CHAPTER 13

The sun glimmered on Palais de la Perpillas, the great residence of House Nazari. The old castle edged a cliff overlooking the ocean; below, waves crashed against the rocky shores. A white stone steeple topped every other structure. Battlements and towers intimidated the little ships on the water and even dwarfed the spacecrafts in the sky. Trees and hedges sprouted in the gardens and down the walkways embedded within the walled stronghold. Yellow-and-purple banners fluttered in the wind, flaunting the insignia of a lavish flower.

Cane Nazari had just returned to the palace from Kosabar where he had won his first match in the tournament. He defeated his opponent, Joshua Port, in record time—nine seconds. When the bout started, Cane sprinted towards his foe and cut him down furiously. Joshua Port was not skilled nor physically adept enough to even block the first strike. To Cane, it felt like competing against a newborn. The training sessions he faced daily were far more difficult. Of course, he was fully aware of his advantages. He had more resources and time to prepare for the competition than the other contestants. That was why it would bring dishonor and shame to his family and the planet itself if he had lost.

Other royal families in the solar system traveled to Lathas to compete in the tournament, but House Nazari must always reign supreme. That was what his father always told him: Nazari over everything.

Cane entered his bedchamber. Piles of dirty laundry were scattered across the white stone floor. A haloed chandelier hung from the high ceiling. In the corner, golden curtains opened to a canopy bed where thick furs covered the mattress. Tapestries glued to the walls exhibited images of previous wars and dead heroes in the Nazari lineage. An electric fireplace burned next to the bed. A desk with three digital monitors floating above the wooden surface stood beside the door to the bathroom.

He freshened up with an icy cold shower, then changed into black sweatpants and a hoodie and lay on his mammoth bed. The rest of the day he had off from training because it was a matchday. He was unsure what to do with the free time.

There was a loud knock at the door.

"Yeah," Cane shouted.

"Can I come in?" his father asked.

"Yeah."

King Bahri Nazari opened the door and walked inside the bedchamber, inspecting the mess on the floor. His hazel eyes then glared at Cane. The king wore a violet ceremonial suit tailored perfectly to fit his broad shoulders. He had the same dark and curly hair as his son, but his facial hair was graying.

Cane thought his father seemed puzzled about something. It was odd for him to come up to the prince's chamber instead of having a servant run the message.

Cane left his bed and walked across the cold stone floor to sit at his desk.

"What's wrong?"

Bahri placed his hands on his hips. "I'm guessing you haven't watched the other fights."

"No, why?"

"The spacer won."

They sat in silence.

"It's just the first round." Cane shook his head. "Did Zokku win?"

"Yes," Bahri sighed. "But that's not the point."

"I know, I know. We don't want the bloodlines of peasants winning any matches in the tournament. It gives the commoners the belief that they can contend against us."

"Yes, we don't want more commoners trying to compete in the tournament. We don't want our tradition to become overrun by insects. Especially filth not even from this system. It is vital that if you meet this Edin Carvosa in the tournament, you kill him."

"Zokku will kill him. I don't even want to think about facing the space trash."

"But if he manages to get lucky—"

"If that fool makes it to the finale . . ." Cane gritted his teeth and clenched a fist. "Zokku is mine to kill. Not Carvosa's."

Bahri glanced around the room and back at his son. "Yes, well, if you didn't go around flaunting your abilities, maybe more respectable contestants would've shown up. Now your only worthy adversary is Zokku."

"Respectable contestants would have been honored to fight me. But he is enough. Zokku is the highest threat to House Nazari winning the tournament since our last defeat. Everyone knows it. His death will bring honor to my name, our name."

"Everyone also knows of the disparity in the tournament this year. The boy is a brute. But you two are the only real competitors."

"So what? The first rounds were weak. The intensity will pick up in the final four."

"I hope you're right." Bahri rubbed the hair on his chin. "It's your tournament, after all."

"In the end, everyone will be satisfied," Cane promised.

"Good." Bahri turned towards the door and began to walk out. "Dinner will be ready shortly." He looked over his shoulder. "Your mother wants to see you, so you have to come down."

"Alright. I'll be there."

The king closed the door to the chamber.

Cane leaned back in the chair and put his feet on the desk. *The space trash actually won*, he thought. Finder Shaw wasn't exactly a leading contestant, but Cane assumed Finder would make it out of the first round. Cane wondered about the training routine of Edin Carvosa. What was the boy from space up to? How was his body adjusting to the gravity on Lathas? *Perhaps someone should be sent to discover more about the mysterious boy.*

There was another knock at the door.

"Come in!"

The wooden door opened slowly, and a young brunette lady entered. Naomi Langley was a few years older than Cane. She was neither ugly nor pretty—very average in appearance. She walked inside carrying a hamper as the chamber door shut behind her.

"Prince Cane, I was sent to gather your laundry."

"My father sent you?"

She smiled. "Yes."

They both knew she wasn't there only to gather his laundry. That was the duty of the house droids, which were overdue on their visit to his room. There was an extracurricular motive to her arrival. She dropped the hamper by the door and walked over to him. The thought of her warmed him. She sat in his lap and put her hands in his curly hair and brought their faces together.

He pushed her away.

"What's wrong?" she asked.

"You promised to bring another girl the next time we did this."

She looked startled. "I didn't have enough time to find anyone."

He tapped her thigh. "Get up."

She left his lap and stood, confused.

He stood as well and looked down at her. "I don't have time for anything before dinner. Bring a friend later tonight."

"If you insist."

"I do."

Palais de la Perpillas sheltered a colossal training chamber underground where the catacombs once existed. Centuries ago, it was fully renovated to serve as an area to tutor the noble family in the art of combat. Increasing the levels of environmental stress helped break physical plateaus. Now the underground chamber could be electronically controlled to alter the strength of gravity and other impeding elements.

The chamber was one large room that extended in each direction, forming a large circle. The walls, floor, and ceiling were smooth gray steel. Cane hated the room. It felt as if half of his life had been wasted in the empty crypt.

Cane had just finished his two-mile warm-up jog in double gravity. It had been three days since his first victory in the tournament. Two combat droids entered through a chute in the ceiling. Then the hilt of a hyperblade dropped from a chute above Cane. He caught it and activated the weapon. It came to life as the infinity plasma buzzed at the edge of the blade. He stared down the two combat droids twenty meters ahead of him. They were humanoid frames of iron painted black with red pinstripes. Both of them carried dummy swords with the ability to block the hyperblade.

Cane rushed towards the droids, trying to mentally disregard the raised gravity level. They charged him as well. Within seconds both machines were shredded into scrap metal. *No challenge.* Cane felt sweat forming under his yellow shirt. The temperature had been raised. Two more droids dropped from the ceiling, resulting in two more piles of charred debris.

The process continued until Cane had destroyed sixteen of the combat robots. The gravity increased incrementally throughout the session, but it returned to normal once he finished. He felt light on his feet. *Time for a break.* He left the chamber through a windowless oval door.

In the wide tunnel, a jug of water and a plate of blackened halofish fillet and fresh vegetables awaited him on a small table—his favorite lunch. He ate the food quickly and then stood, stretching his calves against the rock wall. The afternoon he would spend weight lifting, and then he would be able to retire to his room for the remainder of the evening. Maybe he could sneak Naomi and a few of her friends through his window. He decided to message her later. Training would only get worse until the next match. *Might as well have some fun on the lighter days*, he thought.

Someone was walking in the tunnel. Cane listened to the footsteps and looked down the stony passage lit by thin strips of blue light on the floor. King Bahri Nazari marched towards him, wearing a beige uniform. He was followed by a man Cane had never seen before.

"Are you coming to spar?" Cane asked.

"Unfortunately, I don't have time," Bahri said.

Cane looked at the man with his father. The stranger had long white hair in a ponytail and a creased face. He was shorter than his father and much slimmer.

"Prince Cane." The man curtsied. "My name is Roan."

"Roan dug up information about the spacer, Edin Carvosa, for us," Bahri said. "There seems to be a haze of controversy surrounding him."

"Like what?" Cane asked.

"He is being trained by a man named Ithamar Avrum. But apparently, the two didn't arrive on Lathas together," Roan explained. "And there is no information about Ithamar on the network but for the simple fact that he exists. No real records of him."

"He's probably from some primal planet, worked on farms or something," Cane said.

"What would farmers be doing in the gauntlet tournament on Lathas?" Bahri asked. "Those people work for stability on their homeworld. Why would they come to this planet to die?"

"You don't think they're with the Sheeban Syndicate or Denali Cartel, do you?" Cane asked.

"I can't be sure who they are or why they are here, but there is something deceitful about both of them," Roan said.

"Well . . ." Cane paused. "As long as he doesn't cheat, does it really matter?"

"They might be more dangerous than we presume," Bahri said.

Cane crossed his arms over his chest. "He's nothing compared to me."

"I'm not talking about inside the arena," Bahri said. "They might be a threat outside the arena. There is the possibility they are tied to criminal extremists or some other terror organizations."

"But we do have information on Vanya Waldrip. And it would be odd for someone like her to affiliate with criminals," Roan said.

"Who is Vanya Waldrip?" Cane asked.

"A young blond girl that has been seen with the two," Roan said. "Her family owns a small hotel called the Pebble Inn near the river. It is where Edin and Ithamar stay on match days."

"Maybe we should invite her over to dinner. Investigate," Cane said.

"Maybe," Bahri said. "It would trigger some emotions, at the very least."

Cane grinned. "It shows I have the spine to invite over his girl, and that I have no respect for him."

A breeze cooled the night on the balcony outside of Cane's bedchamber. The castle was lit by torches along the battlements. Only four more days until he returned to Kosabar to fight in the second gauntlet match against Damien Lynch. *Lynch shouldn't be much competition*, he thought. He sat with his mother as they gazed upon the dark sky dotted with winking stars.

Trinity Nazari, the queen of Lathas, had long dark hair running down her back. She wore a lavender nightgown and comfortable slippers. Despite giving birth to three boys, her skin radiated youthfulness, and her amber eyes viewed the world with innocence. Trinity spent most of her time supporting King Bahri, a decade her elder. She was raised in a noble family and never fathomed the world outside of royalty because she never had to dip her feet into those unknown shallows.

"What do you think of spacers competing in the tournament?" Cane asked.

"I don't know," Trinity said reservedly. "Your father wants contestants from this solar system only. But since other systems allow outsiders, it is dynastic law to allow them if they sign the papers."

"But you have no opinion?"

"Not much of an opinion as long as House Nazari wins. Do you?"

"Yeah. I think the royal dynasty wants to lessen the noble families throughout the galaxy until they become just as common as common can get. So the liege pharaoh enforces these galactic laws, like allowing anyone to compete in the gauntlet tournaments, and takes away the power of the rightful rulers, the explorers who conquered planets and built empires. House Heiros gained too much power and feels threatened because everyone knows it all runs through them now. They want control, and they want no other family to touch the throne for the next millennium. Therefore, they allow filth on the same playing field as royalty to make everyone think we are lesser than the dynasty."

"The center of the galaxy is more freethinking on such affairs. More people traveling in and out of certain solar systems. That's why spacers are allowed in the tournaments."

"Yeah, but as a planet and as a system, we should have the right to decide who competes and who doesn't. In these outer systems, we get screwed. The dynasty shouldn't even be bothering us, yet they tax us and tell us what we can and cannot do."

"Well, there's not much you can do about that."

"Yes, there is."

Trinity scrunched her eyebrows. "What?"

"Take over the galaxy. Burn their entire empire to the ground, and watch House Nazari climb summits never imagined."

Trinity giggled. "So, do the same thing as House Heiros?"

"Yeah."

"Oh males, the only gender that has a brain but forgets to use it."

Cane said nothing and stared forward.

Trinity stood up. "I'm going to bed. You should too. Tomorrow you will be training with your brothers."

He continued to stare ahead. "Goodnight, Mother."

She left, and he sat alone in the night.

His mind raced about what would happen after the tournament. He would go to an academy in the First System like most of the victors decided upon after triumph. He would major in economics and diplomacy, and return to Lathas. At that point, he could build a sizeable army with the potential to challenge the dynasty. He just needed plenty of the Gifted beings to overthrow House Heiros. Supposedly the entire bloodline of Heiros was filled with the cosmic wizards. This was the deepest anxiety that plagued him: the Nazari lacked the Gift. If they were ever to rebel against the throne, their family might not be the ones crowned at the end of the rebellion.

All Gifted must die, he told himself. *Use them to conquer, then slaughter the living in the aftermath. The Gift must be outlawed completely once normal beings regain control. For thousands of years we have been dictated to by others because we weren't born with the same abilities.*

Tomorrow would be a busy day. He stood and retreated inside his chamber, walking barefoot across the cold stone floor to his canopy bed. He pulled back the curtains where Naomi lay waiting underneath the warm furs.

CHAPTER 14

Sunbeams broke through the leafy canopy. Humid air thickened as the morning turned to afternoon. Edin followed Ithamar on their run through the dense forest, both covered in scratches from briar bushes they had run through earlier when Ithamar led them the wrong way. Edin ran with his chest out and his head up to avoid looking down at the cuts.

There seemed to be a nervousness about Ithamar. Ever since Edin had woken from the poisoning incident, Ithamar looked obsessively and compulsively for potential dangers but somehow seemed less aware of his surroundings. The anxiety caused more harm than good. It left Edin and Vanya on edge, wondering what was wrong, and it was out of character for Ithamar to lose focus, including the recent incident of running through the thorny patch.

They stopped running by a shallow stream. Ithamar scanned the area and then knelt on the pebbled bank to fill up a canteen he had attached to his belt. The water rushed over his submerged hand, and he brought the full canteen to his dry mouth and gulped.

Edin put his hands on his knees and tried to catch his breath. Sweat dripped from his blond locks to the rocky ground. He straightened up and pushed back his sticky hair with his hand.

"What's wrong with you lately?" Edin asked.

Ithamar lowered the canteen. "What do you mean?"

"Ever since I woke up, you've been acting different."

"There's something"—Ithamar hesitated—"something happening."

"I don't know what that means."

Ithamar studied the ground and then looked up with his mechanical eye. "You're going to start awakening the Gift soon. I wanted to keep your mind off of it so the fear doesn't trigger it."

"The fear. What fear?"

Ithamar stared at the flowing stream. "When you were sleeping, there were signs of the Gift within you. The gravity, the sunlight, the life—all of this is making you mentally and physically stronger." He pointed around the woods and to the sky. "The Gift will reveal itself to you shortly. I just didn't want the thought, the fear, running through your head before the next fight. If you show any signs in the arena, you will be killed by the officials."

"How am I supposed to control something I know nothing about?"

"All I saw were a few sparks around your body. Your conscious mind shouldn't let anything out during this match. It must have been a reaction to the poison."

"A few sparks." Edin's cheeks went pale. "I'm screwed."

"You just need to go in that arena and kill Zokku. End it quickly, then walk yourself out of there."

"So, I do have the Gift? I'm just not able to use it yet?"

"Yeah. You're late in showing signs for a Mizoquii, but you certainly have it."

Edin stared at his hands. He balled two fists and scanned his body. Had he unlocked an evolved form? While in hibernation from the poison, was there a metamorphosis? *No noticeable changes*, he thought. Of course, since arriving on Lathas, he was physically more fit through training, and his skin had tanned from the sun. But he didn't feel like he held any supernatural powers of cosmic energy within.

"I don't notice a difference," Edin said.

Ithamar took another gulp of water from his canteen. "Don't think about it anymore. Like I said, your body was probably reacting to the poison. I'll train you to use the Gift once we get off this planet."

"Okay."

After the break, they ran back to the bungalow. The path they took was downhill, making it easy on the legs. Edin picked up the pace as his rubber boots struck the ground covered by red leaves. Sweaty hair hung over his eyes. He daydreamed of battling against Zokku in a crowded arena. The kill happened fast. He knew the fans would be disproportionate in his opponent's favor and wondered how the spectators would react if he was victorious. For the moment, he pictured them celebrating his triumph. Then he imagined his next fight against Cane Nazari in the gauntlet finale. His mind replayed future fights until the cousins reached the thickets edging the bungalow and left the trail.

"What the flip happened?!" Ithamar yelled.

Edin panicked at the sight. Three windows on the bungalow were shattered, leaving shards of glass on the porch and in the yard. The front door was wide open.

"Vanya," Edin said softly. He sprinted towards the bungalow.

Ithamar rushed behind him. "Wait! Someone may still be in there!"

Edin didn't stop running. He hurried onto the porch and stepped inside. It smelled awful, like tainted fish. His jaw went slack. The walls and furniture were coated with a thick blue slime. The blue goo hung from the ceiling, and weird footprints trailed up the staircase. Edin immediately ran up the stairs and pulled open the doors to the two bedrooms. No one was there. Vanya was gone. The slime was on the door handles and now on his hands. He shook his hands, and the blue goo splattered the wood floor. "What the flip is this?"

Ithamar rushed up the stairs and began searching both the rooms. He opened the tiny closets and peeked underneath the old beds. He came back into the narrow hall and looked at Edin with a frustrated frown.

"There's no blood here," Ithamar said. "She either ran away or whatever creature came inside might have her alive somewhere."

Edin grimaced. He didn't know what to say or do in the current situation. Had Vanya really been captured by something? Was she hiding somewhere else? Sadness rose within him. He missed her.

"Don't worry," Ithamar said. "We can track the beast."

"How?"

Ithamar grabbed a glob of gooey slime. "Follow me."

They went downstairs.

"The Riskplay has a computer with a forensic scanner function. I should be able to analyze this gunk and send the data to my hunter drone. The drone has tracking capabilities."

"You have a hunter drone?"

"Yeah. HD-84 model."

They walked outside where window glass dotted the porch. Ithamar jogged across the dewy grass to the blue starship, and Edin followed, wondering if Vanya was even alive. They entered the cabin of the ship through the metal stairwell leading to the airlock. The inside was as messy as ever, with dirty clothes, electrical gadgets, and books scattered on the beige carpet. Ithamar walked to the back of the cabin, opened the hatch, and entered another compartment. Edin then discovered the room wasn't for maintenance like the sign above the hatch stated.

It was a small armory. Long and short-barrel rifles, a missile launcher, and other ordnance hung from steel racks attached to the bulkhead and ceiling. A computer station in the back had a wide monitor mounted on two metal boxes with cables and wires routed to the wall. Ithamar stood at the computer station and wiped the goo onto a circular sensor pad on the upper electrical box. The monitor flickered on, and a green screen appeared.

Edin gazed over the weapons. "I never knew you had all this in here. I thought it was just a maintenance room."

"That's the point of the sign," Ithamar stated. "Never advertise your hand."

Edin pointed at the largest gun. "Is that a minigun?"

Ithamar glanced away from the screen. "Yes, and don't ever touch that."

"Who just carries a minigun with them?"

"I do."

Edin looked over Ithamar's shoulder at the monitor. The screen displayed scrolling digits indicating the system was analyzing the substance on the sensor. They waited in silence with impatient eyes stuck to the screen. The computer beeped, and then an image flashed—a picture of a massive reptilian beast with blue scales for skin. Deadly eyes looked down a long snout with dagger teeth. The beast stood on two long legs and had two lanky arms. The fingers and toes were elongated and had creepy black nails. An information panel indicated that the creature was called a nistaclar. The nistaclar tended to dwell in swampy ranges, and they built dams and burrows from timber. They were carnivores who thrilled in hunts for large prey.

"That thing has her?" Edin asked.

"Yep. He must be taking her back to whatever burrow he's built."

"But the swamps are on the other side of the mountains to the east. And so widespread. We might not be able to find her before we leave for the match."

Ithamar nodded. "That's why you're staying here."

"What?"

"You have to stay here. Take the Riskplay to the capital tomorrow evening if I have not returned in time."

Edin scowled. "I'm not going to wait here by myself while Vanya is out there."

"You must not care about the gauntlet. If you're late, you will be considered a deserter, and deserters get sentenced to death. You know this."

"I'm coming with you regardless. If it gets too late, I will head back early. But I can't leave her out there knowing I did nothing."

Ithamar looked at the screen and then back at Edin. He appeared to be considering. Eventually, he agreed. "Okay."

Ithamar pressed a few buttons on the keyboard beneath the monitor. A clinking noise came from the ceiling as metal straps released a device in the deadly shape of a missile—the hunter drone. A low hum escaped the apparatus as it hovered in midair. It was painted midnight black with yellow stenciling that read *HD-84*.

"Are you ready?" Ithamar asked.

"Always," Edin promised.

"I sent the data to the drone. It should be able to track the nistaclar. Let's be quick about this."

The hunter drone hummed ahead. They must have jogged seven miles to reach the mountain ridge above the swampland the nistaclar were rumored to inhabit. Edin and Ithamar both carried long black rifles with digital scopes, and both of their stomachs were growling; neither had thought to bring food. Their only goal was to find Vanya as quickly as possible and return the ship.

"Stop," Ithamar said.

The hunter drone turned to face the command, and Edin eyed his older cousin.

"Let's have a look down there. Maybe we can see something from this vantage point before we start tracking in the mud."

"Alright," Edin said.

Ithamar walked over to the cliff where nothing below was visible. The jungle had turned dark an hour ago. One of the moons provided minimal light. Ithamar knelt and laid his rifle on the rocky ground beside him. The rifles they carried, Ion-Tens, were sleek and long, and the scopes were fully automated. Ithamar lay down and looked through the scope with his robotic eye.

"Can you see anything?" Edin asked.

"I can see the land—no nistaclar or signs of anything," Ithamar said. "Your scope should have a night vision feature as well."

Edin walked to the edge, knelt, and stretched out flat on his stomach. Peeking through the lens, he pushed the button on the scope multiple times to access night vision. The glass became very foggy and wet before he could distinguish anything, so he wiped the lens off with his sweaty shirt and examined the ground below. The swamp appeared intimidating at night, as if it were cursed by an enchanted spell. It extended into the distance as far as Edin could see. Muddy land divided multiple bodies of algae-covered water. Thousands of tree trunks twisted out of the murky liquid with skinny branches wrapped in moss. There were no signs of life, but there were signs of death. Edin zoomed in and spotted two putrefying skeletons—one a massive feline creature and the other a winged beast with a crushed skull.

It was the type of place one should avoid, especially in the darkness.

"Doesn't look too pleasing," Edin noted.

"The terrain is going to slow us down." Ithamar grabbed his rifle and stood. "It's going to be a nightmare traversing through that."

"This already is a nightmare."

"True."

They continued down the mountain with the hunter drone buzzing forward about five feet above the ground. A yellow light blinked on the drone; Edin kept his eyes on the light and occasionally checked to make sure he wasn't about to trip on a tree root or slip on a rocky decline. At the edge of the swamp, the smell of the stagnant water overwhelmed them. Then he realized why the bungalow smelled like fish after the nistaclar ransacked it.

"Look." Ithamar bent towards the ground and pointed at the mud. Edin saw two huge footprints identical to the foot indicated on the monitor in the Riskplay.

"At least we're in the right spot," he said.

"I guess the HD-84 was worth the investment."

"How many credits did you pay for it?"

"You don't want to know, and I don't want to tell you."

Edin laughed. "Okay."

"HD-84," Ithamar called.

The drone turned to him and beeped. "Bloop-dee-boo-weep."

"Scan the ground from here on out and make sure we stay on land that is navigable by foot. We don't want to get caught up in the water."

"Beep-weep-boop." The hunter drone turned and zoomed away like a rocket.

"What just happened?" Edin asked.

"I think it's going to go and scan ahead before we start, but I'm not sure. Just because I have a mechanical eye doesn't mean I speak robotics."

"Guess there's no point in being a cyborg."

They waited in the dark for the drone to return. It hurried back a few minutes later and hovered around them.

"Blip-beep-bee-doo," HD-84 beeped.

"What does that mean?" Edin asked.

"I guess it's telling us to follow it," Ithamar said. "It looks happy."

"It has no face. You can't tell if it's happy."

"Just follow the flippin' drone."

HD-84 led them into the swampland. They edged the deep waters by trekking in heavy black mud for hours. They remained silent for most of the nightly expedition. Both should have been asleep and resting for their upcoming trip to the capital. But the silence between them wasn't awkward. They had a mutual understanding of the purpose of the mission, and talking would be a distraction or give their position away to potential predators.

Sleep deprivation crept up on Edin, but he tried to keep his mind on Vanya and to remain alert in case trouble appeared. However, they encountered no trouble through the night. The skeletons lining the mucky embankments were spooky, but the cousins failed to spot signs of living creatures—only the tracks of the nistaclar, which appeared to enter and exit the water in various spots. Edin wondered if Vanya had already been drowned. He prayed for her life, that they would find her, and that he would make it to the capital in time for his match with Zokku.

Dawn arrived with the bright sun glaring off the gloomy water. They continued their hike without a single break since departing. Multiple times they traversed shallow waters to reach embankments further within the wetlands. Edin and Ithamar were covered in swamp sludge from the waist down to their flooded shoes. The Ion-Tens stayed strapped on their backs, the stocks of the rifles covered in slimy filth. They had just exited knee-high water when Edin began examining the muddy shore for footprints.

"We haven't seen any tracks in a while. Are you sure that drone is still on the right path?" Edin asked.

Ithamar searched the ground. "We have to trust it."

"I'm not accustomed to trusting machines."

"Your cousin is a cyborg." Ithamar grinned. "You might want to get accustomed."

Edin stared ahead with dried mud glued to his cheeks and hair. "Well, time is running short, for me and Vanya."

Ithamar nodded. "We're close. I can sense them."

Ithamar's senses were correct. They only walked a few more minutes before discovering the wooden lair of the nistaclar. It was unlike anything Edin had ever imagined. In the middle of the swamp was a massive, cone-shaped structure built of twigs, sticks, branches, logs, and gray mud. The foundation was entirely underwater, but the summit stretched twenty meters in the sky. Edin thought it was primitive and beautiful at the same time.

They hid behind a mangrove tree, standing in low water. The hunter drone hovered behind them as if ready to take more orders.

"Good job, HD-84," Ithamar said.

"Bleep-beso-vlip," HD-84 beeped.

"There's probably more than one in there," Edin said. "I don't see one nistaclar building something like that."

Ithamar scrunched his eyes, examining the timber structure. "I am going to have to swim underwater to get inside of it. There's no entrance above water."

"How are we supposed to see underwater in this sewage?" Edin asked.

Ithamar pointed to his mechanical eye. "I'll be able to see."

Edin dropped his shoulders. "So, do you want me to hold on to you while swimming?"

"I want you to stay here." Ithamar frowned. "Look, you've helped me get this far. But now it will be easy for me to just go in by myself. I don't even need the rifle. I have the Gift."

"But you said I have the Gift too. I might be able to help."

"You know I should go alone."

Ithamar should be able to handle this, Edin thought. There was no reason to doubt his older cousin. He replied, "Alright, but if you take too long, I'm coming in there."

"Okay." Ithamar took the Ion-Ten rifle off his shoulder and laid it against the tree. "I won't be needing that."

CHAPTER 15

I thamar left his cover behind the mangrove and slogged through the muddy shallows until the water rose above his knees. Then he lowered his body beneath the surface to swim toward the nistaclar lair, seventy meters ahead. Algae floated around his neck. It was quiet, so he attempted to swim slowly and breathe lightly to avoid causing a noticeable disturbance.

Composure would be his advantage, he knew. In circumstances like these, he trusted the Gift. *Confidence.* No mortal beast could match a Gifted human. Of course, he was swimming into a wooden burrow with unknown variables lurking within, but there shouldn't be anything the prince of the Mizoquii couldn't handle with his own hands.

At the halfway point to the burrow, his feet could no longer touch the ground. He looked over his shoulder towards the mangrove Edin was waiting behind. His younger cousin waved. Ithamar raised his arm out of the water and returned a thumbs-up. Ithamar felt pity for Edin; the boy had to enter the gauntlet the next day, and they were still many miles away from the ship. It would be a difficult task to engage in combat without proper rest. *With a bit of luck, everything will go as planned*, Ithamar thought. He turned and kept swimming.

The timber structure grew ever larger in stature as Ithamar swam closer. The massive logs were secured with dry mud and rope, which produced a perfectly symmetrical impression. It must have taken some intelligence to create such a fortress. Perhaps he was underestimating the nistaclar. He took a deep breath and dived.

Underwater, he opened his mechanical eye. Visibility lasted a meter. Sunlight was forced to fight through the patches of algae on the surface. He swam alongside the lower foundation of the cone-shaped burrow, searching for an entrance. But he didn't spot an opening before he had to rise for air. He inhaled heavily when he emerged. *Too loud*, he thought. He took a few long breaths before submerging again. He kept one hand on the wooden wall of the burrow while scanning up and down for an entry with his robotic vision.

After a few minutes, he spotted a circular access. He went up for air once more before entering the burrow. Then he swam a few meters to the opening, which turned into a flooded vestibule. The rounded tunnel angled towards the heart of the wooded fortress. Ithamar kept swimming, unable to see anything but blackness, trying not to make noise but also trying to be quick. He assumed that the tunnel would incline upward and that the living chambers would have air. If the creatures lived underwater, then Vanya would have already drowned. He pushed that thought away. *She is still alive*, he told himself. The tunnel was longer than he anticipated. He needed air soon. He swam faster, pushing his arms and kicking at a harder pace.

As he assumed, the tunnel ramped up. He broke the surface with a noisy gasp—a mistake. The sound of his arrival ricocheted in the timber tunnel to the main chamber. Ithamar could only see a light shining from around a bend. He kept quiet, hoping that nothing heard him. But something had.

"Wat wazz that?" a whiny voice asked behind the bend.

"Wut wuzz wutt?" another squeaky voice responded.

"Dripper, you can't hear a thang," a third voice responded.

"Shush it, Tripper. You and Whipper all the time hearing ghosts in yur skrambled brains," Dripper said.

"Ahh, just both of ye shush it. We got a feast tonight. No reason to argue like de oo'mans doo," Whipper said.

Ithamar wasn't expecting the nistaclar to have the ability to speak the common tongue. He wondered if he could negotiate with them to free Vanya if she was still alive. He figured there were a few things back at the ship that he could bargain with as collateral. Surely they could use some weaponry or gadgetry. At least he would be able to offer them their lives instead of jumping directly into a skirmish.

He slowly rose out of the water and snuck into the antechamber. The mud-and-lumber walls were coated in the same blue slime they'd found back at the bungalow. The floor was slick and slippery, and the slime stuck to his clothes and shoes. He crept towards the light coming from the core, attempting to make no more noises. The smell was as awful as anything he had smelled before, like inhaling brackish sewage. His nose started to run, and he wiped his face with his forearm. He crept to the edge of the bend and peeked around the corner.

Hanging from nautical rope, a chandelier made of ivory tusk lit the chamber with hundreds of candles. A round table with three large chairs in the midmost of the room stood on a sprawling blue rug. Dripper, Tripper, and Whipper were on the far side, sitting on a bench with their heads directed at a massive digital display covering the wall. Ithamar only saw their backsides. They were huge creatures with oily blue scales. It appeared that they each held a controller, as if they were playing some sort of visual game. It was the last thing Ithamar expected to find. The nistaclar were fairly advanced and unusual beings.

He looked around the room for Vanya. A body slumped against the far wall, motionless. It was her. Her face was pale, and her blond hair was wet and frizzed. Blue slime stained her yellow gown. *Is she still alive?* He peered closer and believed she was breathing, but he couldn't tell from where he stood. He had to move quickly. He decided that he would talk to the nistaclar first and try to reach an agreement for the girl. But if she was already dead, the three would have to suffer.

He left the corner and moved into the main room. His steps made obvious noises on the sticky ground. Dripper, Tripper, and Whipper simultaneously turned their large heads to see what on Lathas was entering their reclusive lair. Their jaws dropped at the sight of the human, each of them revealing rows of pointed teeth in their long-snouted mouths.

"I tuld yu I had heard sumthin!" Whipper yelled.

They all jumped from the bench and stood to an arresting height. The blue scales glimmered underneath the light of the chandelier. Beads of slime oozed from their scales like sweat, mainly in the armpits and on their large feet. They waddled towards the intruder.

"Ow did yu git here, and wut doo yu come forth?" Whipper asked.

Ithamar stood still with his chest flexed outward. Even though the creatures were much larger than him, he could show no signs of intimidation.

"I apologize for bothering you three lovely gentlemen, especially in your home. My name is Ithamar Avrum, the prince of the Mizoquii."

"Printz of the meso-what?" Dripper asked.

"Methokee! Dumie!" Tripper barked.

"Wut is a methokke?" Dripper asked.

"It is pronounced 'mizz-oh-kwee,' but you don't have to bother with my name or title. I have come to your home to negotiate for the girl. Is she still alive?" Ithamar questioned.

The three of them laughed, for almost an entire minute; Ithamar realized they would never take him seriously.

"Yehs, we don't kill until rih fore we eat. But we hungry. We gunaa eat oo'man gurl," Whipper assured.

"Yu shudn't com places uninvited, littl printz. Wut makes yu tink yu not food too?" Tripper asked.

The three stepped closer with a predatory bearing. Ithamar raised his right hand, and a green orb of cosmic energy emerged. The nistaclar backstepped in shock at the sight.

"Wut iz tat thang!" Dripper croaked.

"I should have told you earlier, but I do have the Gift," Ithamar declared. "Now, let me take the girl and I will not kill you."

They all gasped in disgust.

"De Gifted kilt our ancesturs. Oo'mans tok our land," Whipper said.

"Papa wud be so proud for us to kil a Gifted filth maggot," Dripper said.

"Yez, let's eat hims too," Tripper said.

They rushed at him with reckless aggression, leaping into the air. Ithamar threw the green orb directly at Dripper's face. It decapitated the poor creature, and the body flopped to the ground. Ithamar lunged out the way as the other two snapped their savage jaws down. Tripper and Whipper whipped around and looked at their headless brother, and both quivered with what seemed to be a mix of sadness and boiling fury.

"HE KILT DRIPPER!" Whipper cried.

"THE MESOKEY MUS DIE!" Tripper roared.

The two charged once again. Ithamar formed an energy orb with each hand and threw the two green spheres at his foes. Both missed. The nistaclar evaded with speed that Ithamar wasn't expecting. With blinding quickness, Whipper reached him and grabbed Ithamar's arm with his clawed hand, slinging the human across the chamber. Ithamar landed next to Vanya, his head smashing against the wall. Dizzy, he shook tiny twinkling lights from his vision and looked over at Vanya's body. She was breathing. They would get out of here and return home.

He pushed himself up and brushed the slime off his shoulders and pants. From across the chamber, Tripper and Whipper inched closer with their jaws open and ready to clamp down on their prey at the opportune moment.

"You won't touch me again," Ithamar said. "Let me take the girl, and I will spare your life."

"De mesokey printz iz a fool," Tripper said. "We hungries as eva beens."

"Very hungries," Whipper whined. "Gifted oo'man must tast gud."

"You can't say I didn't try to help you," Ithamar said. "Your loss, not mine."

The three bolted towards a bloody collision in the middle of the chamber where the table stood. Ithamar would wait until they were close enough to strike. He didn't want to miss another target. The nistaclar reached the table first and leapt over it with ease. In midair, they opened their deadly jaws.

That was when Ithamar stopped, stretched his arms forward, and widened his fingers. With only fractions of a second to spare, two green orbs materialized. He mentally pushed the orbs through the mouths and out the backs of his two foes' heads. Their bodies dropped at his feet with sizzling holes in their skulls. Tripper and Whipper had met the same fate as their brother.

Half-wits should have listened to me, Ithamar thought. He turned and rushed to Vanya, lifting her to prop her back against the timber wall. Her eyelids were closed, and her face had gone pale, very pale.

Ithamar grabbed her shoulders and shook her. "Wake up, Vanya."

She remained unconscious.

He shook her again. "Wake up, we have to get out of here."

Her head dropped to the side. Ithamar grabbed her face with one hand and then tugged her ear with the other. "Come on, Vanya, it's me, Ithamar! Wake up!"

Vanya's eyes shot open. "OWWWW!" She pushed Ithamar in the chest and rubbed her ear. "What did you do that for?!"

"You're awake! I thought you might have been lost in a coma!"

Vanya didn't respond. She looked past Ithamar at the three large dead bodies. Then her eyes wandered up to the chandelier and around the wooden burrow.

"Are you okay?" Ithamar asked.

Her pale cheeks went red. "Where am I? What happened?"

"You don't remember being taken hostage by these creatures?" Ithamar pointed at the nistaclar.

"I vaguely remember something, or someone, breaking into the cabin. Those slimy beasts carried me here, I think." Vanya paused, attempting to gather her remembrance. "Ah, I know I was dragged in and out of water. I must have lost consciousness then. I remember one of them speaking the common tongue, and saying that they were going to boil me alive and make human stew."

"That was probably the one called Dripper. He wasn't the brightest character."

Vanya sneezed. "It smells terrible in here."

"We're about to leave." Ithamar looked her up and down. "Can you stand?"

"I'll try. Wait. What time is it?"

"It's probably afternoon. Tomorrow is Edin's match, and we still have to hike back to the ship."

"What? It's been an entire day since I last saw you?"

"Yes."

"Oh my." She pushed herself up and grabbed the wall for support. When she stood, the hand she used to keep her balance was covered in blue slime. "Gross." She slung off the goo.

They stepped over the dead bodies and went into the dark tunnel, plunging into the swamp.

Edin waited, growing worried. He prayed that Vanya was still alive and that she was indeed inside the timber burrow. Time moved extraordinarily slow while he lingered behind the mangrove. Half of him wanted to jump into the swamp and swim to the rescue. The other half of him wanted to fall asleep in the mud. He felt exhausted.

He sat in sludge with his back against the tree. The hunter drone hovered beside him.

"Bleep-boop-beep-beep-beep-sweeeep." HD-84 beeped.

"HD-84! Be quiet! What's wrong?" Edin asked.

The hovering drone trembled up and down with excitement. Edin looked back towards the wooden burrow but saw nothing.

"Is something there? Is it Ithamar?"

"Beep-boop."

"Not sure what that means." Edin raised his hand over his brow to block the sun and squinted. Two human heads popped out of the water. They started to swim in his direction. It was Ithamar and Vanya.

Overjoyed, Edin leapt from the ground and pumped his fist. He never would have expected to be this happy while being sleep deprived in a neglected swamp. But at the moment he was smiling underneath the bright sun. His friends were alive. The smile remained spread across his face until the two of them arrived on the muddy shore.

Ithamar and Vanya walked out of the water covered in algae, mud, and slime. It didn't bother Edin; he hugged Vanya gratefully.

"I thought you were dead," Edin said.

Vanya hugged him back, but the hug felt awkward, especially with Ithamar watching them.

"Oh, so I don't get a hug?" Ithamar joked.

Edin and Vanya split apart.

"Nah, maybe the next time you save my life, you'll be worthy of a hug," Vanya said.

They laughed.

"Well, we better head back to the ship. We're going to have to go to the capital as soon as we get back."

They departed for their return voyage. HD-84 led the way across the wetlands while Vanya told Edin everything that she could remember about being taken captive, which wasn't much at all. Then Ithamar told Edin the story about the three nistaclars named Dripper, Tripper, and Whipper. Ithamar mentioned that he tried to negotiate with them for Vanya, but the large blue creatures were bigoted in their understandings of humans. There was no choice but to use the Gift, he declared. Edin was disappointed that he missed the chance to view the encounter. He knew studying the Gift would become his next task if he won the gauntlet tournament. It would have been beneficial to see the cosmic power displayed in combat.

After the story of the nistaclar, they all grew quiet. It was clear that everyone in the party was fatigued, and talking was a waste of energy. The dense marsh mud never allowed their pace to reach great speed. They were much slower than when Edin and Ithamar had marched through earlier in the morning. Edin noticed Ithamar seemed distant and weary, which was the complete opposite of his cousin's demeanor during training. Perhaps the prince had actually reached his limit. Vanya seemed zombified as well. Her face was incredibly pale, and she mentioned she hadn't eaten anything in at least twenty hours.

It took the rest of the day to traverse the swamp, hike the mountain, and navigate the jungle. They moved faster once they reached the trails they trained on each day. Returning to the view of their homey bungalow was bittersweet. It was refreshing to make it back with all three in the party safe. However, their home away from home had been destroyed by the nistaclar, and it would take time to repair everything. Currently, time was something they lacked. It was midafternoon when they returned.

They showered off the swamp sludge, changed into fresh and comfortable clothes to sleep in, and grabbed their belongings for the trip to Kosabar. The three left the wrecked bungalow and entered the Riskplay, ready to set out, and saw HD-84 hovering in the cabin of the starship. Ithamar had instructed it to return to the armory, but the hatch had been closed. Ithamar twisted it open.

"Come on, buddy," Ithamar said. "You did a good job today. Time to go back to sleep."

HD-84 stayed where he floated and beeped, "Bloop-sweep-beep-peep."

"It looks like he doesn't want to go back to sleep." Edin laughed.

"Come on, HD-84. I can't have you floating around when we take off."

The hunter drone shook its body as if saying no.

"Just leave him out and see how he does," Vanya said. "He won't cause any harm."

Ithamar closed the hatch. "Fine."

"Beep-beep-boop-sweeeep."

CHAPTER 16

O nce the ship launched, they each ate a massive pile of scrambled eggs and buttered toast cooked in the kitchenette by Edin. Afterward, they were quick to settle in their sleeping areas. Edin was on the top bunk, Vanya on the bottom bunk, and Ithamar made a pallet with blankets in the cockpit. Ithamar set the ship on autopilot to land on the roof of the Pebble Inn. They all plummeted into a deep sleep until the morning. None of them even stirred when the Riskplay landed in the middle of the night.

When Edin woke, he was surprised to see the other two had left the ship. HD-84 was hovering in the cabin and facing Edin as if waiting for him to wake up. *It has a funny little personality*, Edin thought, *like a loyal pet.*

"Good morning, HD-84."

"Bloop-beep-boop."

Edin slipped on the formal outfit hanging from a shelf, a green button-down shirt with black pants and leather shoes. He guessed Ithamar left it for him. Edin smiled; it matched the gi he would wear for combat. He grabbed his duffle bag for the arena and swung it over his shoulder as he left the ship for the Pebble Inn.

The surrounding buildings were grimy and lifeless. On the horizon, little clouds drifted in the sunrise. He looked towards the casino and the arena. *Today shall be a good day.* Full of confidence that he would win, he left the rooftop and entered the hotel.

In the elevator, Edin remembered something said when the three ate dinner at Maypoes. Vanya had mentioned that the bottom floor of the Pebble Inn served as a nursing home for three elderly and sick residents, and one of those residents was her grandfather. It was odd to think about. *Why do they just stay in their rooms?*

When he reached the lobby, the old furnishings were covered in a layer of dust. He noticed A-Veetwo behind the reception desk. The droid stood like a statue with his black skeleton frame. But his red eyes glowed, showing that he was activated.

"A-Veetwo, do you not know how to clean?" Edin asked. "This place is filthy."

"Good morning, Mr. Carvosa. I'm sorry, but cleaning the lobby wasn't on my list of instructions left by Ms. Waldrip," the droid responded.

"Someone needs to upgrade your initiative settings."

"Mr. Avrum said the same thing."

Edin laughed. "Well, do you know where Ithamar went?"

"He went to get breakfast and should be back shortly."

"What about Vanya?"

"Right now, she is tending to the residents. They worried themselves that she would never return, or that grave harm had struck her."

"Oh, I guess it has been a while."

Edin went over to the seating area, wiped the dust from a sofa, and sat with his duffle bag placed at his feet. He didn't wait long before Ithamar burst through the front door with a paper bag filled with various fruits and vegetables. Ithamar was dressed in his black cloak and pants paired with a platinum breastplate, gauntlets, and boots—his standard outfit in the city. He pulled transparent containers from the bag and placed them on the dusty coffee table. Most of the produce Edin had never seen before.

"You're going need something light before the match to give your body energy and your mind clarity," Ithamar said.

"Okay. Are we going to be able to go out to eat after the match? Or do you think someone will try to poison my food again?"

Ithamar looked surprised. He must have forgotten about the poisoning incident at Maypoes—forgotten that they had enemies outside of the arena.

Ithamar scratched the back of his head. "We will see when get to that point. Eat up for now."

The berries and melons comprised a rainbow spectrum of fruit. Edin ate them straight out of the plastic containers they came in. He took a liking to a melon that was purple and seedy. The vegetables were a mixed assortment of orangish leaves and stems from several plants. They tasted like grass and left his mouth dry. He set down the containers when he had his fill.

Ithamar had been watching him eat. "We have to leave soon. Better to be early than late."

Edin sighed. "So I'm going to have to sit in that crappy locker room again."

"Unfortunately."

Vanya walked into the lobby from the first floor. She wore a black sleeveless jumpsuit that made her looked older than her age. To Edin's surprise, her makeup was applied and her hair was straightened. She appeared ready to leave. However, she glanced around the room as if she had seen a phantom. As she approached them, her lip trembled.

"What's wrong with you?" Edin asked.

"Have you guys seen the betting odds?" Vanya asked.

"No." Ithamar tilted his head and narrowed his eyes. "Why?"

Vanya placed a round hologram projector on the coffee table. "You might want to see this."

The device blinked twice, and then light expanded from it, forming two nonhuman beings sitting behind an oversized desk. Edin realized it was a recording from a talk show the night before on a channel called

LSHN, Lathas Sporting Hologram News. The two individuals were of an intelligent species called verbandd; they were little, with leafy green skin, and their heads had two small and sharp points like horns. Their bright copper eyes locked onto each other as they spoke.

"Jenkins, what do you think of the first semifinal match? Zokku Rellen against Edin Carvosa."

"Now, Fannin, you know that match is over before it even begins."

Fannin giggled. "Well, we do get paid to discuss these things. Do you think there is no shot for the spacer?"

"None. None at all."

"He was an underdog before and came away with a victory against Finder Shaw."

"Zokku is no Finder. Zokku is a completely different beast, and by beast, I mean beast. His reach is so great that Carvosa won't even be able to land a strike. The strength that Zokku possesses is unrivaled. He is the only threat to Cane Nazari in this tournament. The ONLY threat! There is no way that Edin Carvosa wins tomorrow, and by no way, I mean no way."

"Well, if you were in the shoes of Edin, what would your approach be? Or do you think he is only walking to his death?"

"Run from him when you get in the arena. Maybe Zokku trips and falls and Edin gets a clean strike. That's all I can possibly think of. There's no way he can stand toe to toe and go strike for strike against Zokku. Zokku will attack with such force that Edin won't even be able to hold his hyperblade. They simply are not in the same weight class. That's why the linemakers have set the odds at two thousand to one. We've never seen anything like that in the history of the gauntlet tournament."

"That brings me to my next point. With odds that polarizing, would you not risk betting on the spacer? I'm mean, that could turn out a nice profit if he wins."

"I would be throwing away money, Fannin. There's no shot for him. Zokku Rellen versus Cane Nazari will be your finale. It was set in stone before the tournament even began. They were the only two real competitors. It was nice to see the space boy win one match, but he will be dead tomorrow. His story is over."

Vanya cut off the hologram and picked up the projection device. "Two thousand to one."

Ithamar nodded. "Even if he wins, it will get worse."

"What do you mean?" Edin asked

"There's going to be a lot of money on you losing." Ithamar placed his hands on his hips. "You're going to make more enemies with a victory."

Edin looked down at the floor. "I already have the whole planet against me."

"We'll have to get out of there quick if you win, and we can't stay in the capital for dinner. There might be riots by the radicals."

"I guess I'll pack a bag too," Vanya said.

"Yeah," Ithamar said. "It might be best to leave the Pebble Inn with A-Veetwo again. We don't know who poisoned Edin."

"Make sure you tell A-Veetwo to clean the lobby this time," Edin said.

They laughed, for the moment.

Blue Street was a festival packed with fanatics. Luckily, contestants were dropped off in a private parking area. Edin did not want to walk through a crowd of drunken enthusiasts. After A-Veetwo dropped them off, the three paced to the arena. Vanya slipped Edin a smile when he glanced at her. Then she affected a stern expression. She had complained about waiting alone in the stands for the first match to begin, so now she was getting a behind-the-scenes experience.

They left the parking garage and marched through an underground concrete tunnel lit by glowing light fixtures that arched from the floor to the ceiling. Edin glared ahead with focused eyes, strutting with his chest out and chin up. Ithamar and Vanya followed at each side and did not speak. If anyone saw them, they would appear ready for war.

They continued into the depths of the arena and passed by tournament officials, media personnel, and stadium staff.

None of them had expected to see Edin's opponent before the match.

Zokku Rellen stood in the middle of a corridor with an entourage of three older gentlemen. He was the largest one of the bunch. He had tan skin and black hair slicked back. His biceps were thicker than Edin's thighs. Edin was also half a meter shorter than him and didn't even reach his opponent's shoulders. Edin felt slightly intimidated, but he mainly felt embarrassed. The size difference was evident and discouraging.

"Edin Carvosa," Zokku said in a low voice.

At first, Edin was going to walk by Zokku and not say anything. But he halted and looked up at his opponent. "Zokku Rellen."

Zokku smiled brightly. "Good luck in the match today."

"Thanks."

"Let's give the fans a good show."

"Alright."

It was a peculiar exchange. All eyes within the walkway were on the two of them. There was even a cameraman behind Edin, filming the conversation. Zokku seemed confident, and despite the disparity of physical dimensions, Edin appeared competent.

Edin decided to keep walking. There was nothing more to say. Thankfully, Zokku didn't come across as a jerk. In a way, it made Edin feel cruel in planning a sneak attack at the beginning of the match.

They finally came to Edin's locker room, the same one as before: a square room of nothing but concrete and a single lightbulb. He dropped his bag, sat, and exhaled heavily. It was about to happen again. He was about to enter another match. And this time, he knew if he missed the throw in the opening sequence, then he would die.

"Well, Zokku doesn't seem that bad," Edin said.

"If my odds were that good, I would be smiling too," Ithamar said. "But don't let his smile distract you from your goal. You have to go out there and kill him."

"I will."

Vanya looked at the room with disgust. "This place is horrible. There's not even a bathroom."

"Cane Nazari is to thank for that," Edin said. "There are other locker rooms available, but this is the one I'm assigned."

Vanya shook her head. "This isn't a locker room. This is a storage closet."

Edin laughed. "Maybe one day I'll get revenge on the prince."

"You will," Vanya said.

Edin went to the corner of the room and changed into his gi. The combat clothing felt awfully comfortable. Slipping on a pair of battle boots, he recalled having to pull boots off a corpse on the *Saircor* because the only shoes he owned were too small. Now he had acquired four pairs of footwear.

Once he got dressed, he stretched and bounced on his feet to get his heart rate up. Crowd noise from the stadium had been growing for the past few minutes. Now they could hear chants all the way in the cemented underground.

"It's probably going to be a full house," Ithamar said.

"We might need to head up there," Vanya said.

"Okay. You good down here, Edin?" Ithamar asked.

"Yeah, I'll see you two after the fight."

They both went to the door. Vanya stopped and gave one last smile to Edin. He returned a playful grin as if he had no worries at all. She left and the door closed behind her.

Edin blocked out all thoughts other than the execution of his plan. From above, the chants and drums rose in volume.

Soon, there was a knock on the door. Edin opened it and entered the walkway. The same tournament official as at the last match stood on sharp talons. Edin looked into the tikkino's tan eyes.

"Mr. Carvosa, we meet again. Are you ready?"

"Hey, and yeah, I'm ready."

They strode through the underground tunnels as the noise from the spectators above ricocheted around them. Edin remembered it was fairly quiet the last time he walked these halls. *The entire coliseum must be full*, he thought.

He ignored the armed guards standing watch, tournament officials, stadium staff, journalists, and cameramen and glowered ahead. His stare was viciously cold. He pictured hurling the hyperblade at his opponent's face and hitting with headshot accuracy. They reached the end of the tunnel where the pitch sprawled out in front of them. Chants and screams and instruments and fireworks produced a crowd noise so powerful it irritated the ears. The ground itself was shaking. Only one word ran through his mind. *Kill*.

"Like last time, we still have approximately ten minutes until you walk out," the tikkino said.

"Alright."

"Would you like the hold the hyperblade?"

Edin grinned. "Yeah."

The tikkino pulled out the metal hilt. Edin received it and inspected the handle. It was the same as every other hyperblade he had seen. Last time, he had pressed the silver button on the hilt and activated the weapon. This time he held the hyperblade by his side. He knew what to do with it when the cannon fired.

The cannon fired. Edin pressed the silver button as he sprinted onto the pitch. His heart drummed madly against his ribcage. While he ran, the adamantine blade extended, bending to a sharp point. After it lengthened, the razor edge started to glow from the infinity plasma.

Edin stopped cold in his tracks with the hyperblade buzzing in his hand, unprepared for what he observed. Across the arena, his opponent had walked onto the pitch very slowly. Zokku Rellen appeared to be in no hurry for their blades to collide. He waved at the fans in the seating while blowing them kisses and bowing to them as they cheered for his triumph. Edin had imagined this moment unfolding in a much different manner. He thought they would sprint to the center and he would have the chance to throw his hyperblade unexpectedly.

Edin scanned the crowd. Thousands of spectators were jumping and roaring battle hymns of ages past. Colored smoke rose in the air. Proud banners fluttered in the wind. He looked back towards his tunnel and spotted Ithamar and Vanya in the stands, but he was instantly distracted by a surprising discovery: in a column rising the height of the arena, row after row after row of spectators were wearing black and green. Were those supporters for him? There must have been at least ten thousand people standing on their feet, staring back at him. *The first victory must have gained me some fans*, he guessed.

Zokku strolled out to the middle of the pitch. The brute wore black tactical pants but sported no shirt. His chest and abdomen had been chiseled by years of strength training. He was a walking statue. He smirked as if there were no threat.

Edin wondered if he should still fling the hyperblade at his foe now. Would Zokku react in time? The one benefit of this happening sluggishly was it gave Edin time to be accurate. However, Zokku would have more opportunity to respond.

When the two contestants met at the midpoint of the arena, they paused and glared at each other. Zokku walked to his right, and Edin mimicked him. They circled, pressing glares upon each other. Hollering and howling came from all sides.

"You know how to put on a show," Edin stated.

"Ah yes, someone has to entertain the fans." Zokku winked. "I don't want to kill you too quickly."

"Who said you were going to kill me?"

Zokku laughed. "Ah, spacer, you know your fate has led you here for only one reason. And that reason is to die."

Edin grimaced. "The odds have underestimated me before."

"Not this time." All at once, Zokku quit shuffling to the side and rushed forward. "I am your las—"

Edin flung his hyperblade directly into Zokku's forehead. The hyperblade sank into his skull like a dart thrown in cork. Zokku dropped his weapon and fell to the ground with a solid thud.

The entire stadium gasped.

CHAPTER 17

The hyperblade burned through the flesh in Zokku's face, neck, and shoulders. He twitched in the dirt for a couple of seconds before his massive body went motionless.

Edin didn't reach for the hyperblade. He turned and walked back towards the tunnel empty-handed. The spectators wearing green and black thundered with cheers and fireworks. As he got closer, they only grew nosier and rowdier. He smiled, and his eyes watered with joy. It was the biggest upset in the history of the gauntlet tournament. He would be fighting in the finale. He lifted his arm and gestured at the fans, then pointed at Ithamar and Vanya, sitting close to the front.

The other sections of the stadium remained oddly silent. Most people expected a grand match between Cane and Zokku. He knew his victory wasn't what the people wanted, but it didn't matter. Now he possessed a chance at being the gauntlet champion of Lathas. He walked back slowly, absorbing the scene and pumping his fist to the open sky.

When he arrived at the entrance of the tunnel, the tikkino stood waiting.

"Congratulations on your victory," the bird lady said.

"Thanks, the hyperblade is still . . . out there," Edin said.

She giggled in a high pitch. "It's fine. Happens all the time."

They headed deeper into the buried corridor. The cameramen, media personnel, tournament officials, and stadium staff lining the walls now watched Edin walk by with eyes filled with wonder. He knew they had never anticipated this win. And even though they saw it, they still didn't believe it.

"Is there any way you can get me a new locker room for the next match?" Edin asked.

"I'll make sure you get a proper locker room." The tikkino kept her gaze ahead. "But the one you have has brought you luck. Has it not?"

"I guess you're right." Edin contemplated for a few seconds. "Actually, I'll keep it. Don't worry about it."

"Okay. Remember that you only have one more match to go."

"How could I ever forget?"

When he got back to the concrete room, he changed out of the gi and slipped on his casual outfit. There was a knock at the door, and Ithamar and Vanya entered.

Vanya smiled. "That was quick."

Ithamar smirked. "It should have been quicker."

Edin returned a grin. "He was one for theatrics."

"So were you," Ithamar said. "You seemed natural out there."

"I had fans this time," Edin acknowledged. "Who were those people?"

Ithamar said, "Apparently there are some people fond of spacers on this planet. Not everyone is native to Lathas or this solar system. You seem to have attracted the people that royalty has forgotten or rejected."

Vanya said, "Also, you gained some fans in your first match. A few people won decent money from your victory, so you gained admiration with bettors."

"Well," Edin said, "it was nice to have the support."

They left the locker room and proceeded out of the arena. On the way to the parking garage, many groups of shouting people tried to stop Edin and ask questions. Cameras were pointed at his face with bright lights shining to the point of blindness. He squinted and turned his head away from the filming crews.

He never broke his stride to speak with anyone because he had nothing to say. Most of the questions shouted at him were about the upcoming fight and what he thought of the challengers. Perhaps he should've stayed and watched the next match. However, sticking around the arena didn't appeal to Edin a great deal. He wanted a good meal in a much quieter setting. Then he needed to make his way back to the bungalow to clean it up so he could start training once again. Winning the finale was all that mattered. Watching the fight in person or on film would make no difference to the end result.

When they reached the parking lot, the paparazzi were still following. He turned around and noticed a horde of humans and extraterrestrials lingering behind him.

"Those people are obnoxious," Edin said.

"Welcome to the gauntlet finale," Ithamar said.

A-Veetwo had been waiting for them in the rusty glidecar. The three of them jumped inside, and the droid stepped on the gas as the glidecar sped back to the Pebble Inn.

When they arrived at the Pebble Inn, Vanya went to check on the three residents on the bottom floor and inform them that she would be spending another two weeks away. Edin and Ithamar thanked A-Veetwo for the ride and said farewell before taking the elevator up to the roof. What the two beheld when they reached the cabin of the Riskplay was disturbing.

HD-84 had been destroyed. The outer shell had been ripped off, and the hunter drone was now only a metal frame consisting of ripped wires and crisped circuit boards.

"What happened?" Edin asked, strangely sad.

"Someone was here," Ithamar said. "Don't move."

Ithamar scrambled towards the cockpit. He was in there for approximately a minute while Edin waited by the demolished drone. There were no other signs of destruction in the cabin. When Ithamar returned, he mentioned that it was all clear in the front. The older Mizoquii passed Edin, twisted the aft hatch, and disappeared to the armory. It took longer to search than the front. Edin assumed Ithamar must be doing a full inventory of the ordnance and equipment. Ithamar returned and shook his head with frustration. He looked at Edin with his mechanical eye.

"Do you want the positive news or the negative news first?"

"I guess the negative," Edin said.

"Well, the positive news is that nothing has been taken," Ithamar said.

Edin laughed.

Ithamar grinned. "But on a serious note, someone was here."

He bent down to examine the skeleton of HD-84 and discovered a clue on one of the fragments from the outer shell: a red liquid.

"That's not hydraulic fuel." Ithamar looked up at Edin. "That's human blood."

"Human . . ." Edin said. "Bounty hunter? Or what?"

"I don't know." Ithamar stood. "Most likely this is related to whoever poisoned your soup at Maypoes."

"This is ridiculous."

"Your captain was a man needed by many. It could have been the Sheeban Syndicate, or some other cartel possibly. I don't think the threat comes from Lathas. Too much for anyone to risk because of the tournament rules."

"What do we do now? If they know about the Pebble Inn, there is no point in returning here before the last match."

"We will worry about our return to the capital when the time comes. For now, I'm going to hunt the entire ship for explosives or trackers. I need to check the oil levels in the engine bays anyway. After

I'm done with that, we will head back to the bungalow. However, we'll make a couple of pit stops to make sure no one is trailing us."

"Alright."

"Take all the parts of HD-84 down to A-Veetwo. The droid should be able to fix the drone. If he needs extra parts, authorize him to go out and get whatever he needs and I'll pay back the inn."

"Alright, I'll be back up shortly."

Edin gathered the scraps and fragments of the hunter drone into his arms. It was heavier than he assumed.

They left an hour or so later. Edin was tired and lost track of time. Ithamar fully inspected the Riskplay, and Vanya finished her duties at the Pebble Inn. HD-84 had been left with A-Veetwo, and the droid promised to fix the drone.

The three of them strapped into leather chairs in the cockpit. Ithamar had added an extra seat behind theirs since Vanya had started traveling with them. It was a smooth takeoff. Ithamar launched the blue starship into the sky and flew higher and higher. Edin wondered what Ithamar's intentions were. The ship bolted in an entirely upright angle and accelerated rapidly.

Vanya gripped her seatbelt, her face pale. "What is your problem?"

"We have to leave the atmosphere to shake any potential hunters," Ithamar said.

"But we're going to be the only one up here," Edin said. "Anyone could see us."

Ithamar pushed forward on the throttle controls. "We will lose them on one of the moons. We need to get off the planet."

"Oh goodness," Vanya said.

The ship rattled as it rocketed through the atmosphere into open space. Ithamar slowed down and turned the craft back towards the planet. They beheld the same view Edin remembered from when he was on the catwalk of the *Saircor*: three colorful continents divided by massive oceans; purple auroras danced around the globe, causing the scene to feel like a dream.

"There's a port on the first moon," Ithamar said. "We will buy supplies for the next two weeks and then head back to the bungalow."

"What if the hunters have discovered the bungalow?" Vanya asked.

"Then they will be able to track us anywhere. But away from the city, I can openly use the Gift without fear of destroying things or my powers being discovered."

"So," Vanya said, "there's probably going to be another fight."

Ithamar swiveled his head towards her. "There's always another fight."

It took twenty standard minutes to reach the first moon of Lathas, a blue rock covered in jungles of soft white trees. There appeared to be one area of civilization—a cluster of low buildings and wide hangars. Edin thought it looked primitive, but moon colonies were known to be storage for spacefaring. Air ferries crisscrossed the sky. The affluent in urban areas would take small vessels from planets to moons before setting sail across the galaxy. Larger starships were kept there because of the capacity and price.

The Riskplay descended to the moon, a much smaller rock than the planet it orbited over. The navigation screen on the dashboard indicated that the town below was named Cold Canyon. As they got closer, Edin noticed the highest building was an air traffic control tower near an airstrip. The short constructions making up the town were nestled in a valley with steep ridges. Ithamar messaged the control tower via the communications panel and specified they were approaching the landing strip and requesting permission to park. It was quickly acknowledged and confirmed by the traffic controller in the tower.

"We're good to go." Ithamar grinned.

"First time on the moon," Vanya confessed.

"Really?" Edin asked.

"Yeah, my parents use a hangar outside of the capital," Vanya said. "There never was a need to travel here."

"On the bright side, we might be able to get some food," Ithamar said. "Most moon ports have decent restaurants."

"Thank goodness," Edin said. "I'm starving."

They found a landing spot on the far side of the hangars. Once the Riskplay settled on the airstrip, Ithamar shut down power to the starship. A gust of icy wind met them near the cabin door. It was much colder than what they were accustomed to on Lathas. Ithamar pulled three wool jackets out of a storeroom beside the bunk bed. They donned the thick overcoats and then walked out onto the asphalt.

For the rest of the day, they moseyed around the moon city. First, they went to a little diner near the hangars where they ate eggs and fruit and drank hot tea. It was a quick snack and not very filling. Then they proceeded to the nearest market. The market consisted of low stone buildings, all of the architecture archaic and bare. The pathways they traveled were made of cement and pale cobbles. Edin thought Cold Canyon was more of a community with a spaceport than an actual city. The streets were never crowded, and the shops were never busy. The few beings they did come across wore tattered and stained garments. It was obvious the moon wasn't a place where the wealthy lived, merely a place the affluent owned.

After they had done their grocery and supply shopping, they headed back to the Riskplay. On their backs, they carried large nylon bags filled with food and cleaning supplies. Edin wondered if whoever had destroyed HD-84 would be waiting for them on the airstrip. But when they returned to the ship, no one had been there.

"Can we go eat at a real restaurant?" Vanya asked.

"What do you mean?" Ithamar asked.

"That diner food was horrible," Vanya answered. "We're about to go live in the woods for two more weeks. This will be our last chance to enjoy civilization for a while, even if it is a moon port."

"Yeah, I'm still hungry too," Edin said.

They had just dropped the bags of food inside the ship. Vanya stood with a disappointed glare aimed at Ithamar. Clearly she did not want to leave for the bungalow. It was the one thing Ithamar had promised the two of them: if Edin won the match, they were supposed to get a proper meal.

"Well . . ." Ithamar paused. He rubbed his chin and then nodded. "We're not sure if someone followed us here. But I have an idea."

"What?" Edin asked.

"You two go back to the market and eat wherever you like. I'll trail you by a few minutes and see if I can't spot anyone snooping on you two."

Vanya shook her head. "We didn't see anyone around us all day, and nothing has changed with the ship. The people after us are probably not on this moon."

"We should let Ithamar trail us," Edin said. "He might spot someone that we couldn't. If the threat would pursue us at the Pebble Inn, they might pursue us here."

"Whatever," Vanya said.

Ithamar grinned. "Make sure to get me a plate to go."

Edin laughed. "Will do."

"Wait a second." Ithamar paced to the armory and then returned shortly. "Here, take this."

It was a small circular gadget. Edin grabbed it from Ithamar's hand.

"What is that?" Vanya asked.

"I'm guessing a tracker," Edin assumed.

"Yep," Ithamar said. Edin and Vanya left the ship and walked back to the marketplace with the tracker in Edin's coat pocket. People glanced at the pair of them walking and then glanced away. It appeared as if no one there had watched the gauntlet tournament or even knew who Edin Carvosa was. Edin liked it that way.

A wooden sign hung over a large eatery named Lord of Chow. Looking through the windows, they saw an extensive buffet. They'd passed it earlier, smelling the seasoned aroma from the middle of the street. This time they walked inside with their minds on nothing but curing their deep hunger.

It was fairly busy. There were more people in the eatery than Edin had seen all day while roaming Cold Canyon. Guests traveled from the five long counters in the center to their seats with plates overloaded with random entrees. A human lady greeted them at the hostess stand and took them to their booth right away. Edin salivated at the smells and sights. Once seated, Edin and Vanya both ordered water and headed to the buffet.

Within a single glance over the counters, Edin noticed breads, desserts, fruits, meats, noodles, rice, sauces, soups, and vegetables.

"This is incredible. I've never been to a place like this," Edin admitted.

"You've never been to a buffet?" Vanya asked.

"No, I mainly ate in cafeterias when we landed at spaceports."

"Well, it's all you can eat, so don't fill up too fast."

"I won't. Trust me."

On the first trip to the buffet, Edin piled up a plate of protein, picking what looked most appetizing and paying little attention to which animal the meat came from. Red meat, white meat, blue meat, and green meat were stacked in a pyramid as he returned to the booth. He grabbed a fork, lowered his head, and ate like a famished carnivore.

Vanya took her time at each counter and selected little portions from the healthier options. Her plate consisted of fruits and vegetables. Also, she had a bowl of clear mint soup. She returned to the table as Edin shoved a barbequed kebab into his mouth.

"That's barbaric."

"What?" Edin said with a mouth full of smashed food.

Vanya sat across from him. "The way you're eating."

Edin swallowed. "I killed someone today. I was born to be barbaric."

"I would prefer to eat with a more cultured barbarian."

"Spacers have no culture."

"I thought you were Mizoquii."

Edin glanced around nervously, but the other patrons were preoccupied with eating. "I am."

"Eat like one then."

Edin continued eating until he cleared the dish. Then he got up for his second plate, which consisted of croissants, razzmelon, and more meat. Vanya still had not eaten everything from her first trip by the time he finished.

"Go get some of the kebabs," Edin said. "They're good."

"I'm probably not going to eat much more," Vanya said. "Might get some dessert."

"I thought you were hungry?"

"Yes, but it doesn't take much to fill me up. Plus, I'm more conscious about what I eat than you or Ithamar."

"We're about to go back to the bungalow where the options are limited. You're the one that wanted to come so bad."

Vanya twirled her fork on her dish. "Yeah, I think I just wanted some more time with you, before your training starts."

They looked at each other, and Edin didn't know what to say. *Is she hinting at something?*

CHAPTER 18

While waiting for the match against Damien Lynch, Prince Cane and King Bahri Nazari sat inside the locker room, watching the first match of the semifinals. It was by far the ritziest room below the Kosabar Arena and connected to a washroom with clean showers. The carpeted floor was yellow and purple with an intricate floral design. The area was reserved for House Nazari contestants only.

The battle between Edin Carvosa and Zokku Rellen was displayed on large digital screens in every corner. When Edin slew his opponent with a vicious and unexpected throw of his hyperblade, Cane Nazari erupted out of his chair and threw it against the wall. It clinked loudly when striking the golden lockers.

His father remained seated with an expression of extreme displeasure.

"Can you believe this?!" Cane shouted. "He actually won!"

"Calm down," Bahri said. "Focus on the match at hand. We will worry about Edin later."

"It was supposed to be a finale for the ages!" Cane pointed at the screen. "Now I'll be stuck against that scrub."

"You need to focus on Damien for now. Don't get ahead of yourself."

"The spectators will be disappointed." Cane shook his head. "The bettors too."

They both looked up at the screen. Edin waved to the crowd above his tunnel. It appeared that he had accumulated a fanbase.

"Who on Lathas would cheer for him?"

"Immigrants," Bahri answered instantly.

"Pathetic. Other spacers with no heritage or love for this planet."

"Look on the bright side. He won't be a threat to you in combat. That throw he snuck on Zokku will be pointless to try on you."

"He will have a trick in his mind."

"There's the possibility that Damien will have a trick. Take it one step at a time, as I taught you."

Cane exhaled noisily in frustration. "Okay."

He walked to a locker and opened it up. Inside was his silk combat uniform, a black gi with faded gold trim. He slipped it on, then laced up his battle boots. Once dressed, he began pacing the locker room, anger flowing through his veins. He stopped and started to bounce on his toes and punch the air ahead of him.

"Are you ready?" Bahri asked.

"Forever ready," Cane said with no hesitation.

"Well, I'm about to head to the skybox. See you after the match."

"Bye, Father."

Bahri exited the room. Cane remained standing until the knock at the door.

Cane stood at the end of the tunnel, waiting for the cannon to fire. A worefann, his escort, stood next to him. The little ball of black-blue fur handed Cane the hyperblade.

The cannon fired.

Cane looked at the worefann. "How do you want me to kill him?"

The worefann hesitated. He appeared nervous to recommend something to the prince of the planet. "With a throw," he said with a squeaky voice. "Like the match before."

"I was hoping you would say that."

Cane strolled onto the pitch. The crowd roared at the sight of him, making the ground vibrate. Small rocks scattered in the wake of the energy in the stadium. He smiled.

Damien Lynch sprinted towards him. The noble boy from the planet Lochosh had short ginger hair and a freckled face and wore gray-and-red robes with an armorial bird pinned to his chest. At twenty meters away, Cane pretended to throw his hyperblade at Damien, causing him to flinch.

Cane smiled. He smelled the fear. They got closer and closer, perhaps three meters away when Cane once again faked a throw. Damien flinched for the second time. The spectators gasped as if they had suddenly realized who was the predator and who was the prey.

Cane lunged forward with a forceful downward swing against Damien's hyperblade. The hyperblades whined at the contact.

Damien blocked two more attacks before being cut down by a brutal strike across the abdomen. Blood and guts sprayed from his stomach, and his body dropped face-first, soaking the gravel red.

Despite winning the semifinal match, Cane Nazari was depressed. He failed to eat dinner with his family and retreated to his chamber upon returning to Palais de la Perpillas. The great palace was eerily quiet and cold for the night after a Nazari victory. The entire royal family had wanted Zokku Rellen to be in the finale. Even the guards and servants seemed disheartened as Cane passed them with his head down on his way to his bedchamber.

He lay on his canopy bed and wanted to be left alone. Nothing at the moment would please him, not even Naomi and her friends. Everyone knew he taunted the spacer during the drawing ceremony. It was embarrassing now that Edin Carvosa had conned his way to the finale. *What if someone like Edin wins?* More and more spacers would pour into the arena, taking the tournament away from the nobles. *There is no way I can allow that.* This had to be the end to the spacer's lucky tale.

Countless minutes passed as Cane lay on the bed, thinking about the different ways he would defeat the spacer. There was a knock at the door. Cane didn't feel like getting up or speaking to anyone. A fist then beat on the door like a wild mallet. Cane ignored it once more.

The door burst open, and shadowy figures entered his periphery. He sat up in his bed and realized it was his father and the spy named Roan. The two men looked like exact opposites. Bahri wore a noble suit and had dark hair and a beard. Roan dressed in nothing but black garments and had a white ponytail with no facial hair. They stood beneath the haloed chandelier, which lit the entire room.

"Cane," Bahri said. "Roan has some news about your spacer."

"He's not my spacer." Cane left the bed and strolled to them.

Roan revealed a serpentine smile. "Prince Cane." He curtsied.

"What's new with Edin Carvosa?" Cane asked.

"It appears as if he and his friends are in a little bit of trouble," Roan answered. "We had eyes in the sky watching them when they entered the capital this morning. But we weren't the only ones watching."

Cane leaned closer. "Who else was following them?"

"The Sheeban Syndicate."

The room went silent.

"You can't be serious," Cane said eventually.

"Serious as a plague," Roan said. "And it appears to be two bounty hunters. They searched Ithamar Avrum's starship on top of the Pebble Inn."

Cane rubbed his chin. "So, there is more to this spacer than he shows at first sight."

Bahri stepped closer. "This is a problem for you. We can't have your opponent killed before the finale. It would look disastrous for the integrity of our house and the tournament."

"Are you sure they want to kill him?" Cane asked. "How is he of such great importance that the Sheeban Syndicate is hunting him on Lathas?"

"This is where things get irregular, shady." Roan bit his lip. "We have reports that a Sheeban vessel entered the atmosphere the day before Edin Carvosa signed up for the gauntlet tournament. Apparently, that vessel had a rendezvous which turned sour, very sour, and very bloody. We assume that Edin Carvosa's arrival is a byproduct of that scenario." Roan rubbed the hair behind his ear. "There was a smuggling vessel, called the *Saircor*, that was ambushed outside of the capital. The entire crew was dead when discovered. The intelligence office doesn't like to rush to conclusions, but we think they transported some sort of technology or weaponry and were then slain by the clients, the Sheeban Syndicate."

"Edin Carvosa must have been on that smuggling vessel," Bahri predicted.

"Perhaps," Roan said. "Perhaps he was a deserter on the Sheeban's vessel."

"Whatever he is, he's not the person everyone thinks of him as," Cane said.

"We are going to have to send protection to him," Bahri said. "As I said earlier, we can't let anything happen to him, or it will appear as if we killed the boy and then tried to cover it up. The commoners would riot."

"That's so weird." Cane sneered at the paradox. "Defending the enemy."

"I'm going to send agents to his location." Bahri crossed his arms. "We wanted to inform you beforehand. In case you heard anything, we thought you should at least be knowledgeable of the situation."

"What are they going to do?" Cane asked. "Break his door down and say, 'I've come to protect you from the Sheeban Syndicate'? Because the spacer and his friends might think of that as fairly intrusive."

Roan snorted an odd laugh. "No, no. I'll be accompanying a stealth party that will observe from a distance. Our maneuvers will be entirely covert unless Edin is in imminent danger. We want to know more about this spacer and whatever connections he does have. He could provide valuable intelligence to us about criminal organizations within the solar system."

"Don't get caught spying on him," Cane said. "It would look unethical."

"The boy arrived on my planet by smuggling vessel," Bahri noted. "At this point, I am unconcerned about ethics."

"Exactly, my king," Roan hissed. "We are not dealing with individuals of integrity."

The spymaster reached into his pocket and pulled out a portable hologram projector. He placed it on the stone floor.

Two figures emerged from the projector. Right away Cane could tell it was the two bounty hunters. They wore heavy-plated armor like ancient warriors, but Cane assumed from the sleek edges that the technology of their outer shell was sophisticated. Their faces were covered by thick metal helmets with narrow visors. They looked like they carried death with them wherever they voyaged—the type of creatures who shot first and asked questions never.

"Their names are Lasandro Lightwing and Hagger Condo," Roan stated. "They are both technomancers. They wield the Gift through advanced technology."

"They're insane," Cane said. He had heard the tales of technomancers. "You can die from that. A single mishap and you could blow yourself to smithereens."

"Yes. But it is a risk some are willing to take. Of course, I'm sure they've had years of training if they're the two that the Sheeban Syndicate has sent to Lathas."

"Technomancers." Cane shook his head. "The spacer's story couldn't get any more absurd."

CHAPTER 19

The first week before the finale, Edin trained nonstop. In the mornings, Ithamar ran him through the inclined trails surrounding the bungalow. They would eat a light lunch and focus on calisthenics afterward.

The body exercises left Edin sore each day. The aching grew as the week wore on. His legs turned to rubber from the endless squats and lunges and jumping drills. Ithamar forced Edin to do so many repetitions that the boy would lose count and had to will himself through set after set after set. Upper-body exercises consisted of hundreds of push-ups, and weighted pull-ups while hanging on tree branches. Ithamar would add various workouts to the routine so it was never exactly the same. Around dusk, they proceeded to spar with dummy swords in the yellow meadow. Vanya would watch from the front porch as Ithamar bested Edin in most of the duels. She had focused on repairing the house from the nistaclar invasion during her days alone. By the end of the week, there was virtually no sign that it had been ransacked.

On the seventh day, they had just eaten breakfast of toast and eggs, and they stood in the kitchen before heading out to the woods.

"I can tell that you need a break," Ithamar said. "There will be no workout after the run."

"Will we still spar?" Edin asked.

"No. We'll cancel that too." Ithamar grinned. "Go do something with Vanya today."

Edin blushed and looked away. "What do you mean?"

Ithamar paced around the kitchen. "I see how she watches you when we spar in the meadow."

"You're overthinking the situation."

"I know you two stay up late watching old hologram clips after I'm in bed."

"Maybe you go to sleep too early."

"Well, I'm giving you today off. Feel free to do with it as you like."

Edin smiled and stretched his arms. "Thanks. I'll probably do something with Vanya. She does seem bored around here."

"Take her to the waterfalls north of here."

"I was thinking about that."

They spent the waking morning in the woods. It was humid and misty. They never picked up the pace past a jog, keeping to a slow stride. Edin wondered what Vanya would think about exploring with him. She had started exercising on her own while at the bungalow—there wasn't much else to do in the middle of a rainforest—but had yet to adventure far north. He knew she would say yes to going out with him. But he felt slightly nervous about asking, like he was asking her on a date. *Maybe nerves never really go away when talking to girls*, he thought. Perhaps she would not think much of it, and he was the one overthinking the situation. But she did make him anxious. It was a different anxiety than the one he experienced before a match. Before a match, he felt tense throughout his body. Talking to Vanya gave him more of a mental unease. He tried to avoid both when he could, but he understood the need to fight against the stewing nerves.

Their run seemed to go by faster than normal as his mind raced with thoughts of Vanya and how to manage his composure that afternoon.

They returned to the bungalow with their clothes drenched in sweat. Vanya wasn't there, so he assumed that she was off running on her own. *Hopefully she doesn't run into a nistaclar,* he thought.

He went upstairs to his bedroom and showered quickly, then changed into athletic shorts and a plain navy T-shirt. The front door downstairs slammed shut; Vanya must have returned. *Time to ask her.*

He walked down to the den as Vanya rummaged through the refrigerator for fruits and vegetables to make a salad. Her blond hair was sticky and her skin was wet from sweat. She turned and smiled, her red cheeks lighting up the room.

"What are you up to?" Vanya asked.

"I'm off for the rest of the day."

"Already?"

"Yeah, we just jogged this morning. Ithamar said I needed a break."

"Oh, cool." Vanya grabbed more fruits from the open refrigerator.

Edin shuffled his feet. "I was wondering if you wanted to go to the waterfalls."

She looked over her shoulder. "Yeah, sounds fun."

He grinned. "Alright, well, whenever you're ready, we can go."

She shut the fridge door with her foot. "Okay, I'll eat and shower and get ready. Even though it might be pointless to shower and return outside."

"Take your time."

Edin stepped out onto the front porch and sat on a rocking chair. He noticed Ithamar was in the Riskplay. His older cousin must have been working in one of the engine bays because Edin heard something crash loudly and Ithamar yelled a vulgarity. Edin thought about checking if he needed help but decided Ithamar probably wanted to be left alone.

The warm sun lingered over the surrounding woods where birds sang chipper tunes. It was going to be a good day. Edin felt it in the air. He patiently waited, rocking back and forth with a smile.

Thirty minutes later, the front door opened and Vanya stepped out. She wore a white tank top with her blond hair touching her shoulders, brushing the pink straps of a bathing suit. Black athletic shorts displayed her tanned legs. Edin thought she looked gorgeous.

Vanya smiled and winked. "Hey."

Edin stood. "Ready to go?"

"Yep."

They left the bungalow and entered a narrow trail leading north. The jungle showed all of its colors. Massive golden trunks forked and spiraled and ascended to the heights of the orange canopy lingering hundreds of feet over their heads. The red leaves of the forest floor crackled after every step.

"Do you know why the leaves turn red after they fall?" Edin asked.

"Not sure exactly," Vanya said. "Something with to do with their chemistry and sunlight."

"Science always has the answers."

"False," she said firmly.

Edin gave her an attentive glance. "What do you mean?"

"Science was created by men. Therefore, it is flawed in nature."

"Now you sound religious."

"Science and religion can mingle. Only the narrowminded pledge themselves to one side or the other."

"But the Order of Oracles was created by men. The old text must be flawed as well."

"That's up to each and every individual to decide for themselves—how much they believe in one or the other. Science is too detached for my taste. I prefer religion; I prefer to believe there is something else that controls the universe."

Edin scratched his neck. "I haven't thought much about it."

"About what?"

"If the 'One God' and destiny truly exist. Or are we just living in a simulation that someone else controls?"

Vanya laughed. "This isn't a simulation, sweetheart."

They looked at each other. Vanya's cheeks reddened as if she had accidentally let the word slip. Edin was caught off guard, but then he smiled.

"Who said I was your sweetheart?"

"You're not," Vanya said. "You're my dumb friend who swings a sword."

Edin pushed her shoulder playfully. "Jerk."

Vanya lost her balance slightly. "Woah."

"Don't trip."

She smiled. "Are you ready for your next fight?"

"Yeah. I wish I could've fought Cane first."

"That's not what I'm talking about it." Vanya shoved his shoulder, and he stumbled over a tree root and caught himself on the trunk.

"Hey! That was rude."

Vanya giggled. "Guess you weren't ready."

By early afternoon, they had reached the mountains featuring the aged and secluded waterfalls. If they hadn't been preoccupied with flirting with each other, they would have arrived earlier. Edin grew more comfortable with Vanya as they walked deeper into the jungle. Despite the newfound confidence, nerves still swirled in his body and mind. He wondered if she felt the same, because if she was nervous, she was an expert at hiding it. She always appeared calm and at peace. *How does she do it?*

Ahead of them were three mountains of medium size. Edin heard rushing water before he saw any. At first, they came across streams flowing over smooth boulders and pebbly bedrocks. The canopy was thinner, and sunlight snaked through the leaves and gleamed off the water. They hiked for a few more minutes and found themselves at a large lake where a wooden walkway led towards the base of the first mountain.

"We have arrived," Edin said. "The waterfalls are down this path."

Vanya stared across the lake. "This is so beautiful."

The sun radiated off the flat, wide blue surface. The lake was bordered by massive golden trees overhanging the water. In the middle a group of small birds floated still and quiet. A gentle breeze pushed thin clouds through the sky.

Edin observed Vanya. She took everything in with big eyes as if she had fallen in love with nature at this very moment. It brought him back to when he first met her in the Pebble Inn and had no clue how to speak to a girl. Things had changed since then, if only in minor increments.

"I knew you'd like it here," he said.

"I would have come here earlier if you had told me it looked like this."

"Better late than never."

They continued down the wooden walkway, side by side. Vanya kept glancing over to the left at the water, while Edin eyed ahead.

"The waterfalls are even prettier," he said.

"Really?" she asked. "This area seems magical."

"It's a lot nicer than the swamplands."

"That's true. Don't want to visit that place again."

"Try not to get captured by the nistaclar again."

"I'll do my best to avoid them."

They strolled at a leisurely pace. The planks stood half a meter above the surface of the water. Fish swam between the algae-covered wooden posts.

The walkway turned away from the lake and led to a cave with a slim opening. It was dark inside the mountain, but the cave provided a straight path ahead that looked unnaturally rounded like it was created by men many moons ago. Vanya grabbed Edin's hand unexpectedly, and goosebumps and hairs rose from his toes to his fingers. He gripped her hand with firmness and guided the way. After a couple minutes in complete darkness, they spotted rays of white light entering at the end of the tunnel. A flight of stairs preceded the exit. Edin moved Vanya ahead of him and placed his hand on her lower back, pushing her forward. He wanted her to be the first one out.

They stepped outside to an unforgettable view. The great waterfalls in the distance formed an aquatic network. Near the summit of the second mountain, the highest waterfall plummeted into a pool of cyan water, which flowed to two cascades dropping to a wide gorge running to the shortest of the falls, which lowered into white rapids that flowed back underneath the canopy of the jungle. Everywhere in sight, trees and bushes and flowers clung to rocky edges.

Vanya smiled. "This is incredible."

"Nature." Edin squinted towards the summit. "Sights like this make me think there is truth about the One God."

Vanya stepped closer to him. "How do you do it?"

"Do what?"

"Risk your life in that tournament. There's so much living you have left in you."

Edin turned away. "I've never had the chance to gamble. To make my own decisions. To strive for the betterment of myself. I come from nothing, and the gauntlet was the best option to become something more."

"What if you win but you dislike the academy and the First System?"

"That's doubtful."

"Academia will be a lot different than throwing a hyperblade around. And the First System has a lot of . . . elitists."

Edin turned away from the view and stepped down towards a path trailing to the gorge. Vanya followed him. There was a moment of silence as they walked underneath the canopy.

Edin cleared his throat. "Do you think I'll be the dumbest one there?"

Vanya gasped and shook her head. "No, Edin! You have common sense and a decent work ethic. But schoolwork gets boring and tiring quickly. I think you might lack the patience. Most boys do."

"I have no formal education, and I'll only be accepted due to victory in the tournament." Edin paused. "I think I'll be the dumbest one out of the entire lot no matter where I go."

"Look, I wasn't trying to discourage you." Vanya stepped over a tree root. "Winning the tournament should give you enough confidence to be competitive in whatever your heart wishes."

Edin looked into her eyes. "Come with me."

Vanya raised her eyebrows in shock. "To the First System?"

"Yes."

"My parents wouldn't like that much."

"Your parents haven't been here. I can support you."

"You haven't even won your last match. After that, we can talk."

"Will you think about it?"

"Why would you want me to come with you?"

"Because you're my best friend."

Vanya blushed.

They continued their trek to the lofty waterfalls. The narrow path led down the mountain until it eventually spilled out beside the loud rapids. Rushing water collided and splashed and sprayed in every direction. They walked on the rocky embankments towards the lowest and smallest falls. Not much was said. Both focused on pushing forward and climbing higher and observing the leafy, flourishing scenery that encircled them.

The lowest fall was larger than Edin assumed it would be. He had never ventured this far, always stopping at the vantage point from outside the cave in the first mountain. This had turned into a little adventure. Uncertainty of what he would discover stirred up the excitement. A noticeable stone pathway turned into stone steps rising into the sky.

As they hiked upward, Edin felt the ache of his workouts with each stride. His thighs, calves, and feet burned deep. Pink moss and small lizards clung to the wall of wet limestone where the falls misted nonstop and cooled off the surroundings. The reptiles were unfazed at the presence of humans and remained frozen of movement. The steps led much higher than the high point of the falls. He wondered if the ascension would ever end. It must have taken over ten standard minutes.

Once they reached the top, they stood on flatland above the deep gorge. He looked over the precipice at a stream running sixty meters below.

Vanya stood beside Edin and peeked down the vertical wall of rock. "That's so much higher than I was expecting."

"We should only have one more climb," Edin said. "I want to try to reach the pool at the bottom of the highest falls."

"Do you think it's swimmable?"

"Only one way to find out."

They continued towards the massive falls, now visible ahead, and the two cascades dropping into the gorge. The brightly colored flora clashed with the jagged gray cliffs and peaks. Vanya stared in admiration, as if the landscape had been painted with divine skill, a portrait of temptation.

"I could live here," she said.

"I'll tell Ithamar to move the bungalow," Edin said.

Vanya giggled. "Yeah right. I think he loves the location it's at now."

"No distractions and tons of trails to train on. I wouldn't be surprised if Ithamar makes me stay there after the tournament."

"No, I already know you're going to leave me on this planet by my lonely."

"I asked you to come with me."

"It's not that easy."

"I understand, but think of your future."

"I do. And I see my family in that future."

"When is the last time you contacted your parents?"

"Right after your second match. Neither one of them know about this whole ordeal and my current living arrangement. They would have a heart attack if they knew all that I have been through with you and Ithamar."

Edin hesitated. "What did you tell them?"

"That everything has been well, but the Pebble Inn and Lathas have been boring lately."

"Boring since I showed up?" Edin asked sarcastically.

Vanya smiled. "Yes, you're the root of all my boredom."

They strolled along as the sound of the river running below echoed through the valley.

"But they have heard of you," Vanya said.

"What did you say?"

"Nothing. They heard about the commoner competing in the finale of the gauntlet tournament of Lathas. I guess they heard about you through old friends or the media on the network."

"Do they want me to win?"

Vanya shrugged. "To be honest, I don't think they care that much. They're probably only interested in the scenario."

When they reached the two cascades, it took a few minutes to find the next pathway. The falls both plummeted into the gorge from a sudden drop. Nothing near them indicated a route to navigate higher. They had to leave the water, and they searched the jungle until they eventually discovered another set of stone steps. This climb took much longer than the previous one. The trail weaved back and forth beneath the canopy, so Edin could never be sure of how far they had left to travel. They spotted a large white feline with orange spots lounging on a thick golden branch. It watched the two humans with rounded prowler eyes.

"What is that thing?" Edin asked.

"A gingato," Vanya answered. "Don't worry; they don't attack humans."

A few minutes after seeing the gingato, they reached a dead end—a steep incline of rock looming about ten meters tall. There was a massive tree on the overhang above them, and a plethora of tree roots curled and twisted out of the stone slope.

Edin stepped on a tree root and grabbed another one above him. "You think you can climb up this?"

"Yeah," Vanya said.

They scaled the slope with Edin leading the way. The tree roots were never too distant for comfort. However, they were moist, which made the ascension slippery. Once at the top, Edin assisted Vanya over the edge. Pounding water resounded ahead.

"We should be close," Edin said.

"Hopefully," Vanya said.

The bottom of the largest waterfall was only a few meters in front of them. There was no pathway. They pushed through dense shrubbery and hedges and maneuvered around thorny vines until they came out of the jungle.

Edin's jaw dropped.

Torrents of water poured over rocky pillars at a pace cruel enough to crack steel on the way down. The plunge pool below could drown a large starship if it managed to survive the fall in one piece. The sound boomed and echoed. Mist wandered mindlessly. White water dropped from the summit and exploded against the cyan pool with a continuous roar.

"Wow," Vanya shouted.

"Let's find an area to jump in," Edin yelled.

After a few minutes of inspecting the embankment, they spotted a tree with roots winding and coiling inside of the pool. The current was weak there, and they could hang on to the golden roots in the water. Edin stripped down to his boxers and jumped in first. It was colder than he expected. As the water rose to his ribs, his feet touched the riverbed sediments. He walked deeper into the pool. The current lazily brushed his legs. Small fish swam away in fear. He turned and watched Vanya slip off her tank top and shorts. He thought she looked very fine in the pink bathing suit.

Slowly she entered the plunge pool.

"Come on! There's no current right here," Edin yelled.

"Hold on!"

Edin thought he would go for it as soon as she got close to him. *This is the perfect time*, he told himself.

Vanya walked out into the water with her eyes glued on the ground, checking to make sure each step was safe and some random sea monster was not coming for her. When she finally reached Edin, she met his eyes and smiled. The waterfall in the background was causing too much noise for a casual conversation.

Edin stepped closer to her and placed his hands on her hips. She looked up at him for a brief moment, then closed her eyes as their lips touched.

CHAPTER 20

"You kissed her?"

"Yeah."

"Mistake."

"How?"

"You're already friends with her. That poor girl is going to be in love with you."

Edin and Ithamar were on their morning jog in the jungle. The only thing on Edin's mind was Vanya. It was the first time he had kissed a girl, and he was unsure how things would go next. Asking Ithamar for advice seemed like his only option.

"If I win, should I ask her to go to the First System with me?" Edin asked.

"She's already a distraction," Ithamar said. "She already has your mind wrapped around her instead of your next opponent. This is why I first said no girls were allowed at the bungalow."

They jogged in silence for a few minutes. Embarrassed, Edin knew it was a mistake to bring it up.

"Sorry," Edin said. "I shouldn't have said anything about it."

"Look, she is a sweet girl. But you're both young. Realistically, it's never going to work between the two of you. Life takes people in different directions."

"That's blunt."

"That's reality."

They both jumped over a fallen tree laid across the path.

"Just don't get your hopes up with her," Ithamar said. "Whether you win or you lose, you won't be on this planet much longer."

"I understand," Edin said. "But I feel like I have to put forth some type of effort."

"Will you do me a favor?"

"What?"

"Don't bring it up until after the match. We need to stay focused. You need to be ready for Cane Nazari, because Cane Nazari will be ready for you."

"I'll be ready."

"Good."

The rest of the morning they ran without talking. Edin tried to rearrange his thoughts towards Cane Nazari and picture how the match would play out: Hyperblade striking hyperblade at a blistering rate. He assumed Nazari would start on the offensive and his best shot would be to counter when the opportune moment revealed itself. The match would happen fast, he knew. All matches did.

In the early afternoon he did calisthenics for over three hours. Ithamar pushed Edin to his limit in every exercise, yelling at him when Edin reached his breaking point to provoke more repetitions. Veins and muscles swelled from Edin's biceps and forearms like an overpacked suitcase bursting at the seams. His calves had steadily grown muscular and thick through training. His chest, shoulders, and abdomen were chiseled like inscriptions in stone. He pushed himself to fatigue, knowing his body had transformed into the finest form he had ever been in. At the very least, he would be able to compete with Cane Nazari for the first few minutes of the match.

After jogging and calisthenics, they returned to the bungalow. They ate kulliben and red vegetables in the kitchen. Vanya walked down the stairs from the bedroom and smiled.

"How is training going?" she asked.

"Oh, just lovely." Ithamar flashed a smirk.

Vanya shot a glance at Edin. "Well, that's great."

"What have you been up to today?" Edin asked.

"I've been studying for the GAAT."

Ithamar shook his head. "I'd rather be running through the woods."

"Me too," Vanya replied swiftly.

"Is it that hard?" Edin asked. He knew the GAAT was the Galactic Academy Aptitude Test, the standard test that academies reviewed for acceptance. But he didn't know much about the questions or the format of the exam. Most academies waived the test score for gauntlet victors.

Vanya sighed. "The math portion is a pain. Too many random equations and formulas."

Ithamar placed his hand on Edin's shoulder. "Luckily you don't have to worry about that."

"He could still take it," Vanya said. "Studying for it will help prepare him for academia."

"He will jump that hurdle when he gets there. For now, he must physically train, and focus his mind on the art of combat." Ithamar walked out of the kitchen. "Time to spar," he said, heading outside.

Edin and Ithamar each grabbed a wooden sword by the door and paced out of the bungalow and onto the yellow meadow. Vanya remained on the porch and watched from a distance. In the middle of the meadow, Ithamar stopped and pointed his sword at Edin.

"When you face Cane, you have to start on the offensive."

Edin raised his eyebrows. "Why?"

"I've seen how he fights. Once he gets momentum, he becomes unstoppable. If you get momentum first, you can disrupt his rhythm and alter the fight in your favor."

"I was thinking I would just evade and counter," Edin said. "I think I would leave myself too open if I go full-on attack."

"No, you're going to attack like a madman. Because that is the last thing he is expecting. Plus, we're about to train on this for the rest of the week."

"Okay. I'll try it."

"You don't sound motivated. I'll show you what I mean."

Ithamar lunged towards Edin with a burst of strikes that were indefensible. Edin felt the sting of the wood smash each of his limbs before he managed to block a single strike. He backed away.

"What was that for?"

"ITS TRAINING TIME NOW! LET'S GO!" Ithamar roared. "ATTACK ME LIKE YOU WANT TO KILL ME!"

Three days before the gauntlet finale, Edin's hands were blistered from sparring with the wooden sword. Each evening, they spent countless hours in the meadow, fencing back and forth. Ithamar instructed Edin on how to attack at the first second of the match.

Before, Vanya would stay awake and wait on Edin to complete training for the day, and then they would spend time together in the living area, watching holograms. But Ithamar allowed none of that anymore. They trained until she left the porch and went inside. Edin realized that Ithamar had given them a day to spend together alone because the rest of the week would be completely focused on the upcoming fight. It slightly aggravated Edin, but he understood this was the best way to prepare—no distractions. At least, Edin assumed there would be no distractions.

Edin and Ithamar spent the day sprinting up slopes and completing an intense upper-body routine. After eating a healthy portion of fresh fish and razzmelon, they proceeded to spar in the evening. Edin slipped on a pair of old leather gloves to help with the blisters on his palms, but the skin on his hands had finally started to harden, adapting to the wooden handle. They walked outside to the meadow, and Vanya watched from the porch as usual.

"Are your hands good?" Ithamar asked.

"Yeah, they're getting better. The skin is growing strong under the blisters," Edin said.

"I told you that would happen."

"You act like I've never had blisters before."

"To be fair, your hands are softer than a toddler's bottom."

"Whatever."

Ithamar laughed. "We're going to spread apart and charge like the beginning of the match. So back up some."

"Alright."

The two cousins distanced themselves fifty meters apart.

Ithamar yelled, "Three! Two! One! Go!"

They galloped towards each other with both of their wooden swords itching to land the first blow. When they met, Edin swung furiously towards the neck, leaving Ithamar no choice but to block. Wood splintered off from the collision. Edin spun around low and struck Ithamar on the calf. Edin landed three more hard strikes on the back and both shoulders. Ithamar jumped away to regather himself.

"Dang," Ithamar said. "You don't have to hit me so hard."

"You're lucky," Edin said. "I could have hit your neck if I wanted to."

"You're getting better," Ithamar admitted. "We go again."

As they trotted back to their starting points, Edin realized he had bested Ithamar easily. Perhaps his older cousin took the first round lightly. *The intensity must rise*, he told himself. It was the first time Edin had landed multiple strikes on Ithamar in that manner. Ithamar would be prepared this time and eager for revenge. They regained their positions and looked across the meadow towards each other as the wind grazed the yellow grass.

Ithamar yelled, "Three! Two! One! Go!"

Edin burst forward, gripping the handle like his life depended upon it. His feet pounded against the grass and soft soil, kicking back dirt in his wake. Ahead, Ithamar charged faster than before with his mechanical eye focused on his dueling foe. When they converged,

Ithamar swung first with the intent to smash Edin's left shoulder. The wooden sword sliced through thin air and hit nothingness. Edin lunged in the direction of the swing and dodged the timber blade with flair. Ithamar's entire torso was left exposed as the momentum of the swing carried his defensive guard away. Edin tightened his grip on the handle with both hands and slammed the sword against Ithamar's ribcage. It was a brutal strike. The entire wooden blade cracked, then shattered into little splinters that rained down on the grass.

Clutching his side, Ithamar dropped to the ground and cried out in pain.

Edin looked down at his cousin. "Sorry. Are you alright?"

"I'm fine." Ithamar exhaled loudly. "Go get another sword in the Riskplay. I'll be ready when you get back."

Never had he witnessed his cousin overpowered. In a way, he was proud of himself. If he could defeat Ithamar in quick combat, then he should be able to defeat Cane likewise. *A spacer winning the gauntlet tournament on Lathas. Imagine that. Actually, don't imagine that.* He had to break his promising brainwaves. *Don't fixate on things yet to come,* he told himself. *Concentrate on the present.*

As Edin headed for the Riskplay, he flung the handle of the broken practice sword into the depths of the woods. It disappeared in the tree branches and orange leaves. He entered his cousin's starship through the hatch in the midsection. In the armory, three wooden swords stood propped against the bulkhead. He snagged one and left the ship, the hatch closing behind him automatically. In the meadow, Ithamar stood tall and straight with his mechanical eye and his human eye glued on Edin.

Yep, he's angry, Edin thought. The next round was going to hurt.

"You sure you want another round?" Edin yelled while walking back to his starting position.

"Just one more," Ithamar shouted. "Then we can focus on something else."

Once Edin returned to his spot, he aligned his stance and gripped his new weapon. Ithamar returned to his stance.

"Three! Two! What the—"

A small, gleaming troop transport flew in from the east and hovered over them. The hull was gunmetal gray edged with purple highlights and with a yellow floral crest on the side indicating the ship belonged to House Nazari of Lathas. *They shouldn't be here*, Edin thought. Something odd was transpiring.

The ship proceeded to land. Ithamar walked over to Edin while Vanya left the porch to join them. The three stood between the bungalow and the newly parked ship, awaiting the unknown.

"What could they possibly be here for?" Vanya asked.

"I don't know," Ithamar said. "But I know it isn't good news."

Underneath the forward cockpit, a cargo door opened, and the ramp lowered to the ground. Pressurized air covered the opening in a misty cloud. Silver silhouettes appeared in the fog, and eventually six armored humans walked down the ramp, led by a man in black robes. The man wore his white hair in a ponytail, and his face was pale and wrinkled.

"Good afternoon, gentlemen, and gentlelady." The man nodded to each of them.

"We can cut the chitchat." Ithamar stepped forward. "Why are you here?"

"Unfortunately, you three have a dangerous situation on your hands. Perhaps you know you've been trailed since your last trip to the capital."

"Maybe, maybe not." Ithamar spat on the ground. "I'm going to ask one more time. Why are you here?"

"Okay, okay." The man paused and rubbed his chin. "First, we would like to apologize for intruding on your training grounds. But matters have become very urgent, and your safety is it at risk."

"Apology accepted. Go on."

"My name is Roan Aster. I am the director of the Office of Intelligence, or informally referred to as the spymaster of Lathas. Typically we don't have a great need for spies or undercover work on this planet, but I do take my job seriously."

Ithamar narrowed his eyes. "You know who is trailing us?"

"Yes," Roan answered with a leer. "The Sheeban Syndicate."

Vanya gasped in shock. She put her hand to her mouth, and her cheeks turned red. Everyone standing in the meadow stared at her.

Ithamar broke the silence. "And do you know why the Sheeban Syndicate are after us?"

"I was hoping you would tell me." Roan twisted his mouth again and then turned serious. "But I didn't come for information. I came to offer you protection. You see, House Nazari is in a dilemma. They need the young Edin Carvosa to remain alive for the gauntlet finale. It would be extremely disappointing to the king and prince if Edin disappeared beforehand. Also, there is the reaction from the citizens to worry about. They don't want to be framed for cheating. It would create dishonorable perspectives of the house and the planet."

"How do we know it hasn't been you trailing us this entire time and you're making all of this nonsense up?" Ithamar asked.

"Because Edin Carvosa arrived on this planet amid an illegal smuggling operation."

Edin kept his mouth closed. He glanced at Ithamar and left the talking to him.

Ithamar said, "And that operation has something to do with the syndicate?"

"I assume so. But you two know more about your arrival than I do."

Vanya stepped forward. "How are they supposed to trust you, Spymaster?"

"Miss Waldrip." Roan glanced at the girl and curled his lips. "That is entirely up to them. We won't force ourselves on the three of you. But there are two technomancers by the names of Lasandro Lightwing and Hagger Condo that have had their eyes on your party. When they decide to strike, you would very much appreciate our help."

"I know Lightwing and Condo." Ithamar looked up in the sky. "They're here to kill us then."

"You've had run-ins with these technomancers before?" Roan asked.

"I trained them," Ithamar confessed.

A gust of wind blew across the meadow. Everyone looked at Ithamar, expecting him to explain more, but he just stared at the sky with a frown, as if he might see them coming.

Roan said, "You have the Gift."

"Yes," Ithamar said.

"Now I know how Edin has made it to the finale. Considering that training, he might give Cane a fight for the ages."

"It will be a great fight."

Roan rubbed his chin again. "Can you not ask the technomancers to leave? Or come up with a nonviolent solution to this dilemma, considering you know them?"

"They work for the Sheeban Syndicate now. Their only allegiance is to them. They have no ties to me anymore."

"This is really odd news, Ithamar Avrum."

"The entire situation is odd. I'm surprised they haven't shown their faces yet. Maybe they're scared to confront me. It explains why they tried poisoning Edin after the first match."

Roan glanced away suspiciously. "Why do they want the boy dead so bad?"

"Perhaps they think he knows something about the transaction that happened here. There must have been something important in the cargo. But the boy knows little."

"It was atomics." Edin crossed his arms. "I was an unpaid laborer on the smuggling vessel, and I escaped from my radical captain. I only knew about the warheads, not where they are headed or their plans for them."

Roan nodded understandingly. "Did you kill the entire crew?"

"No, I did," Ithamar said.

"You are insane," Roan said.

"I will kill the technomancers too."

"Do you need our help?"

"Yes, we need to protect Edin and Vanya."

"How do you plan to kill them?"

"When they come."

"And you're expecting them to just show up and fight you?"

"Yes, soon. They must not want us to return to the capital. They're watching us now."

The spymaster and the agents turned their eyes to the jungles in search of irregular activity. But they saw nothing, save for the wind rustling the leaves and birds dancing above the orange canopy.

"I sense them in the jungle," Ithamar said. "They will be here tonight."

"Can your mechanical eye see them?" Roan asked.

"No, I feel them through the Gift. They're in the northern mountains. But it isn't two anymore. There are seven."

Roan's eyes widened. "Seven technomancers?"

"Yes," Ithamar said. "They must have called in backup."

"We can't kill seven technomancers!" Roan roared.

"I can," Ithamar replied.

"You might be Gifted, but you are not capable of that."

"You don't know what I am capable of. I am the prince of the Mizoquii."

CHAPTER 21

"I didn't know the galaxy had any surviving Mizoquii," Roan said.

"Let's keep it that way, and make a deal," Ithamar responded. "If I help you kill these technomancers, then we completely forget about the conversation that just happened and everything else that went on here, forever."

"Okay, I will agree to your deal. We are not exactly supposed to be here in the first place."

"Precisely. Imagine if the citizens thought House Nazari was spying on their opponent."

Roan nodded in agreement. "I guess it's time for us to prepare for a battle."

"Yes," Ithamar nodded as well. "It is time to prepare."

That evening, Ithamar instructed the spymaster and his agents on where to locate themselves and when to fire their weapons. The agents carried Volt700 sniper rifles, with narrow scopes and long barrels that shot skinny blue laser beams. They took their places in the underbrush on the edges of the meadow. Roan hid inside the bungalow along with Edin and Vanya. Outside in the dark, Ithamar sat beside the Riskplay, waiting by his lonesome.

Edin felt uncomfortable about their new guest in the bungalow. He wished the spymaster would go outside with the agents. The old man gave him the creeps with his strange ponytail. *What type of guy wears their hair like that?*

In order to rid Vanya of anxiety from the oncoming onslaught, Edin had an old hologram clip playing in the living room—a historical documentary about the young usurper Plato Bestinger in a distant time before the royal dynasty controlled the galaxy. Edin and Vanya sat together on the couch. Roan watched from behind, sitting on the kitchen countertop.

Roan coughed awkwardly. "Do you think Ithamar can kill these men?"

"If he says he can, then he probably can." Edin turned his head around. "He is in full control of the Gift. He might be the greatest warfighter this galaxy has right now."

Roan burst into laughter. "How many warfighters have you met, boy?"

Edin grimaced. "He is more powerful than you."

Roan bit his lip, then smiled. "Yes, he might be. But he might be dead before morning arrives."

"I've seen his powers in person. They are far greater than the abilities of any technomancer."

"I'll have to see for myself."

"You will."

They remained quiet for a few minutes and watched the hologram in the dark room.

An explosion boomed outside. Plasma rifle fire chattered and burst chaotically. Inside the bungalow, the three dropped to the ground for cover.

"They're already here!" Roan screamed.

Vanya lay flat on her stomach next to Edin and scooted closer. "Don't let them kill us."

"I won't," Edin promised.

The gunfire halted quickly, and the house grew eerily quiet.

Roan crawled towards the window and peeked outside. "I only see Ithamar, no one else."

Edin stood and brushed off his pants. "Everyone else might be dead."

Vanya held up her hand, and Edin grabbed it and assisted her to her feet.

"That was fast," she said.

"Never underestimate the Mizoquii," Edin said.

Roan grimaced at him with distaste. Clearly Roan didn't understand the Mizoquii, nor did he have the desire to show admiration for a man with a separate agenda. The spymaster's allegiance was to House Nazari. Edin could see the hate in his ugly eyes. Roan probably wished Ithamar had been killed or at least injured. It was a look of envy. Someone else was the hero, someone else was Gifted, and Roan was irrelevant to the destiny of the universe. *House Nazari will become irrelevant too*, Edin thought.

Edin walked towards the door and winked. "Told you so."

"We will see," Roan hissed.

Edin and Roan walked out into the foggy night. Ithamar stood motionless by himself in the middle of the meadow as if waiting for them to arrive. Edin thought it was strange. *Where are the agents and the technomancers? Are there still people in the jungle? Did they run away in fear? Did Ithamar kill them all with the Gift?*

"What happened?" Roan asked.

Ithamar turned around. "All your agents are dead."

Roan shuddered. "Did they die with honor?"

"No." Ithamar glared lasers into the spymaster's eyes.

Edin could tell his cousin was furious. "What do you mean?"

Ithamar stepped forward. "Answer me one question, Spymaster."

Roan took a step backward, his eyes watering. "What?"

"Who poisoned Edin after his first match?"

"The Sheeban Syndicate!" Roan cried.

Ithamar raised his hand, and an orb of green cosmic energy materialized. "Wrong answer."

"No! Don't do it! It wasn't me, I promise! House Nazari will avenge my unlawful murder! Don't make this mistake!"

What does this mean? Edin wondered. Had House Nazari broken the laws of the gauntlet tournament and tried to kill him? Who was the other group of people that had been trailing them?

Ithamar raised his fuming voice. "House Nazari attempted to poison Edin Carvosa! Admit it, coward. They tried to kill him before his second match to ensure a finale between Cane and Zokku. They despised the thought of a spacer fighting their beloved prince. Admit to the scandal, coward."

"Never!" Roan took another two steps back with his eyes fixated on the green orb. "Put that thing down, and let's talk like men with integrity."

"I will when you admit to spying on us since the beginning of the tournament."

"Okay! We spied! That's it!"

Ithamar lowered his hand and the ball of energy vanished. "What did you say?"

"We spied. You two came to this planet illegally!"

Ithamar rushed forward and punched Roan in the gut. The spymaster dropped to the dirt, gripped his stomach, and let out a cry. Ithamar kicked him in the ribs, and Edin heard the sound of bones cracking.

"Stop! Stop!" Roan rolled over and tried to stand. But he couldn't. He sat on his buttocks and looked up. "Stop. I'll tell you everything if you ensure I get off this planet alive."

"Speak the truth and you can take your ship and leave," Ithamar said.

"Cane had nothing to do with it." Roan spat blood on the grass. "King Bahri made the call on his own. Obviously they couldn't kill Edin after the second match because the scandal would have been transparent. Bahri thought if Edin died and Zokku was his next opponent, then there would be hatred towards House Rellen, and House Nazari would have likely gained even more supporters." Roan spat more blood out of his mouth. "The truth is that Bahri knows they are losing control over this planet, and this solar system. There're too many immigrants coming in from the center of the galaxy. He fears a revolution. And a spacer winning the gauntlet tournament could be a spark leading to an uncontrollable wildfire."

"A revolution is bound to begin," Ithamar said. "But a revolution for the heart of the galaxy, not this solar system."

"Bahri knows this too," Roan mumbled. "Yet he fears it will start in the outer scopes and make it ways inwards. He doubts his solar system would be able to stand up to a revolution. His kingdom could die and be forgotten in history."

Ithamar raised his hand and once again conjured a green orb. "Don't worry. This planet and these people have no place in history." He pushed the orb forward.

Roan stared at the cosmic power rushing towards him and said nothing while shivering on the mushy ground. The glowing ball burst through his chest and left a gaping hole. He stopped trembling in the charred grass.

Edin looked up at his cousin with jittery eyes. "What about the technomancers?"

Ithamar shot a glance towards the woods. "They weren't going to attack with all of these guards surrounding us. We have to lure them out."

"Are you even human?" Edin asked.

"What do you mean?" Ithamar questioned.

"How can you just kill so many people? With no hesitation?"

"Edin, we have an agenda to upkeep. The rise of the Mizoquii is the only thing that matters. I'm here helping you, on this dumb planet, but in turn, you're going to have to help me one day."

"That's not what I'm questioning. You just killed those agents!"

"They tried to poison you. And I told them who we were. We can't just let the whole galaxy in on our secret. I had no choice but to kill them regardless if it was before or after the technomancers arrived."

Edin shook his head. "There could have been another way."

Ithamar shrugged. "I didn't think of one in time."

"What happens next?"

"We wait until the syndicate comes for us."

Edin and Vanya sat in the Riskplay's cabin. Ithamar told them the metal shell of the starship would be safer from a blast of cosmic energy than the wooden bungalow. The Mizoquii prince was positive the technomancers would strike soon, right after the death of Roan and his secret agents, when the trio were most vulnerable. He walked out into the night, but the other two waited in the ship and played a card game called rooker until they grew tired of the game and started talking about the future.

"You have to come with me to the First System," Edin insisted.

Vanya laid her hand on the metal table. "I don't have to do anything."

"Come on, you know it will be an adventure."

She smiled. "I do love an adventure."

"So that's a yes?"

"That's a maybe."

"Maybe is good enough for now."

"Don't get your hopes up. I'm trying to avoid raising mine."

Edin rubbed his chin. "Why?"

"Because there's still a chance you could die in the tournament." Vanya looked away. "Or maybe even tonight."

Edin laughed. "Ithamar is going to cut down anyone that comes our way."

"Overconfidence has killed many boys."

"Ithamar is no boy. He is a man."

Vanya bit her lip. "I was talking about you."

"I'm not overconfident. I just have faith."

"So, I've convinced you of religion."

"Maybe. Maybe I just believe in destiny. I don't know enough about God or destiny."

Vanya yawned. "We should have this conversation another time. We need to go to sleep. It's nearly morning."

"You're right. I'm exhausted too."

They turned the lights off in the cabin, and both lay down in the bunk bed, Edin occupying the top and Vanya the bottom. Both wore their clothes from the day in case they were woken in the middle of the night and forced to escape or fight—two things neither of them desired to do. Edin knew if Vanya came with him to the First System, her life could never be normal. She would be in severe jeopardy on other planets if the Mizoquii started their own rebellion. Was it selfish to ask her to tag along in these future endeavors? She was the only friend he had known, and he did not want their friendship to end when he departed Lathas. Or were they more than friends at this point? They had only kissed once. *Did it mean anything?*

Edin heard Vanya roll out of her bunk and stand on the floor. He wondered what she was doing but didn't say anything. Perhaps she was thirsty and going to get a glass of water. But instead she climbed up the metal ladder to the bunk bed and lay next to him. She kissed him on the lips without speaking and rolled over with her back facing him. He put his arm around her waist and snuggled closer and closed his eyes.

There was a loud smack against the hull of the ship. The sound ricocheted and woke the two up. They opened their eyes and stirred. Then there was another smack against the hull, and a terrified scream rang outside.

"They're here," Edin said.

"What do we do?" Vanya asked, eyes wide with panic.

"Get to the armory," Edin said. "Quickly."

From the top bunk, they scrambled down to the floor and back towards the armory. Edin twisted the hatch open and stepped through, the overhead light automatically turning on. The weapons and steel walls were polished to the point that Edin could see his reflection. Another loud bang wailed against the hull.

Edin gazed over the weapons, then picked up two short-barrel plasma guns and handed them to Vanya.

"Here, use these two. It's a lightweight gun. The safety is the red button on the side. Just turn that off and pull the trigger."

"I'm way too young to enter a shootout."

The sound of gunfire rattled against the hull like someone outside was trying to shoot a hole through the ship.

"Are they . . ." Vanya hesitated. Her face went pale and her mouth hung open as if she had forgotten that she was about to speak.

"Ithamar will finish them off before anyone breaks in here," Edin promised. "He's probably just busy fighting another one right now."

Vanya said nothing. Fear marked her ghostly face.

Edin turned and scanned the wall for the weapon he would wield. In the back he spotted one that caught his eye: the Almighty War Hero Minigun, which would take two hands to carry. Edin lifted it from the floor. Blood rushed into the veins of his forearms as he gripped the heavy gun. It must have weighed one hundred pounds.

"You can't carry that," Vanya said.

"We need a lot of firepower," Edin said. "We have no clue what type of advanced weaponry they're using along with the Gift."

"You can barely walk with that thing."

"Whoever stands in front of this won't be able to walk after this hits them."

Vanya shook her head.

They walked out of the armory, and Edin closed the armory hatch. They waited by the airlock where the sound of gunfire had recently halted. There was someone on the other side, and they knew it wasn't Ithamar.

A circle of steel around the hatch started to glow bright orange.

"They're trying to melt their way through," Edin said. "Stand behind me."

Vanya huddled behind Edin while he kept the minigun aimed towards the intruders. The circular spot moved slowly, and smoke filled the room.

"To the eternal abyss you go, syndicate imbeciles!" Edin thundered.

The barrel started rotating rapidly before the first round fired. Once the first plasma beam left the spinning minigun, multiple shots per second burst through the airlock, destroying anything and everything on the other side. The cabin was clouded in smoke, and the smell of burning metal made his nose run. Edin took a few steps forward and kept firing. He assumed he had killed the invader because there was no return fire, but he kept shooting anyway.

Vanya hit him on the shoulder. "Stop!"

Edin laid off the trigger. The minigun stopped firing but remained spinning until gradually slowing to a complete stop.

"We need to move," Edin said.

"Where?" Vanya asked. "If we go to the cockpit and you shoot that gun aft, you're going to be firing towards the armory and the engines. The whole ship will explode."

"And if we go into the armory, they will fire towards us."

"Yes."

"I'm going outside. Stay here."

"Edin! Ithamar said for us to stay here!"

"I've waited long enough!"

Edin moved forward with the minigun. He stepped through the old airlock, which was now a giant hole in the side of the ship. Outside, two dead bodies lay by the door. Edin gazed over them in the moonlight. They wore so much armor and were so charred and mangled by the minigun that it was impossible to see their skin. He wondered if the technomancers were humans.

He walked along the hull of the ship, scanning in all directions for more technomancers. He saw no one else and heard nothing but the low hiss of the wind. Where was Ithamar?

There was a large explosion of green energy far off in the jungle. Edin's jaw dropped. The flare-up lit the dark sky like lightning. He never imagined anyone could muster that much cosmic energy. Was it Ithamar, or was it the abominable abilities of a technomancer? The light died down, and then another one went off. It was like an atomic blast. When the green light erupted again, Edin assumed the massive discharge was visible from orbit.

Then the night became dark, quiet, and still. Edin assumed the fight was over but was unsure of who had won or what exactly happened. He waited with the minigun pointed across the meadow towards the jungle.

Beneath the second moon, a figure emerged over the canopy, flying like a winged beast towards the Riskplay. *What in the world?* Then Edin remembered technomancers had jetpacks. He gripped the gun tighter and his heart raced. *Has Ithamar really been defeated?* The figure flew closer, and Edin realized it wasn't a technomancer flying on a jetpack. It was his older cousin, somehow using cosmic manipulation against the force of gravity.

Ithamar landed on his feet in front of Edin. He was covered in sweat, and his armor was dirty from battle.

"You can fly?" Edin asked.

"Of course, I can manipulate cosmic energy."

"Are you kidding me?! Why haven't you done it before?"

Ithamar pointed to his mechanical eye. "I had an accident once. Don't want to talk about it."

Edin shook his head. "You never want to talk about anything."

CHAPTER 22

They left for Kosabar the day before the gauntlet finale. There would be no training that day or the day of the match. Ithamar had faith in Edin and feared overtraining would be futile at this point. The three decided on dining somewhere ritzy in the capital that evening, considering it could be their last meal together. But there was a problem. There was no way to fix the gaping hole in the side of the Riskplay caused by the minigun and the technomancers.

When Edin walked downstairs after sleeping in until late morning, Ithamar was waiting on the couch in the den.

"We're going to have to use another ship to get to Kosabar," Ithamar said. "And that ship will likely be what we use to travel to Morhaven IV after the match."

"So, we're going to need something that can go parabolic across solar systems," Edin noted. "I haven't seen the syndicate's ship yet, but I bet it's more reliable than what Roan flew."

"I haven't seen it either, but it should be more suited for space. Let's bring it back here, and we can transfer some of the cargo and equipment from the Riskplay. I think I have a hunch on where it is."

Vanya opened the door to her bedroom and walked downstairs. "Can I come along?"

Ithamar grimaced. "You were spying on our conversation? Do you know what we do to spies?"

"Unfortunately, I know what you do to spies, technomancers, and filthy swamp creatures."

Edin laughed.

"Come along then," Ithamar said. "We'll need another set of hands."

They left the bungalow and walked north towards the mountains that held the cascades. Below the orange canopy, Ithamar led the way while Edin and Vanya followed. The older cousin strode with a purpose. He kept his head forward with eyes scanning everything.

"You don't think there's someone still out here, do you?" Vanya asked. "Or someone still inside their ship when we get there?"

"Doubtful," Ithamar answered without pausing his constant surveillance. "If there was anyone still here, they would have departed the night of the fight. No starships have taken off from around here, so their ship should be here."

"Will you be able to fly it?" Edin asked.

Ithamar turned his head back. "Don't ask stupid questions. I can fly anything."

Edin and Vanya laughed, then smiled and looked at each other. Ithamar's confidence was always reassuring.

After a couple hours of hiking, Ithamar raised his hand and then pointed between two golden trees, towards more orange and yellow shrubbery. "The ship is that way."

"I can't see anything," Vanya said.

"It's his cyborg eye," Edin said.

"Oh, sometimes I forget we live with a cyborg."

Ithamar shook his head. "Let's move forward. But don't get in front of me and don't touch anything that looks out of the ordinary. There's no telling what traps they might have left behind."

They pushed through the shrubbery. When Edin first saw the

starship, his mouth stretched from ear to ear with a giddy grin. It appeared much newer and finer than the Riskplay. The hull was midnight black with gunmetal-gray highlights on the sharp wings. Frightening cannons rested above the tinted cockpit and below the underbelly. It wasn't much larger than Ithamar's previous ship, but the wingspan was noticeably wider. The exhaust thrusters merged with the hull cleanly so they were veritably unnoticeable. It was an aerodynamic and violent creature in hibernation. They would soon be the ones to wake the beast.

"That thing looks like a monster," Vanya said. "Wild."

"That monster is called a Valorwraith," Ithamar stated. "A newer model based on an old starcraft used centuries ago."

"Amazing." Edin walked forward. "We've got to fly that thing."

Ithamar grabbed Edin's shoulder. "No, let me go first."

It took an hour for Ithamar to finally permit Edin and Vanya to come aboard the Valorwraith. He must have checked every nook and crevice three times. They stood waiting impatiently as the eldest of the party made sure no tricks or traps lurked within or around the starship. They sat by a tree, and Vanya listed the places to eat in Kosabar where she thought Edin would like to visit tonight. He made no choice. There were too many options, and his stomach had yet to tell him what it desired.

Ithamar strolled back from the ship. "It looks like they were absolutely positive they were going to win against us. They made no attempt at all to rig the ship against intruders."

Vanya rose from the ground. "Probably because a group of technomancers never fears loss."

"Fear might have prepared them better." Edin hoisted himself up.

"I wish I were more intimidating," Ithamar admitted. "Everyone underestimates me, so I never get their best shot."

"They just don't get close enough to see your cyborg eye," Edin said. "That thing is scary looking."

Ithamar glared at his younger cousin. Vanya chuckled.

They entered the Valorwraith up a dark gangway. The interior was lit by ruby-colored lights and smelled like sweat and oil. It reminded

Edin of his times in the engine bay on the *Saircor*. In the aft section of the cabin were three bunks, but each held three racks, making a total of nine sleeping spots. Black carpet blanketed the flooring, and the bulkheads were made of dark metal.

The reddish lighting irritated Edin's eyes. He rubbed his eyelids and then opened them slowly. It was an unnatural radiance, and he had grown fond of normal sunlight. In the forward zone was a kitchen area and a large access that led to a compartment below.

"Armory and maintenance room," Ithamar said when they walked over it.

They continued on to the spacious cockpit. All the controls and knobs on the overhead and side panels were painted jet black. Ruby backlighting illuminated the instruments. The monitors on the forward panel were curved and wide. There were five large leather seats, with flight control sticks next to three seats in the front row. The two seats in the back row had switches and joysticks for weapons delivery. *The creature appears just as deadly on the inside*, Edin thought and smirked. *Such an upgrade.*

"Well, I'm going to crank her up," Ithamar said, "and see if she runs as good as she looks. We're running late too. Should have already been back at the bungalow by now."

"Yeah, it's getting late," Edin said.

Vanya sat in the back row and grabbed a joystick for the upper cannons. "Time to go hunting."

"Right," Ithamar said. "You couldn't hit the widest wall on the Pebble Inn."

"Go stand in front of the ship and let's see how good my aim is," Vanya responded.

Ithamar smiled and said nothing.

It took a couple of hours to transfer the computer systems, arms, and gear from the Riskplay to the Valorwraith—an easy but mundane task. None of the components or weapons were too heavy, but there were a lot of random items. Edin wondered why they were bringing anything at all. It felt as if they had everything they needed and Ithamar was simply hoarding his old and unneeded possessions. Of course, maybe he flew more comfortably with his personal data systems.

Waiting for Ithamar to find the right sockets to attach the cannon plugs to and then boot up the computers took longer than Edin expected. But eventually the three of them were buckled into their seats in the cockpit with all of their belongings packed in the cabin. It was a glorious feeling. It was the last time Edin would be at the bungalow. Before the engines turned on, though, it twisted into a bittersweet feeling. He'd made just as many memories in the orange jungle and wooden bungalow as in the fancy arena and the capital city. *Training sucked*, he reflected, *but I've come a long way*. His scrawny arms had grown twice as dense with muscle, and his dull mind had sharpened to adeptly absorb the art of combat and swordsmanship. Physically and mentally, he had matured into a different person. He glanced at Vanya as she watched Ithamar go through the preflight checklist. Edin smiled and was glad she had stayed beside him this long.

Ithamar pressed a button, and the engines sparked to life. The ship let out a low growl from the exhaust and rattled slightly before hovering off the ground and ascending over the bungalow and the trees. The ship rotated southward, then sped forward with Ithamar on the controls. The engines roared as the ship accelerated at an alarming rate.

"LET'S GOOOO!" Edin yelled.

Vanya laughed. "This is too fast!"

Ithamar kept his expression serious, but Edin knew his cousin was enjoying himself.

It happened unexpectedly and out of nowhere.

A missile exploded against the starboard hull. The starship jerked and whipped wildly and threw them around in their seatbelts. Vanya shrieked and started crying. They were going to crash, Edin knew. He gripped the armrest with all his might. The ship was spinning so fast he couldn't tell what was happening through the windows. Another rocket detonation jolted the ship in the opposite direction. *We're going to die*, Edin realized. He didn't even think about who had shot them down. All he thought about was how he would die in a random crash landing. The ship collided with trees, and the dark glass window shattered.

Edin closed his eyes and covered his face as the world around him collapsed into chaos. *This will be my final memory*, he told himself. His head snapped front to back. He blacked out when the starship impacted the ground, coming to seconds later to find his left arm ablaze. The cockpit was full of smoke and so were his lungs. He coughed and his eyes watered. His arm was in deeper pain than he had ever experienced in his life. He screamed like he was melting. He unlatched the seatbelt and rolled on the ground, bawling and screaming. It didn't go out. He ran out of the cockpit with his sleeve on fire and kept slamming himself against the metal bulkhead in the cabin where Ithamar and Vanya had escaped and were coughing.

"OH MY GOD!" Vanya shrieked when she saw Edin.

Running towards a glass case next to the cockpit, she pulled out a small yellow fire extinguisher and drenched the burning arm in violet foam while Edin choked back his sobs. The fire was smothered. But he knew his entire arm was ruined forever. He knew if he even made it to the capital with one functional arm, he would die in combat against Cane Nazari. There was no way he could compete crippled. The physical pain was dreadful, but it was nothing compared to the mental torture of knowing he would soon face unavoidable death.

A fiery explosion boomed from the cockpit.

"Get back to the middle of the cabin near the racks, Edin," Vanya said. "And Ithamar, go get me a first aid kit. You searched this ship; you should know where that is."

"There's bandages and medical supplies on the level below." Ithamar dashed towards the ladderwell. "I'll be back in a second."

Tears ran down Edin's cheek as he hobbled to the back. He kept his chin tilted up because he didn't want to look down at the burn. His stomach couldn't handle it. When he reached the back of the cabin, he lay down on the bedding on a bottom rack. *Get ready to die*, he thought. *Get ready to die*. He noticed Vanya beside the rack, looking down at him.

"It is going to be okay. You're going to be fine."

Edin didn't respond. He finally looked at his arm. It was the nastiest burn wound he had ever seen—a gross mess of charred flesh. He wanted to vomit. He closed his eyes, but tears escaped and streaked down his cheeks.

At least Vanya and Ithamar are safe, Edin thought. *At least they will be fine*. He heard Ithamar return with a bag and start speaking to Vanya about the injury, but Edin didn't pay much attention to the words spoken. He was lost in a confused consciousness, and none of their words mattered at the moment. While his eyes were still closed, he felt a needle enter his arm.

After Vanya finished washing the burn, she wrapped the limb with an elastic bandage. Over her shoulder, Ithamar watched the process unfold in silence. He'd completely put out the fire after sticking his younger cousin with a shot to put him to sleep. The cabin smelled like burnt wires, flesh, and wet chemicals from the fire extinguisher. The two looked down at their broken gladiator with wide eyes of gloom. Once she was done wrapping the arm, she looked back at the older cousin.

"Will he still fight?" Vanya asked.

"He has to," Ithamar said.

"What if House Nazari were the ones who shot us down? That is completely against tournament rules."

"But we don't know what happened. Does he need to go to a hospital?"

"Probably for medication."

"Painkillers?"

"Yes."

"I have some morph extract."

"Should we give it to him now?"

"No. We will wait until he wakes."

Vanya frowned. "Okay."

"We need to get to the Pebble Inn."

"Do you have a comms device?"

"Yes." Ithamar pulled a black gadget out of his pocket. "Do you know who to transmit to?"

Vanya grabbed the transmitter. "I know the number for the Pebble Inn. I'll buzz A-Veetwo and tell him to find us a shuttle immediately."

"Alright."

When Edin woke up, he assumed he was still dreaming. He was in his old room, 607, at the Pebble Inn. The room was dimly lit, but he recognized Vanya sitting on the foot of the bed and Ithamar in the armchair in the corner. They smiled at his return to consciousness, but all he felt was tremendous pain. He looked down at his left arm wrapped in a beige bandage. *What happened? Did I already fight?*

"I'm guessing I won?" Edin asked.

Vanya and Ithamar looked at each other as if neither had expected him to ask that.

"No," Ithamar said. "We were shot down on the way to the capital. Your arm was burned by a fire in the cockpit. Do you not remember anything?"

Edin pushed himself upright using his right arm. They had been flying into the city, and then his memory faded. He remembered nothing. Nothing at all. Then he started to panic. He still had to fight. How long had he been knocked out?

"What time is it?" Edin demanded.

"It's the same day, closing in on midnight," Vanya said. "Don't worry; you didn't miss the finale."

"Don't worry?" Edin questioned. "I'm about to fight Cane Nazari with one flippin' hand!"

The room went silent.

Edin dropped back down in the bed and threw the white sheets over his head.

"There's still a chance you will win," Ithamar said. "You just have to start strong and land a solid strike quickly."

Edin didn't respond. He stayed under the covers, frozen in thought.

"Vanya, go warm up his food," Ithamar said. "He needs to eat."

Vanya walked out, and the door shut behind her. A few minutes later she returned without knocking and sat on the bed. Edin was still hiding underneath the sheets.

"Hey," Vanya said gently. "Earlier we went out and brought back the most delicious meal in Kosabar just for you."

Edin could smell the red meat and pepper. He moved back the sheets and positioned himself with his back against the pillows and headboard. Vanya placed a serving tray across his lap and then rested the hot plate of food and a glass of cold water on it. Edin grinned despite himself and bit his lip. It was bunruj steak. The uncommon meat came from a large herbivore mammal known to dig in the ground and graze on deep-rooted vegetables. The steak was seared with a tender pink center. As a side, mashed spuds were buttered up along with a slice of brown toast.

"This looks good," Edin said. "Thanks."

He glanced at the silverware, then realized he couldn't cut the steak with both a knife and fork because he could only bend one arm.

Vanya must have read his expression. "Here, let me cut that for you."

She sliced the steak into tiny cubes. Edin watched her and knew he was lucky to have someone like her around. He wanted to win the tournament for her as much as he wanted to win for himself and the Mizoquii.

He grabbed the fork and stabbed one of the meat cubes. Juices flowed. He took his first bite and swore that it was the best thing he had ever eaten.

"This is amazing," Edin said.

"Better be," Ithamar said. "Two hundred credits a plate."

Vanya laughed. "Well, he needs the energy. This is a great meal for the night before a finale."

"True. Thanks, Ithamar."

Edin ate the rest of the meal faster than he would have liked. He just couldn't help but devour it. He was hungry, and the taste took his mind off his broken wing. Once he cleared the plate, he sighed and stretched his back.

"I have some morph extract you will take before the fight," Ithamar said. "That will numb your pain and maybe give you a boost of energy."

Edin laughed sarcastically and shook his head. "I can't take that. I'll throw up."

"What?"

"My stomach doesn't react well to painkillers. Must be allergic."

CHAPTER 23

To his surprise, Edin slept well the night before the finale. He assumed his body must have been exhausted from trying to recover from the burn wound. Or there was the possibility that Ithamar had sedated him again with a drug in his food or water. Edin didn't think much about it. He didn't think much about anything in the morning when he woke. He tried to block all of his thoughts because they grew darker the longer he stayed trapped within his own consciousness.

He climbed out of bed, supporting himself with his healthy arm, and freshened up in the washroom, trying his best to avoid wetting the bandage. Then he changed into a casual outfit that had been laid out for him: khaki trousers, a dark-green shirt, and a pair of shiny new boots with reptilian scales. He wondered who had picked out the boots. He had told both Ithamar and Vanya about how he struggled to obtain new boots when on board the *Saircor*.

After slipping on the scaly shoes, he took the elevator down to the first floor. Walking to the lobby, he heard coughing from the sickly residents. He wondered what Vanya's grandfather would say to him if he knew the dilemma Edin had gotten himself in. *Walking into a gauntlet finale with one arm to clash against someone with Nazari as their family name. Insane.* That's what her grandfather would say, the same as anyone else on the planet.

Ithamar was seated in the lobby when Edin entered.

"Finally up! It's almost noon!" Ithamar yelled.

"Really?" Edin sat on the couch slowly to avoid irritating the burn.

"I swear on all the stars and moons."

"That means it's time for lunch."

"Well." Ithamar paused. "Time for you to eat fruits and vegetables, nothing heavy."

"Come on, it's my last meal. I'm going to get killed."

"Why do you assume you can't defeat Cane? Why are you so full of confidence in your own defeat?"

"I have one arm, Ithamar. I won't be able to do anything at full speed. My lone hope was to match his pace, and with any luck, I might have gotten a clean strike early on." Edin rubbed the back of his head. "Everyone knows he's far stronger than me and much more skilled with a hyperblade. It's over. I know it, you know it, Vanya knows it, and everyone else does too."

"You're wrong."

Edin clenched his hand into a fist and glared into the mechanical eye of his older cousin. "It is impossible."

"Are you going to make me give you a motivational speech?"

Edin laughed. "You're my trainer. I thought you would have something written down already."

"I don't have anything written down."

"Make one up."

"Okay." Ithamar sighed and thought for a few seconds before speaking. "You know the character of a man isn't determined by how fiercely he swings a blade. The character of a man isn't even determined by the intellect he possesses." He tapped his skull. "Some of the most intelligent beings in the galaxy are also the laziest in existence. Some of the strongest warriors are the first to die in war. You see, character comes from a place utterly different. It is simply perseverance." He poked Edin in the chest. "Perseverance is in your heart, your spirit, your soul, whatever you want to call that motivating force to be more than just a man. By now I've been around you long enough to know your heart pumps the same blood as me, and my father, and our grandfather as well. And the Mizoquii have blood that never surrenders, that never abandons hope. Right now, it is not a matter of winning or losing; it is a decision between quitting or transcending your own limitations. Either die as a forgotten dream, or grow into a myth the galaxy remembers for generations."

After a long pause, Edin managed to ask, "That was the best you could do?"

"Um . . . yeah."

Edin laughed. "It was actually pretty good, thanks."

Ithamar shook his head.

Edin understood what he had to do. This was his tournament to spoil, his tournament to win.

Purple auroras wavered, and two moons emitted blue hues in the dark sky. Starships with their blinking lights flew between the glass skyscrapers and reflected afterglows. It was custom for Lathas to host the last gauntlet match at night underneath the stars.

On the ground, Edin and Ithamar rode in the back of the glidecar while Vanya sat in the front seat next to the A-Veetwo. In the distance they saw the white glow of the stadium, the floodlights shining brighter than the billboards and the starships and the moons. The four spoke no words on the way to the arena. Edin had a look in his eyes that verbalized he didn't want to speak with anyone nor hear anyone speak. It was the hard glare that men possessed in moments of immense pressure—a glare that signaled death waited in the air.

When they arrived at the drop-off point at Kosabar Arena, hundreds of reporters and cameramen were waiting for Edin's arrival. Violet velvet ropes and golden stanchions lined a clear walkway to the tunnel. Security personnel held back the crowd and carried plasmas rifles.

"Good luck, Mr. Carvosa," A-Veetwo said.

"With the fight or with the media?" Edin asked.

A-Veetwo chortled mechanically. "Both."

Edin broke his hard glare and laughed. "Thanks, A-Veetwo. Take care."

Edin, Ithamar, and Vanya stepped out of the glidecar. A-Veetwo drove off to the parking garage. Cameras flashed as the three made their way towards the long underpass leading to the underbelly of the coliseum. Edin had his black duffle bag slung around his healthy shoulder. He kept his chin up and stared straight ahead with cold eyes and a grimace, trying his hardest to not look left or right. His left arm was conspicuously wrapped in the bandage, and every reporter hollered something about it as he pressed forward.

"What happened to your arm?!"

"His arm is broken!"

"The spacer is going to fight with one arm!"

"Edin Carvosa is injured!"

"Edin! Edin! Why is your arm in a wrap?"

Edin tuned out the shouts and the flashing lights. He glanced down and saw his reptilian boots glistening from the flashes of the cameras and the overhead lights of the arena. He remembered back when his greatest desire was a new pair of shoes because his haggard kicks were too small and caused bloody blisters on his heels. His desires had grown exponentially. He wanted so much more now than back then. He questioned if human nature was a dry throat thirsting for more than it had, and no matter what it obtained, it could never satisfy that endless thirst. Then he considered whether he was walking to his death and all of his expectations would die along with him.

Approaching the tunnel, Edin grew nervous. The arched lighting fixtures formed a semicircle from floor to wall to ceiling. The media personnel inside the arena carried themselves more professionally than outside, but Edin still stared forward and disregarded the questions about his arm. Ithamar and Vanya marched behind him with the same warlike approach.

They made it to the locker room without being stopped. Edin sighed in relief when he opened the door. The cameras in his face made him feel uneasy, like the entire galaxy was observing and waiting for him to make a fatal mistake. He paced to the center of the empty locker room as the door shut behind him.

"You have two hours until the fight. I'll find us some chairs," Ithamar said and then left.

Edin dropped his duffle bag on the concrete. "Are you ready?"

Vanya smiled. "Shouldn't I be the one asking you that?"

"Watching the matches has to rattle your nerves as well."

She nodded. "They do, and I only grow with anticipation as you keep advancing."

"Same."

Ithamar entered with three foldable chairs. "Found some." He set them up, and the three sat in a triangle.

"Thanks," Vanya said.

"Do you think the officials will ask about my bandage?" Edin asked.

"They'll come knocking any moment," Ithamar answered. "They'll have to inspect your arm before allowing you on the pitch."

"We are here fairly early," Vanya said.

"You should have brought a book to read," Ithamar said.

"Yes, that would have been wise."

"Tell us a story," Edin said.

Ithamar raised his eyebrows. "About what?"

"About a woman," Vanya said. "It is strange a man your age has no woman. There has to be a reason. Was there ever a girl in the life of Ithamar Avrum?"

"There have been many ladies in the life of Ithamar Avrum."

"Tell us about your favorite."

"I guess we do have time." Ithamar rubbed his chin. "When I was twenty-four, by standard years, I met a girl named Helen Kotorm on the planet Tallaham in the Forty-Second System. It is a planet dominated by rural areas, but the capital, Bethedere, is one of the most gorgeous cities I have laid eyes upon. Anyway, I had just finished up at a small academy, studying governance and leadership. It was more of a training program than an academy when compared to the schools in the epicenter. I took a position working as an assistant to an assistant to an assistant of the king on the planet."

He paused and bit his lip. "I met Helen at the biggest tavern in the city, and at first sight, I thought she was the most striking female I had ever seen. I talked to her fairly easily. We had mutual friends, so the conversation carried naturally. Of course, I wanted to keep talking to her after the tavern, so I planned a date for us. Then one date led to another until I eventually lost count and I looked forward to seeing her more than seeing anyone else. To me, it was like being in a fairy ta—"

Bang! Bang!

The three jerked their heads up at the knocking. Ithamar stood and went to the door to open it. King Bahri Nazari stepped inside as Ithamar bowed. Edin and Vanya stood and bowed as well, but privately, Edin freaked. *Why is Bahri here?*

Two bodyguards armed with plasma rifles stepped inside, and the room felt overcrowded.

Bahri glared at Edin. "What happened to your arm?"

"It was burned in a crash."

Bahri shook his head in disgust. The king wore a white quilted jacket with a purple-and-gold flower embroidered on the chest. He was taller and wider than Ithamar standing next to him.

"King Bahri, why have you come?" Ithamar asked.

"How about I ask why the two of you have come to my planet?"

There was a moment of silence as Edin and Ithamar shot glances at each other.

Bahri continued, "And how about I ask why the Sheeban Syndicate follows the two of you around like you're creatures on a chain?"

"Look," Ithamar said, "we were trying to get rid of them just as much as you. We have no connections with them."

"Kill the absurdity." Bahri placed his hands on his hips. "You two are in a mess and have brought this dilemma to my planet and jeopardized the safety of my citizens!"

"Roan confessed you gave the order to poison Edin. Don't lecture us, King Bahri."

Bahri stepped back with a contorted expression. "Where is the spymaster?"

"The same place as the technomancers sent by the Sheeban Syndicate."

Bahri shook his head in disgust again. "So, there are no more of them on this planet?"

"None that I know of."

"Will they send more?"

"I doubt the syndicate wants to start a war with your whole solar system."

"Good. So, it is over."

"That part, yes—that part is over."

Bahri looked around the barren locker room. "I'm guessing you decided to take the Valorwraith after your little skirmish?"

"Yes, and I'm guessing your people shot us down."

"We didn't know who was on that starship."

"That makes it twice that you have attempted to kill a contender in the gauntlet tournament."

"There's no reason to hold grudges. It will all be over soon."

"Promise me just one thing, King Bahri."

"What?"

"If Edin wins, there is no further conflict between your house and us."

"He wouldn't defeat Cane with both arms. There is no hope for the boy."

"Just promise me, we get off this planet alive if we win, and no one has to know about what has happened outside of the tournament."

"I can promise you that. But Cane will not lose."

"I understand your confidence. He is a fine lad."

"Indeed." Bahri turned and left the locker room, followed by his two bodyguards.

After the door shut, Edin said, "Certainly not a fine lad."

"I only said that to get him out of here." Ithamar returned to his seat. "He's just as ugly as his son."

A few moments later, another knock came at the door. Four tournament officials entered along with the gamewarden. The officials were two tikkino and two worefann. Edin, Ithamar, and Vanya greeted the five with more authentic joy than their last visitor.

"Edin Carvosa! The spacer who shocked the solar system!" the gamewarden said.

"Gamewarden, how are you?"

"Great, great." The gamewarden bobbed his big, bug-like head. "There is one thing different about the finale that we must go over. Also, we heard the rumors about your bandage, and that must be inspected and rewrapped in front of an official."

Edin looked at his arm. He didn't want to take the bandage off and reopen the wound. But he understood why the rules were in place. "Okay, yeah, we can do that."

"I will go ahead and let you know the procedural change. Before the match begins, you will walk to the center of the pitch and greet the other contender. Both of you will be introduced to the crowd by myself. You will return to the tunnel and wait for the cannon to signal the match has begun."

"Okay. Simple enough."

"Good. Well, I'll leave you with the officials." The gamewarden left the locker room.

"We brought more dressing cloth in case you didn't have any," one of the tikkino said.

"Okay, thanks," Vanya said. She grabbed the roll from the tikkino. "Edin, sit down. I'll take off your bandage."

Edin sat, and Vanya grabbed his arm. He stared straight ahead while she unwrapped the bandage, starting at the wrist. Pain slithered up his limb. Ithamar and the officials looked at the wound from a few feet away. Once she had the dressing off, Edin glanced at his arm and saw nothing but raw, burned, and blistered skin.

"That's worse than I had suspected," one of the worefann squeaked.

"Yes, that is disappointing," the other said.

"Now, are we good to rewrap it?" Ithamar asked.

"Yes, go ahead," the tikkino closest to the arm said. "We have seen enough."

Vanya cleaned the injury with a damp washcloth and rewrapped it with a black bandage. She hurried as if being watched by the strangers made her anxious.

"Has a contender ever fought with this sort of injury?" Edin asked, trying to get his mind off Vanya doctoring him.

"I'm sure there have been contenders in the gauntlet who have fought injured," the nearest tikkino said. "But I have never seen anything like that."

Edin nodded and looked at the ground.

"However, you have proven to be one who beats the odds," a worefann squeaked.

Edin raised his chin and smiled. "True. I pray destiny stays with us."

Vanya finished with the wrap and stood. "He's all good."

A tikkino said, "Good luck, spacer."

The other officials said their farewells and left the room, leaving Edin alone with Ithamar and Vanya. Steady noise had been growing above them, in the grandstands. The spectators were arriving in droves, and the sound of chants and drums had only just begun.

"Time is closing in on us," Ithamar said.

"Yes, it is," Edin said. "I need to change into my gi."

Edin stripped down to his underwear and slipped into the black gi tied at his waist by the green belt. It felt loose and comfortable. He stretched his arms and back, then bounced on his toes and threw jabs with his right hand.

"You look confident," Ithamar said.

"The only hope I have is matching his confidence and intensity," Edin said.

"It's about time for us to go. Is there anything else you need?"

"You didn't finish your story about that girl. Hurry up and finish it."

"No. I'll save that for another time."

Vanya walked to Edin and wrapped her arms around him in a suffocating embrace. "Go out there and win."

Edin hugged her tight. "I will."

Ithamar said, "Good luck, trooper."

Ithamar and Vanya exited, which left Edin by himself. He jogged around the locker room in circles, his heart rate steadily rising. The crowd noise had quadrupled, and the vibrations of the arena made the concrete chamber quiver. *This is the last fight I have to enter*, he thought. After this, all of his dreams would be a few spaceflights away. Or they would be gone forever.

CHAPTER 24

Edin walked with the same tournament official, the female tikkino, who had escorted him in the past two matches. They navigated the underground maze towards the pitch. Security sentries massed at every corner and guarded with plasma rifles. A few media personnel had gained access to the area. Again, the cameramen and reporters tried to capture comments from Edin about his wrapped arm, but he said nothing. He scowled with irises that flickered emerald flames. He thought of winning and he thought of killing and he thought of nothing else, as if his mind had isolated itself from everything other than combat. As he neared the field, the noise from the grandstands amplified.

They turned the last corner, and the light from the pitch seeped in from the end of the tunnel.

"You should walk onto the pitch at any moment for the prefight introductions."

Edin did not respond.

They stopped where the concrete of the tunnel met the soil of the field. Chants and drums rumbled the ground so hard that specks of dirt bounced and glittered under the bright floodlights. The gamewarden was standing in the middle of the pitch on a podium. All four of his arms gestured downward, urging the crowd to quiet down. This lasted for nearly a minute before the gamewarden finally spoke.

"Ladies and noblemen, welcome to the 292nd Lathas Gauntlet Finale!"

The crowd applauded deafeningly.

"Now, I will introduce you to the two contestants who will be battling for money, prosperity, and glory that will last a lifetime." He bit his lip and nodded. "Our first contestant, battling out of the west tunnel, is a home planet favorite, the son of King Bahri, the prince of Lathas, and arguably the most overpowering participant in recent memory of the tournament: it is none other than Caaaaane Nazariiiii!"

Cane Nazari swaggered onto the pitch from the opposite side. Purple smoke rose from the stands above his tunnel. Gold fireworks shot into the sky and burst into lavish, fiery flowers. The prince of the planet waved at his supporters and then stepped on the stage next to the gamewarden.

"Our second contestant, battling out of the east tunnel, is arguably the biggest underdog in the history of our tournament. The unexpected boy from space, Ediiiiin Caaarrrrvosaaa!"

Edin Carvosa stepped out into the open stadium. Dozens of drones hovered, recording his every move. He believed the whole solar system was watching. As he made his way to the center of the pitch, he glanced back and above the tunnel he had departed. Green smoke clouded the seating while war drums beat intensely and half of the stadium cheered in a frenzy. He didn't think he would gather this much of a following. Ascending to the podium, he stood beside the gamewarden. He swiveled his head, scanning the crowd, and noted nearly half of the grandstands' seated spectators were dressed in green and black. They had come to support him against the terrible odds.

The gamewarden allowed the entire grandstands to cheer for a few minutes. Once the crowd started to quiet down, he said into the microphone, "Contestants, you may now return to your respective sides and await the sound of the cannon."

"Space simp!" Cane yelled across the podium.

Edin ignored the insult, pivoted on his foot, and walked back to the tunnel. He skimmed over the spectators until he located Ithamar and Vanya. They were standing and clapping. The sight made him feel warm, but he refused to smile. He raised his healthy arm and waved and kept a stern expression drawn across his face. Time had run out, he knew. This was the moment that each decision in his life had led to. The next time Cane and he walked on the pitch, only one of them would walk off alive.

"In five minutes, your match will begin," the tikkino said when Edin entered the tunnel. "Here is your hyperblade." The tikkino handed over the hilt with its talon.

Edin grabbed it. "Thanks."

The hyperblade was slippery in his hand. He had started sweating, and his palms grew clammy. As his heart raced, he wondered if it could erupt from anxiety. The confidence he once possessed had slipped into a pit of fear where his deepest insecurity revealed he was afraid to fight frightened. He only had one arm. *Will this be the last few minutes of my life? Probably*, he answered himself.

On the field, the podium was carried off by stadium personnel. It felt like they were moving in slow motion and everything was a blurry daydream. Edin needed the fight to start as soon as possible. Thinking about death was driving him mad. Finally, the field was cleared. His mouth went dry. His face paled until all color was lost. He clenched his fist, the knuckles as white as his face. A bead of sweat streaked from brow to cheek to the corner of his lip. He could taste it. *Any moment now*. He bounced on his toes and breathed deeply.

The cannon fired.

He rushed onto the pitch and pressed the silver button on the hyperblade. Everyone in the stadium stood screaming at the spectacle of the two boys charging to kill one another. Across the pitch, Cane Nazari activated his hyperblade as well.

When the two collided, glowing hyperblades sliced air and bounced off each other. Startling to most, Edin started on the offensive, but all of his strikes were blocked. The pressure kept Cane on his heels and unable to make an offensive push of his own. Edin almost forgot he was fighting with only one arm; then Cane clutched the hilt of his hyperblade with both hands and smashed into Edin's blade. The impact sent Edin's weapon spiraling out of his hand to land twenty yards away. They looked each other in the eye.

Edin spun around and ran for his life to pick up his weapon. Cane hounded from behind, gaining ground. Edin felt the air move as Cane swung at his back.

Cane giggled insanely. "Come back here, spacer!"

The hyperblade lay in the dirt a few steps away. Edin dived headfirst, stretched out his arm, and grabbed the hilt, raising the weapon as Cane struck downward. *Escape.* Edin kicked the ground frantically to push himself away and rolled over. Cane's blade made contact with the ground on the next swing. Edin leapt to his feet. There was a bombardment of strikes from his opponent. Then it happened once more.

Cane swung powerfully and knocked Edin's hyperblade away. Before the weapon had landed, Edin was sprinting towards it, realizing this was not sustainable; he would have to fight with both arms. This time, he slid on the ground, picked up the weapon, and stood much quicker than before, both hands gripping the hilt. Cane remained on the offensive as the blades continued to clash.

Edin was overwhelmed by the adrenaline of the situation. He did not have the time to take the discomfort and pain of his burned arm into consideration. Of course, it was a matter of life and death.

Cane stopped swinging and stepped back. "I could have killed you already."

Edin remained on guard and said nothing.

"When you were running after your blade." Cane spat in the dirt. "I could have thrown my hyperblade right through your empty skull."

"Maybe you should have killed me when you had the chance," Edin said.

Cane laughed. "This finale is already dull because of your broken arm. It is up to me to give the spectators their worth."

Edin shook his head. "Your vanity will be your death."

"Maybe you're right, spacer. But my death won't come at your hands."

Cane lunged forward. He held his hyperblade in one hand, and the speed of his strikes seemed to have doubled. Edin could not keep up with the pace. He lost sight of his opponent's weapon. There was a sting on his burned arm, and Edin jerked back and spun away.

"No!" Edin screamed.

There was a cut on his tricep. The blade had grazed the arm, and the bandage was burnt. Blood soaked the bandage and trickled down his arm. It wasn't a deep wound, but a pain wave fizzled through his fragile limb, reminding him that he was still awfully impaired.

"You scream like a woman," Cane said.

"You dress like a woman," Edin said.

Cane smiled. "Speaking of women, how is Vanya Waldrip?"

"How do you . . ." Edin shook his head. "Just shut up and fight."

"After I kill you, I plan to invite her over to my palace."

"That won't happen. She hates you."

"Now, maybe you're right. But after I show her things that you could never, I'm sure your little blond girlfriend would be very fond of a prince."

"Not a dead prince."

Edin charged. His next few strikes were with both arms, and Cane blocked them with little effort. But Edin stayed on the offensive. He was uncertain what would happen if Cane landed another hit. Edin swung faster and vaulted from side to side, praying for an open path to the torso. Yet there was never an opening. Cane was too large and too swift for Edin to get close enough to implement real damage.

Sweat drenched them both. Blood coated Edin's left arm. The two boys danced, both locked in tunnel vision with eyes following the movements of the twirling blades. The crowd roared and the drums beat loudly, but neither of them heard it. They were absorbed in killing the other. Neither gained an offensive edge, and both were slowly being drained of energy. The hyperblades hummed and sparked at contact.

In an aggressive stance, Edin lunged forward. The attack was parried. Cane riposted quickly. Edin barely dodged the counter.

Edin stepped back and out of striking range, considering his options. It looked as if there was no way for him to land a strike on his foe. Throughout the match, his blade had never come close to touching skin. However, Cane had difficulty striking as well. Even nursing the injured arm, Edin was slim and elusive.

An idea emerged in Edin's head. It was dangerous. But it could trigger the weakness of his rival. A false temptation.

"Come on, Carvosa," Cane said. "It will all be over soon. I can tell you're fading."

"You're moving slower too."

"Does it really matter? You have no chance. Everyone in this stadium has noticed that you won't be able to land a single hit."

Edin spat in the dirt and said nothing.

"But I give you credit," Cane admitted. "You fought better than expected."

"I will land a hit."

Cane laughed and raised his arms in a taunt. "Bring your best."

The time was now. All or nothing. Edin charged ahead, holding the hyperblade with one arm. Cane noticed this and grinned. He clenched his hyperblade with both hands and reared back for a powerful swing.

Edin eased the grip on his sword as the two weapons collided. Like before, the hyperblade went soaring across the pitch. It landed thirty standard yards away. Edin was defenseless. But this was what he had anticipated. He sprinted.

It was at this moment that the crowd screamed the loudest. Cane had teased the spectators earlier; now they must have assumed there would be real bloodshed. Edin didn't feel Cane at his heels like the last two times. It meant one thing. He ran faster, his feet pounding the gravel beneath him.

Cane watched his prey scramble across the pitch. He smiled, then focused his eyes. The hilt of the hyperblade hummed in his hand. He drew back his arm and threw the buzzing sword savagely. It cut through the air in a quick blur, spiraling rapidly, blazing across the field like it had been launched out of a cannon. The accuracy was faultless.

Edin spun around and snagged the hilt midair, in an instinctive maneuver that seemed humanly implausible.

All together, the grandstands gasped, then went utterly still and silent.

Edin scooped up the other sword. Now he was dual wielding hyperblades, and Cane was weaponless.

Cane stood frozen in shock. With an energized sword at each side, Edin stalked toward him.

"How did . . . you . . ." Cane stepped back. "What . . ."

"It is over," Edin said. "Time to kneel, Prince."

"You fool! You dare to challenge a prince!"

Cane lowered his shoulder and charged with no weapon. Edin lunged and slashed the right arm off, right below the elbow. Blood sprayed the air. Cane screamed and tried to dash away. Edin cut off the left arm at the shoulder. The limb fell. Bright-red liquid fanned the ground and stained the soil.

Cane dropped to his knees, spitting red saliva, and Edin Carvosa beheaded the prince of Lathas with a quick slash.

Edin felt nauseated as Cane's body slumped and his head hit the ground. He stared at his victim as a sign of strength, then looked up to the grandstands. He walked away from the body, to the side of the stadium that seated his supporters. Those wearing emerald jumped in cadence as fireworks burst and light-green smoke fogged the night air. Drums started to beat in an aggressive and victorious rhythm. Then a chant started.

"CAR! VOS! AHH! CAR! VOS! AHH! CAR! VOS! AHH!"

Edin glanced at the other side of the arena. The fans in gold and purple stood motionless and demoralized. Then they started to trickle out of the grandstands. He turned and ran up to the seating near his tunnel, hopping on the concrete wall where the people in the lower rows were bouncing up and down in celebration. He stood on the wall and raised both hyperblades to the sky as if he had just conquered an entire solar system. The chanting grew louder, and the fanatics jumped higher. He looked for Ithamar and Vanya, but it was too hard to determine faces in the crowd fogged with clouds of green smoke.

There was a tap on his calf. He looked over his shoulder and down on the pitch.

"Come down," the gamewarden said, then smiled. "Time for your reward."

Edin nodded and dropped to the gravel. He deactivated the hyperblades and tucked the silver hilts in his belt. As the gamewarden and Edin walked to the center of the field, the supporters quieted down behind them. Hovering drones lingered around the victor, their cameras recording and transmitting the event.

"I wasn't expecting you to win, Carvosa," the gamewarden said. "It shocked all of us, and it infuriated the nobles, but as a whole solar system, we are proud of you. It has shown the commoners there isn't much different from a spacer and a prince."

Edin ran his fingers through his sweaty hair. "You're more right than you know."

"What do you mean?"

"Before I die, I might become a prince."

The gamewarden laughed, then looked thoughtful as he realized Edin wasn't trying to be sarcastic. "Stranger things have happened in this galaxy." The gamewarden raised his head and browsed the stars. "And with an education from the First System, you could unlock doors to any pathway you desire."

They halted and waited as the podium was rushed out to the center of the pitch. Edin eyed the glass skybox above the grandstands. He wondered what was running through the head of King Bahri Nazari in the moment. The thought made Edin grin cunningly. The stadium personnel swiftly staged the wooden podium, and the gamewarden stepped onto it, Edin following suit. The crowd went silent as the gamewarden spoke into the microphone.

"We have a new gauntlet champion of Lathas! Edin Carvosa!"

The remaining spectators cheered and whistled and hollered.

"Now, Edin, I know you're not big on answering questions from the media, but there are a few questions I must ask you now that you're the champion."

"That's fine," Edin said. "Just don't ask me questions about mathematics."

Chuckles came from the crowd.

The gamewarden smiled. "Can you go into detail about your training process? You do appear to be in much better shape now than when you arrived on the planet."

"All the credit goes to my trainer, Ithamar Avrum. We trained up in the jungle north of the city—pretty much isolated ourselves and focused on the mission, which was getting in the best physical shape possible, and learning how to wield a hyperblade, of course."

"Nice, nice." The gamewarden nodded. "Now, your last match against Prince Cane, did you expect that to happen? Was it your plan to entice Cane to throw his hyperblade?"

"Yeah, actually it was. I was having a lot of difficulty with my burned arm. He was a strong contestant, and I knew I would be in trouble if I didn't think of something quick. I purposely eased up on my grip the last time our blades made contact. I figured he'd tried to kill me with style, so I made him think he had the perfect opportunity to earn flair points."

"Interesting strategy. Everyone noticed your arm is in a wrap, but you haven't given an official statement on the injury. Would you like to tell us about it?"

"I just got a little burn in an electrical fire. A little pain but nothing too drastic."

"I see, I see. Well then, you've earned around a million credits in prize coin, and most academies cut tuition for gauntlet champions. What are your future plans? Do you have any academies in mind?"

"I'm going to talk it over with my family before making a decision."

CHAPTER 25

The morning after the gauntlet finale, Edin waited for Vanya in the dusty lobby of the Pebble Inn. They planned to get breakfast somewhere in the city, but she was currently visiting with her grandfather.

Vanya walked into the lobby. "Hey, Edin, I have a request."

Edin scrunched his eyes. "What?"

"Well, my grandpa has been following the gauntlet, and he was wondering about the spacer who defeated Prince Cane. I think it would make him happy to meet you."

"Really? Yeah, I could that."

"Are you sure?"

"Yeah, why not?"

"Okay, well, he's sickly. He doesn't look the best."

"That's fine."

Edin followed her down the hallway lit by dim wall sconces.

"This is the room," Vanya said at the door marked *121*, and they entered. The small space was in the same layout as Edin's room, furnished with a bed, writing table, armchair, and a floor lamp. On the wall a digital display streamed the local news channel. Beside the bed was a bulky machine with tubes attached to an old man lying on his back. Liquids flowed into his neck and stomach. Vanya's grandfather wore a white T-shirt and blue sweatpants. His ghostly face was skinny and pale, yet his gray eyes appeared bright with energy. He smiled at their arrival.

"I didn't believe you, Vanya," he said kindly.

"Why would I have lied?" She stood next to him and put a hand on his shoulder. "Edin, this is my grandfather, Trevor Waldrip."

"How are you doing, sir?" Edin asked.

"Good, I saw your fight last night," Trevor said. "I knew a Nazari would die in a gauntlet match again; I just didn't know if it would happen in my lifetime."

"Oh, I take it you're not a supporter of House Nazari."

"Lord no. Has Vanya not told you what happened to me?"

"I didn't want to bore him with the full history of our family," Vanya said.

Edin laughed. "We have time, if you want to tell me."

"It isn't a pretty story," Trevor stated.

"Pretty stories are boring."

"Well then, I guess I'll share my ugly story."

Edin nodded. "Please do."

Trevor heaved a sigh. "Before I was injured, I was a pit worker, mining epiglass. The two other gentlemen that stay at the Pebble Inn and I got contaminated by radiation, from a radioactive explosion we didn't even notice at the time. It happened on Rahg Latharitt, an entirely unhabitable planet mined for its resources. We were drilling over two miles from the incident. We had no idea what had happened. At first, our wonderful local government tried to cover it up. They didn't tell us about the radiation. They let us work for five standard years in those conditions." He frowned. "But a few of the crew started getting sick. We thought it was a virus at first. We eventually discovered what had happened and we returned home. House Nazari gave us credits to keep our silence about what occurred. But the damage was already done. Now, it's impossible to move the muscles in my body, and my bones have grown desperately weak over the years."

"Wow, that's a tough situation," Edin said, unsure how to respond to someone who had been through more than himself.

The old man grinned. "With the credits from our government, my son got to start his own business and live a better life than I did. Then he can pass it along to my granddaughter. I guess that's all you can hope for in this galaxy—something positive to pass down to the following generations."

"Yes," Edin said, "I think that would be my goal, if I ever have children."

Trevor eyed the two. "Have you guys talked about it yet?"

"Grandpa!" Vanya yelled playfully. "No! I'm way too young to even be thinking about children!"

"Well, you have been spending a lot of time together the past few weeks. By the way, leaving your grandfather with no one to talk to but a droid is no way to treat an elder."

"I said sorry already, but they needed an extra person for their training."

"I still don't see how you could have helped. All you know of is hospitality, and maybe you have some clerical skills."

"She did help with preparing food and upkeeping the grounds," Edin said. "I couldn't have done it without her."

Edin and Vanya smiled at each other.

"Yeah," Trevor said. "There's definitely something going on between the two of you. It's what us old folks like to call young love."

"Grandpa," Vanya said, "you're embarrassing me, and probably Edin as well."

Edin laughed. "It's fine."

"Are you going to go off-planet with him?" Trevor asked seriously.

Vanya's jaw dropped and her eyes widened. "No! My parents will be here any day now! I can't leave Lathas with a random boy!"

"A part of you wants to leave with him. I can see it. He's your age and has a solid future ahead of him. I'm not dull, Vanya. I know most girls dream to leave this planet with a gauntlet champion."

"Things have changed since your day. I have my own future ahead of me, and I don't want to bother Edin on his forthcoming endeavors."

"What if I want you to bother me on those endeavors?" Edin asked.

They smiled at each other again.

"This is making me cringe," Trevor said.

"You're the one that started it," Vanya said.

"You have my permission, though, if you want to leave with him. I'll tell your parents that I approved, and all the blame will be on me."

Vanya smiled. "If it comes down to that, I will let you know."

Ithamar Avrum woke up to a dry throat and a throbbing pulse in his scattered brain. Between the dehydration and the hangover headache, he was unsure which caused the most discomfort. He stretched in bed, then looked around the space, illuminated by bars of morning light filtering from the window. He was inside a room at the Pebble Inn and unsure how he'd ended up there. Also, he was unsure of the young lady sitting on the armchair, watching him.

"You finally woke up," she said. "Do you remember anything about last night?"

"Not really," Ithamar confessed. "I'm guessing—"

"Yeah." She smiled sinisterly. "That happened."

"Well, why are you still here?"

"That's rude to ask."

"That's honest to ask."

"Last night you said you would pay for my cab back in the morning."

Ithamar groaned. "Okay, fine. I'll pay for your cab. But first tell me what happened last night."

The lady smiled, her sweet expression radiating youth. She wore a red dress exhibiting long, tan legs. Ithamar figured she was a few years younger than himself. And he slightly remembered talking to her the evening before, but it was a hazy blur. He had entirely forgotten her name.

"Do you even remember my name?" she asked.

"Umm . . ." Ithamar paused, then shook his head. "No. I was just trying to think of it."

"That's fine." She giggled. "We'll keep it our secret."

"Okay, well, go on with the story. How did 'we' happen?"

"After your cousin won the gauntlet, you decided to party in the university district. A surprising choice, but considering Edin is a young spacer, it makes sense. The uni district is a little more accepting of spacers than most. You were pretty tipsy when we met at a tavern called the Study Hall."

"The Study Hall?" Ithamar scratched his chin. "We must have been very studious."

"Not so much. You were very ludicrous."

"So, we met there? And you came back home with me?"

"Yes, we met in VIP. The bouncers let you in for free. We spent most of the night talking by the railing above the dance floor. We were people watching. But it was odd, considering everyone stared back at you and Edin Carvosa all night."

"Oh, that doesn't sound too bad."

"Yes, but when we got back you admitted something to me."

"What?"

"That you were still in love with a girl named Helen Kotorm and the only reason you talked to me is because I reminded you of her."

"Okay, that is embarrassing. Please, I don't want to know anything else I said. Please forget that."

The girl smiled. "But you said—"

"I said I don't want to know what I said." Ithamar's cheeks reddened. "It is time for you to leave."

Her eyes darted to the floor. "Okay, sorry."

Ithamar rolled out of bed and gave the girl some coins from his pants pockets. "Where are you headed?"

"Do you really want to know?"

"Uh, I mean sure. I apologize for coming off rude. I know how I can be when I'm drunk, and it's embarrassing to hear about it from a stranger."

"I live on the residence on campus, and that's where I'm headed. I'm in my first year at Lathas University."

"Oh, cursed moons. You're younger than I thought."

"I won't tell anyone."

She stood and walked out the door without either of them saying goodbye. Relief swept over him as soon as she disappeared. He shook his head, then smiled. It had been a while since he'd gone out and enjoyed a night. He wondered what Edin and Vanya had planned for the day. His goal was to get off the planet and head back to Morhaven IV before nightfall. Too many strange incidents had occurred on Lathas since his arrival, and he feared his younger cousin would not be safe on the planet much longer. House Nazari and the Sheeban Syndicate were now both enemies to avoid.

He got dressed in the same clothes he wore the night before and left the room. The elevator dropped him off on the first floor. He walked into the lobby. No one was there, but he heard people talking in the hallway. A few seconds later, the corridor door opened, and Edin and Vanya entered.

"Hey, Ithamar, we're about to get breakfast," Vanya said. "Want to come?"

"We need to get a starship first," Ithamar said.

"Are we leaving today?" Edin asked.

"Yes, we both know we need to get off this planet. It is time for you to meet the sapa khan and the rest of the Mizoquii."

Edin frowned for a second. "Yeah, I understand."

"Look, you come with me to get the ship now, and you and Vanya can go out for a little while tonight while I set everything up for the flight."

"Okay. Does that work for you, Vanya?" Edin asked.

"Yeah," she said. "That's fine. If you need to leave sooner, don't let me hold you up."

"Don't worry. As long as we get away tonight, we're good," Ithamar said.

"I'll be here. Just come back whenever, Edin," she said in a voice that sounded soft and sad.

Edin and Ithamar left the Pebble Inn in the old glidecar. A-Veetwo chauffeured them nearly an hour outside of the capital to a fancy suburb. On the ride, Edin told Ithamar about meeting Vanya's grandfather and how the old man said Vanya should travel with him off Lathas. Ithamar listened but didn't say much in response. Edin was too young to commit to a girl. Commitment was a nuisance and distraction. Plus, Ithamar didn't feel like talking because his hangover lingered.

On each side of the street, short glass buildings stood with aesthetically oriented gables. The pale clouds in the sky reflected off the glass. Ahead was a hangar bay that towered above and sprawled wider than the surrounding structures. When the glidecar pulled into the parking lot, the cousins spotted a glowing neon sign that read *Chipper's Starships*. A-Veetwo drove up to the huge hangar and halted at the entry.

"Mr. Avrum, we are here," the droid said. "The best hangar to buy a starcraft on the planet."

"Thanks, A-Veetwo," Ithamar said. He unbolted the door and stepped out. Edin followed, and A-Veetwo drove off, the muffler rattling loudly.

"This place is gigantic," Edin said, gazing up at the hangar.

"They'll have a few pricey starships inside there, but most are parked on the flight line. Have you never been to a hangar that sells starships?"

"No."

"Well, let's go in."

They walked inside to an elaborate showroom with a secretary desk at the front and glass offices along the walls. The secretary welcomed them, but they did not respond, distracted by the beautiful black starship taking up the display area. Their decision on which starcraft to purchase was instantaneous because they were staring at a brand-new Valorwraith.

"That's the one," Edin said.

"That's why we came here. I knew you would say that."

The Valorwraith was pricey, but Ithamar had wagered on Edin to win the entire tournament before it began and earned quite a bit of extra coin against the improbable odds. After the paperwork was finished, the Valorwraith was transported out of the hangar and onto the flight line by a maintenance crew. Then Edin and Ithamar scrambled up to the cockpit and flew back to the capital where they parked on the roof of the inn.

When they landed Ithamar said, "Look, I'm going to the market to get a few things for the flight. You can take Vanya out one last time here on Lathas. And we will meet back here later tonight. No rush."

"And what if she wants to come with us?" Edin asked earnestly.

Ithamar shook his head and sighed. "If she wants to come with us, I'm not going to be the one to tell her no. But you do realize you're going to meet your people, the Mizoquii, for the first time. It might be odd taking a stranger with you."

"She's not a stranger. She'll be good company, and you know it."

"Okay, suit yourself. But don't say I didn't warn you. Sometimes the sweetest things turn sour."

Edin laughed. "I'll be ready for that day when it comes."

"That's what all boys think."

They left the ship and took the elevator to the lobby. On the couch, Vanya sat scrolling through an electronic tablet, reading something on the network. She looked up from the screen when they walked inside.

"Hey, guys. Back so soon?" she asked.

"Yeah," Edin said.

She looked down. "Ah."

"Ithamar has to go to the market and pick up some supplies. Why don't you and I go grab something to eat?"

"That sounds nice."

"I'll see you two later." Ithamar walked away.

"Where did you want to go?" Vanya asked.

"Why don't you decide?" Edin replied.

"You know I hate making decisions."

"Want to walk on the riverwalk and get gyros at that one spot?"

"Sure, I love that place."

"I know."

They left the Pebble Inn on foot and strolled along the river leading to the center of town. The riverwalk was made of ancient cobblestone between short brick walls. The sun dropped in the background, the waterway reflecting the many tones of dusk. Humans and other species walking along the path stared at Edin when passing by. They wanted a glimpse of the spacer who butchered a prince.

"How does it feel?" Vanya asked.

"What?"

"Knowing you accomplished what you set out to achieve."

"Life isn't over yet. This is just the first step."

"Yeah, but now you have a greater opportunity than the other ninety-nine percent of beings in the galaxy."

"There's still a lot I have to do with the Mizoquii. And you still haven't given me an answer yet. I want you to come with me."

"Edin, I can't."

"I understand." Edin looked to his feet. "I guess this is the last time we will see each other."

"Keep in contact with me on your comms. I'll visit you in the First System or wherever. I swear."

"Okay."

"Don't be sad. You will make new friends and so will I. We'll be fine."

"Alright. Yeah, it makes sense that way." Edin wanted to say more, wanted to beg. But he couldn't bring himself to ask again. They kept strolling along as the red sun disappeared in the distance. Even though he was disappointed, he wouldn't let it ruin the night.

Indistinguishable shouting erupted behind them, which they both ignored at first. When it became apparent a certain name was being yelled, they both turned their heads.

"Vanya!"

Two middle-aged people, a man and a woman, ran towards them. Vanya gasped.

"Mom! Dad!" She dashed in their direction with a huge smile, leaving Edin standing by himself. He watched them meet and hug each other lovingly. They spoke to each other for a moment, but Edin was too far to hear what they said. Eventually they all looked over and moved to join him.

"Hey, Edin," her father said. "I'm Ross Waldrip, and this is my wife, Vessa."

"Edin," Vessa said, "Vanya has told us all about you."

Edin said, "Vanya has told me a lot about you two as well. How was your trip?"

"Nice," Ross said. "We found our new home in the Altoyy system. Already purchased four new hotels."

"That sounds wonderful," Edin lied.

"We watched the gauntlet finale," Vessa said. "You fought bravely."

"Thanks."

"Edin," Vanya said, "let's all go eat together in the city, and when we get back, we can introduce my parents to Ithamar."

The situation felt awkward. Edin knew he should give her space with her parents. They had just returned, and he was only a boy she had met by chance. It was time to leave, he felt.

"Look, I don't want to intrude on your family's homecoming. How about you go out with your parents, and I'll just leave when Ithamar is ready."

No one spoke for a few seconds. Vanya and Edin looked at each other unhappily.

Vanya turned to her parents. "Will you two give me a minute to speak with Edin alone?"

"Sure," Ross said.

"Nice to meet you, Edin," Vessa said.

"Nice to meet you as well," Edin said.

Her parents left them, and they stood next to the wall overlooking the river. Edin looked at Vanya, and her eyes revealed her sadness.

"It was always going to end this way, wasn't it?" Edin asked.

"Yeah," Vanya said. "Or you were going to die in the tournament."

He smiled. "I'm glad that didn't happen."

She smiled back. "Me too."

A tear rolled down her cheek. Edin raised his hand and swiped it off before it left her face.

"Don't cry. I'm glad I met you, Vanya Waldrip."

"I'm glad I met you too."

They hugged, but it was not how Edin imagined a goodbye hug would feel like. It was a graceless and stiff embrace that felt as if it lasted too long while also not lasting long enough. Then again, they both knew her parents were watching. Edin and Vanya let go and spun away from each other, too upset to look the other in the face, finally understanding their paths were always destined to part. He stepped away from the riverwalk, wiped his cheek, and hurried to a nearby alleyway where a streetlamp flickered before it went dim.

CPSIA information can be obtained
at www.ICGtesting.com
Printed in the USA
LVHW091752110322
712904LV00012B/377